Gloam

Jennifer Withers

Also by

Jennifer Withers

The War Between

ISBN: 978-0-7961-6274-8 (Paperback) 978-0-7961-6275-5 (ebook)

Published by Jennifer Withers in 2024

Postnet Suite 1214

Private Bag X1007

Lyttelton

0140

Email: author@jenniferwithers.com

Website: www.jenniferwithers.com

Cover Design: Cathy Helms of Avalon Graphics

Author Photo: Ania Kamerski

Edited by: Ace Slaughter

For my Dad – Mark Fysh.
Gone suddenly and too soon.
This one is for you.

'Gloam is defined as the time of day immediately following sunset. Synonyms include dusk, evenfall, fall, gloaming, nightfall, twilight.'

vocabularly.com

Prologue

THE TAP HAD BEEN running for days. Was it days? The maddening *drip drip drip*. Then, as if someone had put something underneath it to catch the water – *plink plink plink*. She pushed against the wall at her back, her throat raw from screaming. Why had he put her here? Why was he doing this? Matt was friends with her family. He knew her. Knew them. Why was she down here?

She closed her eyes and thought of Keren, the girl from Gloam who always saved the day. A mercenary Pop had made up, and then created fantastical stories around, as if normal fairy tales just wouldn't do for his children. There were plenty of real mercenaries in the city, of course, many of whom they'd passed on the street during their time in Gloam. But Keren was different. She belonged to them, somehow. In Pop's stories, she was someone who could right every wrong, who made the idea of corrupt cops seem less terrible, because she was there to dispense justice. She tried to imagine she was Keren. A bad-ass merc who wasn't afraid of anything or anyone.

The door opened then, squealing on its hinges, startling me. The boy stood there, a full tray of food in his hands. A sandwich. An apple. Two small squares of chocolate. And a bottle of water.

1

He smiled at her, his teeth a flash of white in the muted yellow glow of the single hanging lightbulb. He set the tray down on the small table nearby.

He stepped away, his eyes moving to hers. He seemed to be searching for something to say. She waited for him to say something that would explain why she was here.

"How are you doing?" he asked.

She wanted to scream, but fear had closed her throat, until it felt like she were breathing through a straw. "Fine," she croaked.

She tried to muster a smile. Out of all of them, he was the only one who'd been nice to her, as weird as it was.

She shuffled to the edge of the bed. "I want to go home." He flinched back a little, as if she'd raised her hand to hit him. She forced herself to stay where she was, even though instinct screamed at her to move closer to him. Closer to the door. "When can I go home?"

He looked at her as if it were obvious. "When Matt says you can."

She shook her head vehemently, tears making her eyes burn. "Please. I don't know why I'm here. I didn't do anything wrong."

He stared at her mutely, and she thought she saw something in his eyes. She reached carefully for his hand. He didn't resist, and the warmth of his palm against hers felt like an anchor, something to hold on to for dear life.

They stood like that for a long moment, before he gently pulled his hand from her grip. "You should eat."

He turned away and disappeared through the door, the sound of the lock turning causing her legs to turn to jelly.

***

The note was on his desk. Casually sitting there among the other debris of his case files, notebooks and stationery. The only difference was that it was tacked to his desk with a strip of tape, as if its sender wanted to be sure it would be found.

I have her. Don't do it. You can come back, and all will be forgotten.

The world dipped beneath his feet, and he sank into his chair, gripping the edge of his desk until his hands ached. He should've known this would happen. Should've seen it coming. He'd hoped for a different outcome, another way to undo years of duplicity. He pictured having to come clean with Lena. With Rich and Charlie. He buried his face in his hands.

Carter looked up from his laptop. "Frank? What is it?" He raised his head, taking in the concern in his partner's face, knowing he didn't deserve it.

He wished he'd done things differently. He wished he'd told Carter before, so he wouldn't have to tell him like this. It was too late for that now.

"I need your help."

***

Frank stood in the shadows of the house. A place as familiar to him as his own. Light spilled from the windows, and Frank caught the movement and sounds of the people inside. He kept to the shadows, waiting.

Carter was circling around the back, following the detailed instructions Frank had given him. Matt would've put her in the basement. They'd conducted all their business in there, although there'd been no need. Matt's family knew who he was. He'd had the luxury of honesty with his family.

When Frank was sure Carter was where he should be, he walked up to the front door, and knocked, as if this was some social call, and not his attempt to negotiate the safe return of his daughter.

Matt himself answered the door. He smiled and stepped back, inviting Frank in, as he'd been doing for all the years they'd conducted business.

Angie and the boy were nowhere to be seen. Matt waved a hand at the kitchen table. "Have a seat."

Frank couldn't bear it a moment longer. "I'll do whatever you want. I'll stay your contact. Please. I won't leave. I just want her back."

"I'm sure you realise I can't just take your word for it. I need insurance."

Frank heard the quiet creak of the back door, but willed himself to keep his eyes on Matt. He watched for a sign that Matt had heard it too, but he remained fixed on Frank. Behind Matt, Frank caught the brief outline of Carter as he headed for the basement, his footsteps quiet on the tile floor.

"Insurance?"

Matt opened a drawer and withdrew his pistol. "A daily reminder, you know? Of this conversation. Of whom you work for."

Frank felt like someone had chopped his legs off at the knees. They couldn't hold him. He bent and flattened his palms against

4

the smooth wood of the dining table in an effort to stay upright. He had to give Carter as much time as he could.

"Don't kill her. Matt. Please. She's my only daughter. This is between us. She's only a child."

"I'm not going to kill her, Frank." Matt's knife sat on the kitchen counter. Frank thought of how many people he'd watched endure the agony of its blade in their flesh.

Matt followed his gaze. "I could use a blade instead. It'll leave a pretty nasty scar but that would be a mercy compared to being maimed, don't you think? A shot to the kneecap could mean she'd never walk again." Matt moved towards him, slinging a companiable arm around him. "It's a shame, you know? Trust is so easily broken, and she's like a daughter to me, too. I don't want to do this, Frank, but you've forced my hand." The smooth barrel of the gun touched the underside of his chin. There and then gone. "I'll take you to her, shall I?"

Frank had been so focused on Matt he hadn't listened out for Carter's departure. Were they gone? Had he found her?

The sudden scuffle of feet and then a thump, as if someone had fallen, drew Matt's attention from him and towards the kitchen door. Frank caught a brief flash of white before the footfalls increased.

Matt ran for them, but Frank reached for his sidearm, the one Matt had neglected to take from him, and drew it. "Stop."

Matt paused in the doorway. He turned slowly with his gun still in hand. There was the sound of a door opening and slamming shut. Frank knew if he survived this, if they all did, that he would owe everything to Carter.

"Frank, put the gun down. You know who you're dealing with? You'll be ruined. You'll never work as a cop again. Not in Gloam, not anywhere else."

Something gave way in Frank. The understanding that he'd never been the person his family thought he was. That the man he'd wanted to be, the one he'd imagined himself to be, was buried beneath all the things he'd done for the past few years, the things he'd told himself were justifiable.

He pointed his gun at Matt and fired.

Chapter One

Harlow

WE'D WAITED TOO LONG to leave. The streets were all but deserted, with only the occasional streetlight to dispel the dark. Chloe leaned heavily against me, giggling and oblivious, and I had to quell my irritation. I'd joined her in Gloam on the spur of the moment on this night out, and now, dragging her drunken deadweight, I wished I'd had the sense to say no.

The city was shuttered for the night. The only people out were carousers like us or homeless people littering the street like confetti, their sleeping bodies curled against the cold.

Chloe stumbled again, her high heels catching on the pavement. She staggered into me, nearly toppling us both, which only made her giggle harder. I swore under my breath.

"What?" Chloe asked in a stage whisper, her mouth so close to my ear I felt a damp spray of spittle. "Chloe. I need you to walk. Can you take those ridiculous shoes off?"

She looked down at her feet dumbly, as if she'd forgotten she was wearing shoes at all. "Gross," she said. "Do you know what's on these pavements?"

Right. Of course. She'd thrown up in a dumpster not ten minutes ago, but walking barefoot was unimaginable.

I thought of the man in the bar who had watched us the whole night. At first, Chloe had enjoyed it, returning his gaze, smiling demurely. We'd waited for him to approach us, to offer a drink, or a lame pick-up line, but he'd remained in his booth, unsmiling and watchful. I'd wanted to leave then, having found what I thought of as the perfect excuse to do so, but Chloe had vehemently protested. When he'd finally left, he'd walked by us, close enough for us to inhale his scent – soap, beer and sweat.

We rounded a corner onto an unfamiliar street. I'd been so preoccupied with keeping Chloe on her feet that I hadn't noticed the direction we were going in.

"Chloe," I hissed. She'd slumped to her knees, swaying a little. "Get up. We need to keep moving. Do you know where your car is?" I slipped my arm around her waist, hoisting her up with a grunt.

"Heeeyyyyy." I turned towards the voice. A group of men were watching us, their faces garishly lit by the streetlight they stood beneath. The man who had spoken was leering at us, the sheer bulk of him making me take a step back, dragging Chloe with me. "You ladies look like you could use some help." He motioned to Chloe with the cigarette he was smoking. The scent from his body washed over us. Soap. Beer. Sweat. *Fuck.* We'd been followed.

"She looks lit, man. You need a lift home?"

At this, his friends broke into knowing laughter.

My hand went instinctively for my Sauer. I groped nothing but air. I pictured it sitting on my bedside table where I'd left it, embarrassed by Chloe's teasing in my thinking that we'd need it.

I silently cursed myself for letting her convince me to leave it at home, instead of listening to my own instincts.

"No. We're fine."

I turned away from them, hoping but knowing, that my rebuff wouldn't be enough. "Chloe. We need to get out of here. Where's your car?"

She pushed against me, coming to her feet unassisted. She glared at the group of men. "Fuck off!"

The leader of the group took a step forward, his buddies crowding behind him. I scanned the street rapidly, but it was deserted.

"What did you say to me? Huh?" He was close now. Too close. I could make out the colour of his shirt, the white gleam of his sneakers.

"Nothing." I said. "We just want to get home, ok?" The man licked his lips and considered me, his eyes traveling the length of my body, taking his time. He turned to his buddies briefly. "Isn't that what I just offered to do?" More laughter.

"Chloe! For fuck's sake! Where's your car?" I hoped the quaver of fear in my voice had gone unnoticed.

She looked around, her eyes slitted and heavy with drink, then shrugged. She tugged at her ridiculously tiny evening bag, rummaged around and sighed a deep, heavy exhalation. "You know, I really don't know. And I don't seem to have the keys, either." She gave a hiccup followed by a grin. It was the first time in my life where I could ever recall wanting to hit her.

"Ah. You see. You really do need our help." The man smiled around the smoking cigarette in his mouth. I wanted to shove it all the way into his mouth, picturing the cramp of pain on his face when it seared his tongue.

I forced myself to look at him, straight into his bloodshot eyes. I had to tip my face upwards and tried to recall every moment I'd watched Chloe manipulate a man with just a curl of her mouth and that gleam in her eyes.

"Well. Of course we would need your help if we were lost or couldn't find our car. But as luck would have it – there it is!" I pointed down the road, at a car I'd just noticed, parked some way down the street.

"Your friend just said she doesn't have the keys."

I laughed and hoped it didn't sound as fake as it felt. I leaned a little closer to him, trying not to breathe in the stink of him. "She's drunk. I've got the keys." I waited for him to ask to see them. The blood was pounding in my ears, and Chloe shifted next to me, as if she was about to correct me. I squeezed her arm, hard, and she went still.

The man stared at us. I turned, taking Chloe with me, resisting the urge to run. Over my shoulder, I called, "Thanks though. Such gentlemen!"

I started walking further down the dark street, dragging Chloe along, wondering if they would follow us, if we were in exactly the kind of trouble Pop had warned me about.

I could feel the heat of their gazes on my back, but I forced myself to keep going, willing them to turn away before we reached the car I'd claimed was ours. Finally, the welcome sound of their retreating footsteps came, and then, only when I was sure they were gone, did I stop and turn back. The street was silent and empty. Somehow, the silence was worse.

I eased away from Chloe. "Can you walk?" She nodded, her face ashen. "What the hell was that?"

"I'd rather not find out. Have you really lost the keys?"

She rummaged around in her bag, coming up empty-handed for the second time. "I really have. I might've left them at The Dive. When I was looking for my lipstick."

I sighed inwardly. Nothing to be done about it. At least the men were gone.

"We could walk?"

I stared at her. "Are you insane? Have you forgotten where we are? Look at what just happened! We can't be walking on the streets at night. Not in this city."

Chloe looped her arm through mine. "The only reason we drove here in the first place is because your Pop was so damn uptight about us coming here. Otherwise we would've called a taxi."

"A taxi? To The Sands? You know no one comes all the way out there unless they live there or they're lost."

"I would've convinced one of your brothers to take us, then."

I snorted. "As if Rich would."

"Oh, but Charlie would." She grinned slyly. "I think he's sweet on me."

"You think all men are sweet on you."

"That's because they are."

We laughed.

"Anyway." She tossed her hair, the smell of smoke mixed with her shampoo filling my nose. "Your Pop knows you're a grown woman, right?" She stumbled in her high heels. She let out a curse, paused, and ripped the shoes from her feet, her revulsion at the idea of walking barefoot forgotten.

"He's told you too many stories about this place. Plenty of people live here, and they're just fine."

Drip drip drip. I shuddered, closing a mental fist around the memory and snuffing it out.

"There's nothing wrong with having a reliable, loving family, Chlo. Some would say it was a blessing."

Chloe glanced at me, her eyes soft. "Not when their love implies that the only place of safety is with them."

I opened my mouth to retort but stopped. Chloe didn't get it. She never would. I changed the subject, still stinging from her barb.

"So why The Dive?"

"Huh?" Chloe turned to me.

"There's like a bar on every corner in Gloam. Why The Dive?"

Her eyes twinkled, and before she opened her mouth, I knew the answer.

I sighed, smiling a little. "The barman, right?"

"Well, not specifically. I mean, there was plenty of potential there tonight."

"Who? The one with all the piercings, with the terrible pickup line, or the one whose beer breath was so bad we smelled him before we saw him?"

Chloe laughed, elbowing me in the ribs. "Okay, you got me. He was really cute, don't you think?"

I thought of the barman Chloe had introduced me to. Tousled hair, like he'd fallen out of bed just minutes before. Eyes that seemed brown, until closer inspection revealed they were hazel, bordering on green. His casual outfit of jeans and a close-fitting, impeccably clean white shirt.

I shrugged. "Cute enough, I suppose." I brought my attention back to the street.

"Well, since we don't know where the car is, I guess we'll have to walk. The question is, do you know which way's home?"

She pointed vaguely down a side street. "I know it's more or less in that direction."

We walked for what felt like forever, passing buildings which all looked the same, save for the number of broken windows in each. A breeze came up, turning the night air icy and swirling the trash along the sidewalk around our feet.

Light bloomed up ahead. Several braziers were lit, a small crowd clustered around them, huddling together for warmth. Chloe stiffened against me, and I realised that for all her bravado, she too had been shaken by our earlier encounter. I straightened my back and stared straight ahead, willing them to ignore us, hoping we'd pass through without incident. A drunk had fallen asleep right across the path we were taking, and we were forced to step over him. I thought of him waking and reaching up, grabbing my ankle like in those old horror movies. A woman approached us, hand held out, palm facing upward. She said nothing, but stared at us with eyes that seemed to look both at and through us. We moved around her, doing our best to ignore her. She shrieked something unintelligible at our backs. I walked faster, Chloe matching my pace.

I'd never wanted the familiarity of The Sands so badly before. I only had vague memories of Gloam when we'd first lived here, and those were all overshadowed by the reason we'd left in the first place.

I turned my attention back to our surroundings. Chloe was leaning against me again. I glanced down at her feet, now filthy, and noticed she was limping. I slid my arm around her waist, and she did the same, giving me a gentle squeeze.

The first shacks appeared. We were now on the periphery of Gloam, and I estimated we'd need to walk for another half hour or so before we reached The Sands. The shacks on either side of us were lit from within with lamps or hanging torches. The promise of electricity had never happened here. The sound of shouting was drifting through the open window of one, and a brief glance inside revealed a swaying man standing over a cowering woman, her hands clutched protectively over her head. I shuddered and looked away, hating my cowardice and my singular focus to get home.

The city streets gave way to smaller pathways, and then, just as I thought we'd never get there, the cool comfort of sand gave way beneath our feet. We came to the street where we both lived, the crossroad leading left and right, taking us to our respective homes. I pulled Chloe closer for a hug, then held her away from me so I could study her face.

"You okay to walk from here by yourself?" She shook her head. Her eyeliner had smudged, leaving a thin black trail outside of each eye. "Could I come to you tonight? Just for one more drink? Brad'll be home." She twisted the ring she still wore, a habit she'd picked up since things had gone sour between them.

I slipped my arm through hers. "I don't think you need another drink. But of course you can come. Stay the night, if you want."

She smiled, and we turned left, the welcome sight of my home coming into view. It took all I had not to sag against Chloe with the force of my relief. That would be the last time I ever set foot in Gloam.

I took the three short stairs to the front door, rummaging in my bag for my keys, when the door opened from the inside and

Pop stood in the dim light from the kitchen, dressed in his usual plain blue pyjamas.

"Good. You're home." He glanced over my shoulder at Chloe and smiled warmly. "Nightcap?" he asked.

I hugged him, harder than I meant to, and when he stepped back and held me at arm's length so he could study my face, I knew he could read the apology there. He'd been right about Gloam. He was always right.

"Just keep it down, okay? Your mother and brothers are asleep." I nodded, relieved that he didn't ask about Chloe's car. Tomorrow, we'd have to solve the problem of getting her car back, but for now, all I could think about was basking in the familiarity of home. Maybe a nightcap would do us both good, after all.

I turned to Chloe. "How about that drink?" She grinned and then nodded.

"I'm going to just hang out here, if you don't mind. Breathe in the night air and rest my feet." She lifted a foot to show me. It was black with the detritus of the streets we'd walked. "I'm going to have blisters tomorrow."

I walked into the kitchen, taking care to only switch on the lights I needed, and to step as lightly as I could. Pop was standing at the kitchen counter, already making drinks. He reached into a high cupboard, one only he could reach, and pulled out our one good bottle of gin from its depths.

"Pop!" He smiled at me and carried on pouring, then motioned to the fridge. "Grab the mixers, will you?"

When I emerged from the coolness of the fridge with three tonics in hand, Pop was gone. I called for him but got no reply. I popped the seal on one can and poured, and it was only as I set it down, empty, that I heard Pop shout. Alarmed, I swung towards the noise, and accidentally swept the full glass of gin and tonic to the floor, the crash reverberating in the quiet of the kitchen. In my haste, I stepped into the pool of liquid, and I slipped, grabbing for the counter to keep myself from falling.

Before I could move towards the door, another shout punctuated the air, this one higher than the last, shrill with fear. I finally managed to find my feet and bolted for the door, rocketing through the open doorway. Someone was running from the yard, their retreating form briefly lit by the outside light. My mind scrambled to make out the details of the strange insignia of their jacket. They disappeared from view, dropping over the fence into the neighbours' yard.

Chloe lay silent and unmoving. Pop's neck was twisted at a strange angle, the skin at his throat oddly purpled. I screamed, all the air leaving my lungs, my knees buckling, my body toppling down the three short stairs to the sand below.

I got to my knees, my arms trembling beneath my weight.

It was only when I felt their hands on me, pulling at my arms, and the ring of their voices in my ear, that I found the will to rise. I pointed in the direction I'd seen the attacker go, but they were long gone, the night enveloping them into its inky embrace.

Richard shoved past me and rushed to Pop, his hands fluttering over him as if not knowing where to land. I couldn't look at Pop directly. The image of him lying there had been burned into my eyelids, and every time I closed them, all I could see was his unmoving form.

I ran to Chloe instead, kneeling beside her, whispering a long stream of nonsense syllables. I pressed my thumb into her wrist, and nearly cried with relief when my touch was met with the throb of her pulse.

"Chloe?" I patted her cheek gently, brushing her hair from her face. Behind me, Ma wailed. I couldn't turn. I didn't want to see. I closed my hands around Chloe's shoulders and shook her. "Chloe. Wake up. Wake up. Wake up!" My voice rose until it drowned out my mother's screams.

Chloe's eyelids fluttered, and finally opened. She stared up at me blankly, and then, seeming to hear my mother's weeping, she sat up abruptly, knocking me back.

I pulled her into a suffocating embrace until she squawked in protest, pushing me away.

"Low." Her eyes were huge as she stared over my shoulder.

Instead of turning and facing my family, I fumbled for my phone in my pocket, willing my shaking hands to still as I punched in the number for the cops. I waited as it rang and rang, unable to do anything but listen. I hung up and dialled again, the maddening ring tone on the other side droning on until I wanted to scream.

A robotic voice answered. *Your call is important to us. We are experiencing unusually high volumes of calls. Please hold.*

A warm hand dropped on my shoulder as Charlie came up behind me. I couldn't look directly at him. I would read it all there and I didn't want to know. A sob closed like a fist in my throat, choking me. I swallowed hard, forcing the tears back. "Is Pop…"

Charlie pulled me to him, hugging me hard enough to bruise, and in that embrace, I knew everything he couldn't say.

Chapter Two

I SAT IN THE kitchen, wrapped in a blanket and nursing a scalding cup of coffee. Despite the heat, I couldn't stop shaking. A short, sharp warble sounded outside. No one had spoken a word for so long, that the noise made me jump, like an electric current had run through my body.

Chloe stirred long enough to get up and go to the door. When she opened it, a whirl of red lights filled the room, painting it a sickening scarlet. Two paramedics stood in front of the open doors of an ambulance, their faces tired and drawn.

They took one look at Chloe's face – the bruise that had ripened against the paleness of her skin, the imprint of finger-prints around her throat, and the rising bump on her temple where she'd hit her head, and they stepped forward, already trying to usher her out of the door.

"Ma'am you need to come with us." The shorter man took her arm, ready to escort her into the waiting vehicle, but she planted her feet, adamant.

"No no no. I'm fine. I don't need to go to the hospital." I rose and went to stand beside her, turning her towards me so our eyes met.

"Chloe. Go. Just get checked out. You could have a concussion." Her shoulders slumped, turning inward. "I want to stay here with all of you." Tears turned her eyes luminous. I pulled her into me for a long moment, forcing myself not to clutch at her.

"I'll come see you later, okay? I promise. But please just go. I can't worry about you, too."

She nodded against my shoulder, before pulling out of my embrace to follow the paramedics into the ambulance. As it pulled away, a cop car came into view, pulling to the side to allow the ambulance through.

Two cops got out of the car, their black and navy uniforms neatly pressed. A third followed, dressed in jeans and a plain blue button-up shirt, his shoes scuffed but clean. I motioned them inside wordlessly. The uniformed ones passed me without a glance or a word. The plain clothes cop had to turn to fit through the doorway. His eyes were a rich nut brown, small and mean. His eyebrows arched over them, thick and unkempt, meeting in the middle of his forehead. Already there were small sweat patches beneath his arms.

"I'm Detective Madden. These are my colleagues, Corporal James and Corporal Mackenzie."

Corporals. The lowest ranked cops in the city. The amateurs, the beginners.

Their questioning took all of five minutes. As they made for the door, I stepped in front of the detective, blocking his path.

"You're done? Already?"

The corporals glanced briefly at me before moving around us, the click and then clunk of the door punctuating their departure.

"There isn't much to go on."

He brushed past me, his bulk impossible to halt, and I felt a wave of heat sweep through me, an eruption starting at my toes and filling my mouth, hot and metallic.

"That's it? That's all you have to say? My father is dead! He was murdered in our backyard. My friend was attacked. Doesn't that mean anything to you?"

He paused before turning back to me. Instead of the anger I'd expected, his expression was sympathetic. It made me want to close the distance between us and punch him. To keep punching him until the hollowness inside me was gone.

"Murder happens all the time. Do you know how many murders we deal with on the daily in Gloam? Between the constant gang wars and the general lawlessness, there are dozens of case files of unsolved murders cluttering my desk every day. I don't mean to say that your father's death doesn't mean anything, but we're in over our heads."

I blinked, taken aback by his honesty. "So what you're saying is we shouldn't have any hope that you'll catch whoever did this?"

"I'm saying that we'll do what we can." He paused. "There is one thing. That insignia you mentioned on the jacket of the intruder – you're sure it was an eagle?"

I stared at him. "It was a bird, for sure. A big one."

He nodded. "That's something, at least." At my blank stare, he sighed. "It's a gang insignia. The Natives." His words made no sense. His mouth was moving, but the words falling from his lips was nothing but gibberish.

"I don't understand. What would they want with my father?"

Detective Madden considered this. "Is there any connection between your family and Gloam? Any history?"

"Sure. We used to live there. A long time ago now though."
I paused. I actively tried to keep my kidnapping locked away in
the deepest recesses of my mind. I deliberately kept the memories
hazy. Clarity meant reliving it, and I had no desire to do that.

Detective Madden studied me. "Why do I feel like there's more
to it than you're saying?" When I said nothing, he shrugged.
"Anything you keep from me will only make the case harder to
solve. It's in your best interests to tell me what you know."

I forced the words out, one painful syllable at a time. It felt like
spitting out razors. "I was kidnapped by a friend of my father's.
Years ago, now. He and his partner got me back, but we left
Gloam that same night. We've never been back, until tonight."

I glanced at him. He appeared to be listening but hadn't taken
any notes. His hands were in the pockets of his coat. He appeared
to be mulling over my words.

"Gloam is the Natives' playground. Drugs, kidnappings, murder – you name it. What puzzles me is why one of them would
come all the way out here unless they had specific business in these
parts." He waited, as if I should know the answer to his unspoken
question. When I said nothing, he nodded at me, turning to leave.
"We find anything, we'll let you know."

I watched him walk away, fighting the urge to yell at his
departing back.

This was my worst fear – that the cops would be no help at all. I
stood in the doorway as they piled into their car and drove away,
sure of only one thing. We were on our own.

Chapter Three

"WHAT DO YOU MEAN, we can't bury him here?" My voice was loud in the small room.

"There's no soil," the man said shortly. "You've lived here a long time, haven't you? You know this. You know we can't bury our kind here. Too much sand." His voice wasn't without sympathy, but I could still read his impatience, his expectation that I was too old for these theatrics, that I should know better.

Ma laid a hand on my shoulder. She had to reach up to do it, and when I turned towards her and took in her face and the deep lines that hadn't been there yesterday, I forced myself to breathe.

"Where do we go then?" Charlie asked. He was so pale. So utterly spent. I wanted to hug him, but his posture was so stiff I knew he was only just holding it together.

The man regarded us. "There's a number of places. You could drive south to the Badlands. They have cemeteries there. Or to Southport, which is a bit further but will probably be able to offer you more in terms of funeral services, if that's what you're after."

He paused. The silence grew heavy in the room, stifling and full. "Or you could go the other route." We mulled this over. Plenty of families within our community had *gone the other route.* An outsider from Gloam had helped a neighbour of ours when one of their relatives died. He'd snuck the corpse into the cremation centre where he worked one night and brought the resulting ashes back the next day. He'd charged what I considered an exorbitant amount of money, but it was still cheaper than transporting to the surrounding towns or cities and paying for a funeral. How could we do it? How could we send him with a stranger, and stick him in an oven, like a pig to be roasted? No ceremony. No memorial. Just a body to be burned.

My hands were shaking, and the room felt small. Heat was forming at my hairline and traveling along my body in a blaze that left me sweating and swaying. I reached out a hand for the nearest armchair for support, only faintly aware of my mother's voice, and my brothers' hands on my arms as they steadied me.

I breathed until I could stand again. "The other route isn't an option. We need to bury him properly, send him off…" I had to stop to swallow, my throat feeling like it had a burgeoning fist within it. "We'll arrange a funeral."

I turned abruptly for the door, unable to bear being in this room one moment longer. I burst out into the growing heat of the day, the sun already high and bright, and let out a scream so loud, so shrill, that the birds who'd been tittering contentedly in a nearby bush took flight.

"Low." Rich came to stand beside me, wrapping an arm around my shoulders. "You know we don't have the coin to bury him. We could take him out to Northside, and—"

I turned on him, my fury mounting to such a pitch point I could feel my fingertips throbbing with the strength of my pulse. "And what? Bury him like an animal in the plantation?"

Rich's arm dropped to his side. "This isn't just hard for you. Ma is carrying the heaviest weight. She has no income now, nothing.

You can't add this to her burden, Low. She's already cracking. I don't want Pop buried anonymously in some plantation, so far from home, or burned in an oven by some backstreet quack, but we don't have a lot of options."

Ma emerged from the funeral home, Charlie following in her wake. Her pallor was even worse in the harsh sunlight, and I felt my heart close like a fist, my stomach clench with grief.

"Ma. I'll get the money for the funeral. I just need a few days."

Rich grabbed my arm in a sudden, uncharacteristic display of fury. "Pop won't wait a few days for fuck's sake! We have nowhere to-to-to..." He couldn't finish. His shoulders heaved, and the sobs that came from him were loud and shocking. His uncharacteristic display of vulnerability felt as intimate as if he'd stripped naked in front of a group of strangers.

I turned without answering, unable to bear his grief, unable to reach for him and enfold him as he had done for me since this had happened. I marched back into the funeral home, startling the man we'd been speaking to minutes before.

"Can you keep him here for a few days?" The man started to speak, but I cut across him before he could say what we both knew. "I'll come up with the money. You have my word. I just need a few days." The man's face closed, and I felt as if I was standing at the entrance to a tunnel, the blackness ahead impenetrable, the light behind me closing off with the finality of a slamming door.

"Please?" To my horror, I felt the sting of oncoming tears, but I refused to look away, to give this man a moment to breathe, to consider all the reasons he shouldn't help me.

The silence stretched on, and the heat of the room was closing in on me again. I willed myself to persist, to withstand.

Finally, the man spoke. "You have until Friday. That's all I can do. And it'll be added to the cost of the funeral if you choose to have one. It's a substantial cost to store a body." He paused. "If you're not back by then with the money, I'm afraid I'll have to remove the body myself."

I bit my tongue so hard my mouth filled with blood. I knew what that meant. Pop would be dumped at the nearest convenient point and left to rot.

When I spoke, my tone was even. "I understand. Thank you. I'll be back by then with the money."

I joined my family. My brothers had formed a protective cluster around Ma, their arms around her as she keened quietly.

"Ma." They turned towards me. "They'll keep Pop until Friday. I'll have the money by then."

Rich opened his mouth to protest, but I was already walking away.

***

The house felt suffocating in its grief. It was a relief to leave, to get into our family car with its wheezing engine and rusted doors, and leave The Sands behind. I thought of my vow, just a few hours ago, that I'd never step foot in Gloam again, and didn't know whether to scream or cry. My body thrummed with anxiety, my mind full of questions I had no answers to. I pictured Pop's body, covered with an old, yellowed sheet for the time being. A boulder of grief rose in my throat, choking me, and I pulled over to the side of the road, the tears coming at last, flowing down my face until my skin was tacky with salt and I'd run dry.

I pulled back onto the road, driving with blind indifference until I reached the outskirts of Gloam a few minutes later. I followed the directions of the map on my phone, until I arrived at Gloam's largest public hospital, pulling into the parking lot.

Once inside, I followed the signs to the general ward. I approached the nurses' station and gave Chloe's name. The nurse lifted her chin to indicate I should go down the hallway before saying, "Room twelve. But you'll have to wait. She's got visitors right now, and we don't allow more than two at a time."

I nodded and took the seat she indicated in the waiting area, mindlessly picking up a tattered magazine and flipping through it without taking in a single detail. I closed it again, keeping hold of it so I had something to do with my hands.

Two more nurses joined the one I'd spoken to. The room was otherwise quiet, and I could hear their conversation clearly, even though they'd taken the pains to lower their voices.

"Just back from room ten. Did you see that girl when she came in?"

The other two nodded, their expressions grave. "Cut to ribbons. Her face will never be the same again. He stabbed her eight times."

The smaller of the three shook her head, her blonde curls bobbing. "What about that guy who came in yesterday? Gunshot to the shoulder. Rumour is he's a mercenary."

"Nothing but vigilantes, mercs," the second nurse retorted.

The blonde one snorted. "At least they clean up the streets."

I'd leaned so far forward that my chair moved with my weight, producing an ear-splitting shriek as its metal feet dragged against the tile floor.

All three nurses turned, all looking like they'd either forgotten I was in the room or hadn't seen me in the first place.

"Harlow?"

I looked up, grateful to be saved from explaining my blatant eavesdropping. Chloe's parents stood there, smiling down at me, their faces alarmingly pale beneath the garish yellow of the hospital lighting.

I rose and embraced them both, breathing in their scent of home.

"You here to see Chloe?" Josiah asked when we pulled apart.

I nodded. "How is she?"

"The doctor said she's going to be fine." Rachel squeezed my hand gently. "They're concerned about the bump on her head, so they'll keep her overnight for observation."

Her grip on my hand tightened. "Honey." When I met Rachel's gaze, her eyes were bright with tears. "I'm so sorry about your father." Josiah took my other hand, holding it tightly. Was he trying to anchor himself, or me?

"He was such a good man, my closest friend. We will miss him," Josiah added

I gently pulled my hands from their collective grip. "Thank you."

I looked beyond their shoulders, at the nurses. "Can I go see her now?"

The blonde one nodded. "Ten minutes, you hear? She needs to rest."

Josiah and Rachel waved me off. I forced my feet to take slow, measured steps, despite my burning need to run. Was this going to be what the next few weeks would be like? Accepting condolences, observing the grief of others, while trying to keep a lid on my own?

I made my way down the short corridor to Chloe's room. I'd meant to just keep going, but when I saw the number on the door, something compelled me to go in. Room ten. The woman who lay in the only occupied bed was swathed in white, with only her eyes, nostrils and mouth visible. Red spots discoloured the otherwise pristine bandages. *Stabbed eight times,* the nurses had said. Would she be home now, instead of in this hospital bed, if someone had been there to help her? Someone not bound by the law, but someone who upheld it anyway. Like a mercenary.

I touched her hand lightly, holding my breath against the possibility of her waking. She didn't stir. I glanced at her one last time before leaving the room and making my way further along the corridor, finding Chloe's room three doors down.

The muted lighting was just bright enough for me to make out four separate beds, all empty and neatly made. Chloe grinned when she saw me, waving me over. The bump on her head seemed to have grown and had turned an ominous purple. I perched on the edge of her bed, taking her hand and squeezing it hard.

She laughed. "You look so worried. I'm going to be fine, you know."

I nodded. The tears I'd been trying so hard to keep at bay came. A torrent of grief and disbelief. Chloe's hands moved to my hair, her fingers gently smoothing back the strands, the repetitive sweep of them calming me.

When I looked up at her, she too, was crying.

"Why did this happen?" I asked. She shook her head, swiping at her face with one hand and mine with the other, her fingers clumsy and tender.

"I wish I remember more, but I didn't even see whoever it was. They came behind me, and it's only when they grabbed me that I realised they were there at all. And then I was waking up to you shaking me."

"The detective told me that insignia I saw on the attacker's jacket is the mark of a gang called the Natives. Why would a gang member be all the way out in The Sands? For Pop?"

"What do you mean? That he thinks your Pop had something to do with a gang in Gloam? That makes no sense."

"He didn't say that specifically. He asked about our connection to Gloam."

Our eyes met briefly. I silently pleaded with her. *Don't bring it up.* She hesitated, then reached out to squeeze my hand.

"Think the cops are going to catch who did this?"

"No." I paused. Could I say aloud what I'd been thinking since overhearing those nurses? Since seeing that woman just three rooms away?

"Chloe. I've been thinking. What if they don't catch the attacker? What if he comes back? He knows where we live now."

"Low. Don't think like that. It could've been random." Even as she said this, I could see she didn't believe it herself.

"The cops aren't going to be much help. That seems pretty obvious after they interviewed us."

Chloe was watching me, realisation dawning, her face pinching with concern.

"What are you saying?"

"I don't know exactly. All I do know is I need a job. One which makes money. Fast. We don't have any to bury Pop." I buried my face in my hands, the tears trickling between my fingers.

Chloe's hand was on my back. "You mean come to Gloam?" I nodded without looking up. "But you hate this place." Even without looking at her, I heard what she didn't say. *And you're afraid.*

Chapter Four

THE NIGHT fiNALLY CLOSED in, the stars winking against the black of the darkening sky. I stood on our deck, listening to the hum of insects, wondering what the hell I was going to do. I'd promised the money for Pop with only a half-baked plan in mind. And the plan was insane.

I paced, muttering to myself. I knew Ma had no savings and had relied heavily on the income Pop had brought in doing odd jobs for the neighbourhood. We'd had money once, but that had been when we'd still lived in Gloam. When we'd fled, we'd only taken what we could carry.

Rich and Charlie worked too, and contributed, but everything we made went into our living costs. It had never mattered before. We'd always had what we needed. Until now.

I thought of how I'd left Chloe, of the look on her face when I'd told her my plan. She was right about my hatred of Gloam. And my fear. Would that be enough to stop me?

I stopped and pressed my palms into my eyes until I saw stars. Tears were of no use now. Grief would not produce the money we needed, and for once, my brothers were at a loss. They seemed paralysed at the catastrophe that had befallen our family. What had been our lives now felt like a simple stack of cards. It would only take one wrong move to bring it all down.

Could I really do this? Who would hire me? What skills did I have, beyond knowing how to fire a gun? I thought of Pop's maddening dialogue about Gloam. How dangerous it was. How he'd lectured me the night before when I was on my way out with Chloe. How his concern had irritated me. My eyes burned with the memory. I would give anything now just to hear him lecture me one more time.

The back door opened, and Rich joined me, a pack of cigarettes in his hand.

"Rich. You worked so hard to quit."

I expected him to snap at my admonishment, but he nodded, meeting my gaze with glassy eyes. He tipped the pack towards me.

"You know I don't smoke." He shrugged, still holding the pack out to me. "Exceptional circumstances, and all that."

I pushed the pack back towards him, shaking my head.

He extracted a cigarette and lit it. The lighter in his hand was Pop's, one of the few items from our previous lives in Gloam. There'd been an engraving on it once but use and age had worn most of the details away. I remember running my fingers over it as a little girl, trying to imagine what the engraving had been. All that remained of it was the ghost of its previous face.

I fought the urge to snatch it from his hand and hold it against me like a talisman to ward off the grief. He inhaled deeply, then exhaled a sigh of satisfaction.

"What's your plan, Low?"

Funny you should ask.

I gripped the narrow railing of the deck and stared out into the dark, broken only by the few house lights in the neighbourhood. Several candles flickered in nearby windows. I thought of the extravagance of electricity in Gloam, the monied areas lit at every corner. The constant supply of power for those who could afford it.

"I'm going to Gloam."

Rich's hand stilled in mid-air, the smoke curling between us. "To do what?"

"To make coin, obviously."

"Doing what, Low?"

The word stuck in my throat, and then clung to my tongue. If I couldn't even say the word, then how was I actually going to play the role?

"Merc jobs."

He laughed, then stopped when I didn't join in. My face was as stiff as granite, frozen in this moment. I was on the precipice. I could jump or bring myself back from the edge, one toe at a time.

"Come on sis. You can't do that."

I lifted my chin, hoping the doubt I felt didn't show on my face. I pictured Pop as he'd been last night, his face a mix of pride and concern as he'd seen me out, the warmth of his arms as he'd hugged me goodbye. Another followed – a sheet covering his body, his bare feet exposed.

"Why? I know how to use a gun. And not just my Sauer. I can shoot just as well as you or Charlie."

"I'm not arguing that." He took another drag, tipping the ash over the side of the railing. "But Gloam isn't like here."

The clawing rage within me formed wings and caught flight. "The only thing you know about Gloam is what Pop has told us. He liked to fear-monger because he never wanted us to leave home."

The betrayal of saying those words about Pop when he'd barely been dead a day burned my traitorous tongue. I hadn't meant it.

Rich's gaze was steady when I finally dared look at him.

"You know that's not true, Low."

"Which part?" I snapped. I knew I was acting like a child, but my anger and grief were warring inside me, a witch's brew of poison.

"All of it. I have many more memories of our lives in Gloam. You were still little, and I think you've blocked out so much because of what happened." He sucked hard on his cigarette, the tip glowing scarlet in the dark. "I remember that night as if it were yesterday. That moment when Pop came home and told us you were missing. Told us about the note."

He tapped his ash into the ashtray he held, one of the few possessions we'd brought along from Gloam. It seemed odd, to leave so much behind, but bring this ugly, rarely used item.

"Ma went crazy. She actually hit him. He had a shiner for days." He smiled a little at the memory. "Gloam wasn't the same back then. The city *was* the same, sure, but *we* were always safe."

"Until we weren't."

"That was revenge. You know that. Being a cop in a place like Gloam doesn't win you many friends. But Pop had contacts. The kind that kept you safe, just by association."

I thought about that, and realised he was right. Pop had known a lot of people in Gloam, and yet, we'd had few visitors to our home. The people we'd seen the most of were Matt and Angie. I shuddered.

"Then what's the plan, Rich? How are we going to bury Pop? And how are we going to live? Pay our bills?"

My words were defiant, but deep down in that shameful part of me I kept hidden away, I wondered what I would do if he had, in fact, formed a plan of his own.

"Remember Keren?"

Rich gave a short laugh. It sounded sad, like it was filled with the knowledge that we would never hear another Keren story again, even though Pop had stopped telling us her stories years before.

"I think he made her a girl so she would feel like a kindred spirit. So you would feel like anything is possible – including the world being a fair place." Rich glanced at me, his eyes softening. "Pop always wanted to make the world a beautiful place for you. Even if it was only in the stories he told."

Rich stubbed out his cigarette, holding it between his fingers. I wanted to laugh. A grown man, still afraid of being yelled at by his mother for littering her backyard.

"You could tend bar, you know. Or waitress."

I sighed. The moment had passed.

I shook my head. "For minimal wage, sure. But we need the money, fast. Like, now. It'll take weeks to get up the kind of money we need for Pop. The longer they hold him, the more it's going to cost. We can't just leave him to rot."

"I could find more work. So could Charlie. We'll make do."

I snorted. "How? How are we going to make do?"

"Low, that place isn't for you. It's why Pop moved the whole family from Gloam. So no one could hurt us. So no one could hurt *you*, ever again."

Plink plink plink. I shook my head hard, trying to shake the phantom sounds from my head. My stomach clenched, forming a boulder of tension so taut it made me feel sick.

"Yeah? And look what happened. Right here, on our doorstep, outside of the city. What if it happens again?"

Rich looked stricken. As if this notion had never occurred to him.

I reached for his hand and gripped it. "I want to do this. I need to. You must see that."

His face was a mass of worry. "You have nothing to prove –"

"I have everything to prove!" I yelled, snatching my hand back as if the press of his skin against mine had burned me.

"I want a life of my own. I want a semblance of a life that doesn't involve The Sands, or any of you hovering over me like I'm still ten years old and still in danger of being snatched by some unknowable bogeyman. I'm a grown woman." I stepped back from him, wanting nothing more than space and to breathe my own air. "I'm not asking."

Rich's expression morphed into fury. "All we've ever tried to do is protect you. From yourself, a lot of the time. You can't just leave us. Pop is dead. Ma is shattered. Charlie is barely lucid. And I—"

"You what, Rich?" He said nothing. His hands were shaking, but my fury was mounting. "It's your job to take care of all that, remember? The oldest son, and all that? What do I know anyway? I'm simply the stupid little sister."

36

"Low." We both turned. Neither of us had heard Charlie's approach. He stood in the doorway, his features backlit by the kitchen light. He wore his favourite shirt – the faded green one which was too narrow for his shoulders and cut too short on his torso.

"Please don't leave us." He held onto the doorway with both hands, as if afraid he'd fall without the support. "We need to stick together. We need to be together now, through this. We've already lost Pop." His words were like hot needles against my skin. I looked away from him, his anguish and grief too much to bear.

"Guys, you know how much I love you all. How much I love Ma. How much I loved…" I couldn't finish. The finality of speaking the words of our loss aloud made it real. Undeniable. "We need the money. And fast. How else are we going to get the funds?"

"Pop wouldn't want this," Charlie said.

"Pop isn't here. I want him buried, or cremated, legally. Not by some hustler who promises families the proper rites and then dumps his body in the river."

I twisted my hands together, my knuckles growing white with the strain.

I turned back to face them, looking long and hard at each of them. They stared back, wordless.

I nodded, as if they'd given their assent. "That's settled then."

Chapter Five

I WOKE THE FOLLOWING morning from a restless sleep. My dreams had been haunted by the sound of gunshots ringing out, over and over again, and my fear as I screamed and screamed but couldn't move, my limbs frozen and my body unresponsive to my panic.

I got up and padded to the kitchen with bare feet, the rising sun already pouring into the kitchen, hot and blinding.

I flicked the kettle on, then turned at the sound of approaching footsteps. Ma stood in the doorway, her eyes dull with exhaustion, her skin looking paper-thin in the harsh light.

"Coffee?" I asked.

She nodded, slipping on to one of the high stools at the kitchen counter. There was only the sound of the kettle boiling, and the occasional melody of birdsong outside, but even though Ma said nothing, I knew she had something on her mind. I left her to think, knowing that when she was ready, she'd speak her mind.

I made the coffee and took a seat beside her. She finally turned to me. "I know you're planning to go to Gloam." Of course. My brothers had told her, even before I could choose the moment to do it myself. I waited for her to protest, for her to try to convince me to stay, and I braced myself for the onslaught.

"I won't try to stop you." I stayed silent and still, afraid that any word or movement on my part would somehow change her mind. "But you can't go without a plan. Pop and I..." She trailed off, closing her eyes and pressing her lips together. Despite her best efforts, a tear slipped from her right eye. She wiped it away savagely. "We don't have any contacts left in the city. We left too long ago, and we cut all ties because of.... Well, you know."

Yes, the unnameable thing we all took pains to work around. My conversation with Rich the night before had been an anomaly.

I took her hand. It was hot and clammy, but I held on anyway.

"You may be able to contact one person."

"You just said-"

"Listen." She clamped my hand hard, grinding my fingers together. I winced but said nothing.

"Your father's old partner in the city. Remember him? Carter Reach?"

I didn't want to admit I had only vague memories of him, and none at all of his involvement in my rescue.

"Pop seemed to lose touch with him when we left the city, but we've seen him on the news many times since then. He's a private investigator now."

I shook my head, confused. "Ma – why would I need a PI?"

"You'll need contacts, Low. He's the only one I can think of. Maybe he can help you find work, put you in touch with the right people."

"How will I contact him?"

"You'll need to ask around. I don't have his details, but I know you'll figure out a way to find him." She looked at me for a long time, communicating something she didn't have the words for.

I hugged her tightly, holding her until she gave a small laugh and gently pushed me away. "Go love. Before your brothers wake."

***

My conversation with Ma gave me the courage to leave. I quietly lifted the bag I'd packed with a few measly belongings – three changes of clothes, shoes, and some other essentials. My Sauer was right at the bottom, wrapped in an old pair of jeans, and several clips of ammunition had been shoved into multiple pairs of socks. I knew it was ridiculous to hide the gun, especially because where I was going, guns were as common as trashcans, but it still felt like something I needed to keep hidden. I hadn't touched it for months because I'd had no use for it. I'd been handling weapons since I was old enough to walk. I thought of it there, of the moment Pop had given it to me, of Ma's disapproval, and Pop's insistence that one day I would need it. I was thirteen years old when my father gave me that Sauer, not long after we'd arrived in The Sands. Ma had scowled at him, saying I was too young, but when he pressed it into my hand, he held my gaze in a way that I knew what he was giving me mattered. It wasn't the gun itself; it was what it represented to Pop – a means of defence against the certain violence of the world.

The tears came and I stood there, watching my murky room blur and shift, feeling like the ground beneath me would never again be stable, or trusted. My chest tightened, and I forced myself to breathe, to focus only on my breath as it entered and left my body. Ma was there then, wrapping me in her arms, holding me against her. A memory surfaced; one which had faded to the recesses of my mind. Her holding me just like this when Pop had come home with me. Her arms around me the anchor I'd needed to keep myself together. I gave her one last squeeze and left my room, willing myself not to look back.

I slipped outside and into my car, turning the key. Click. *Shit.* I tried again, willing the car to start, and when it didn't I thumped the dashboard, the tears coming again. I sat in the quiet of the car, cursing and crying. I popped the hood open and got out of the car. I stood next to it for a long moment, knowing it was hopeless. What did I know about cars? There was no one who could drive me. Chloe would only be discharged today. Walking would take me hours. I considered the possibility of hitchhiking, and then pictured being picked up by a madman, my body tossed from their car and left to rot in the sun.

"Car trouble?"

Rich stood in the doorway, arms crossed, watching me. *Ah fuck.*

"Statement of the obvious."

"Need some help?"

I eyed him suspiciously, unsure of whether he meant it or was having me on.

He sighed and came down the stairs, his feet bare and his ragged white shirt tinged a faint shade of yellow.

"Move," he said shortly, and I shifted out of his way, watching him bend over the hood, his hands working quickly.

"Battery's dead."

He glanced up at me. "Check if we've got any aspirin in the house."

"What?"

"Just do it. I'll need about a dozen. And a cup of water."

I came back with the items and watched him dissolve the tablets in the water and carefully pour it into what I could only assume was the troublesome battery.

He straightened. "Try again." I slipped behind the wheel and turned the key again, expecting nothing more than the dreaded click, but instead the car roared to life, and I stared wide-eyed at Rich.

Rich came to the window, leaning in. "Trick Pop taught me. Leave it running." He motioned for me to get out, and when I did, he caught me in a bearhug, holding me so tightly to him that the air left my lungs with an audible *woosh.* I was washed in the smell of him, and the scent made me homesick, even though I was yet to leave.

"Low, do you really have to do this? We could find another way." I sighed. How many times could I convince not only others, but myself, that I was doing the right thing? "Anything could go wrong. You've never lived away from home. What if you need us?"

I wanted to laugh, if only to lighten the moment. But I found I couldn't. That the effort of it lodged in my throat and kept me silent.

He grabbed my arms then, clutching them in a way that forced me to look at him, to really take him in. His eyes looked sunken, the circles beneath them more pronounced than ever before. More than the look on his face, it was the panicked quality in the tightness of his grip which made me want to squirm away, which made me irrationally angry.

"Let go, Rich." I tried to yank my arms from the prison of his fingers but he clamped down harder, and I kicked at his shin instinctively and without forethought. He yelped and finally released me.

"What the fuck Low?" he yelled.

"Stop trying to scare me! Stop trying to make me stay. This is hard for me already. Why help me with the car if you're just going to stand there and try to stop me from leaving?" I was panting with rage.

I couldn't see his face as he bent over, rubbing at the spot on his shin where I'd kicked him. "We can't lose you, too. Ma would never come back from that. And neither would I."

My lungs felt constricted, making it painful to breathe. Was I making a mistake? Was I abandoning my family when they needed me the most?

Rich finally straightened, and to my shock, he was crying. He pulled me to him, my face against his chest.

"I don't want you to go, but I know you're going to, anyway. Be careful. We'll be here when you come back." He stepped away and was gone before I could thank him.

I watched him go, wincing as the screen door slammed behind him.

I climbed back into my car and sat for a moment longer. Now that I had Rich's and Ma's blessing to go, I found myself unwilling. The sound of birdsong through my open window was so familiar, a comfort of home. The sound which had woken me every morning of my life here. The grief came at me and hit with a force that felt physical. My breath left my body with a gasp, and I sat there, trying to catch my next breath and found it impossible, as if the air had turned to clay. My throat was a fist, and I only became aware of my tears when they ran down my face, wet and hot.

I swallowed and finally managed a small, shallow inhale, my hands clenching the steering wheel until my fingers ached, and when my tears had dried and I could hear the outside world again, instead of just the ringing in my ears, I pulled at my seatbelt and buckled myself in. I glanced one final time behind me, wanting to imprint the sight of my home in my mind. It seemed ridiculous that this short departure would seem so permanent, but Rich was right – I'd never been away from home since we'd left the city.

Moving mechanically, I put the car into gear, telling myself that this wouldn't be the last time I saw my home, and not knowing if that was true.

I drove, and within half an hour, the scenery had changed from dirt roads and sparse housing to badly tarred highways and the fading dunes of The Sands. Soon enough, the landfills which edged Gloam appeared, the debris piled so high it looked like rolling hills. Trash hills.

I arrived in Gloam around midday. The sun beat down relentlessly, my car's aircon barely able to keep up. The research that I'd done on apartments had yielded pitiful results. The ones I could afford on the little money I'd taken were no more than rat-infested holes with trash lining the stairs and the pavements outside. The ones that looked only slightly better (less trash and rats, and better graffiti) were asking for the kind of money that required a job. And the only plan I had for that, was a name.

Chapter Six

Markham

HE SAT ON THE lumpy couch in the reception area, waiting. The skin of his arm itched where it rested against the rough fabric, and he shifted, watching the blonde receptionist talk on the phone, her voice high and grating. She met his gaze, briefly, and smiled, displaying even white teeth, her hand moving to smooth her hair.

He stood, registering her surprise. If he left now, he wouldn't have to go through with this.

A voice spoke behind him. "Markham. Won't you come in?" He turned to face Dr Black, wondering if the indignity of running now outweighed the torture that awaited him in her pleasant, sun-drenched office.

She motioned behind her to the artificially lit corridor. Markham willed himself to move but found that the action of rising from his seat seemed impossible, as if the couch had turned to mud and he was mired in it.

Dr Black waited, her face impassive, showing no surprise at his hesitation. Did he do this every time? He couldn't remember. His sessions often faded into the black of forgotten memories as soon as he stepped out of the building, buried deep beneath the other things he couldn't look in the eye. He wanted to run, and his limbs burned with the need, the first tingle of panic inching up his spine.

"Markham?" How he hated that name. The sound of its syllables always brought a feeling of entrapment, of the dread at what followed every time it was spoken.

When he finally looked at her, she smiled, gesturing in the direction of her office. "Shall we?"

Markham forced his body into motion, rising from the couch and following Dr Black down the short passage to her open door, closing it behind them as he stepped inside.

He sank into his usual seat while she perched on her armchair, her hands resting neatly on her knees, her plaid skirt ridiculously girlish.

She waited, her gaze steady on him. His tongue felt thick in his mouth, as if it were expanding with every second of silence that passed between them.

He rose without realising he'd given his body the command to move, and strode for the door, his hand on the door handle before Dr Black had a chance to react.

"Markham." The way she said his name. Calmly, without even a hint of anger or irritation. He paused. The handle felt slick in his hand, the wood impossibly impenetrable.

"Why are you here today?" She asked his back.

All he wanted was to be out of this office, out in the welcoming smog and chaos of the city, but that voice inside him, the one who wanted him to *Be Better,* like some damned marketing slogan, made his feet move back to his chair.

He said the first thing that came to mind, surprising them both. "My stepfather wasn't always this way."

Dr Black nodded, her attention fixed on him. She never took notes. It was unnerving, being beneath her gaze for fifty minutes, her unwavering attention feeling like a spotlight over him.

"The first time my mother brought him home to meet me, he gave me a soccer ball."

"So he knew you liked soccer?"

He laughed. "I never played. Who was going to kick a ball around with me? Her?"

"Did it make you feel unseen?"

"What?"

Dr Black smiled patiently, as if waiting for him to arrive at the same conclusion she'd already drawn. "The fact that your mother didn't know you didn't play soccer?"

"Oh, she knew."

He stopped, unsure where he was going with this. "But Matt played with me that day. He spent more time with me than her, and he didn't care that I missed the ball more often than not. It was the first time I ever felt like I had a father."

He shifted, suddenly badly wanting just one of the cigarettes from the box he kept hidden in the cubbyhole of his car. It was another habit he hadn't been able to entirely kick.

"Then they got married, and everything changed. They got into a fight at the wedding. My mother danced with a friend of Matt's, and he didn't like that. They went into a room together, Matt dragging her there, and when they came out...she had a black eye."

Dr Black's expression didn't change, and she betrayed no emotion. Maybe this was why he'd chosen her out of all the therapists he'd seen since he'd become an adult. Because she seemed both intensely focused and professionally disinterested, giving him just enough space to say the things he thought he'd locked away.

Harlow

Even after looking up the address of the nearest police station and following the directions, I'd now circled the block three times without finding it. Frustrated, I settled for pulling into the nearest available parking, which earned me several blaring of horns as I pulled out of traffic without warning. I didn't have an address for Carter's home or office, or know if he even operated out of one, and so, I stood where I'd finally managed to park my car, amid towering skyscrapers and a street already teeming with people. Where the hell was I to start looking for him? I studied the buildings around me, staring along the street, hoping by some miracle I'd happened upon a street Chloe and I had walked just two days ago, desperately searching for a beacon of familiarity.

A cop car drove past, and I watched until it turned a corner a block up. I opened the boot of my car and rifled through my bag for my gun, slipping it into the waistband of my jeans, beneath my light leather jacket. A bit of insurance. Just in case. I moved in the same direction as the cop car, making slow progress as I weaved between people. A beggar sat on the corner where the cop car had turned, his dirty palms upturned. He stared up at me with blank eyes, his face haggard. I turned away, swept up with the momentum of the crowd.

As I came around the corner, I spotted a small, faded sign just ahead. Black, with white lettering, faded and peeling from the heat of the sun. *Police*, it announced. Finally. No wonder I'd kept missing it – it was barely visible even when I stood almost right outside the entrance door. I stepped through, surveying the near-empty room. A lone cop sat at a long and scarred desk, slumped over his phone.

"Excuse me?" He looked up, regarded me with hostility. His thumbs hovered over his phone's keyboard, and he barely looked at me when he spoke.

"What?"

"I'm looking for Carter Reach."

The cop snorted. "He hasn't worked for the force for some time. He's gone *private.*" His emphasis on *private* made it sound like a dirty word. The gleam in his eyes as he regarded me made me feel unclean.

"I know. I was hoping you would know where I could find him?"

The cop eyed me. "I look like his secretary to you?"

His raised voice reached several more cops sitting at their desks behind him, despite the panel of glass between us. They looked up from their work to stare, their gazes penetrating me until I felt stripped, naked and vulnerable. I fought the urge to turn on my heel, find my car, and drive back to The Sands. What the hell was I doing here?

I placed my hands on the surly cop's desk, palms down, and leaned in until only he could hear me. "I need to find PI Reach. So the way I see it, you can help me now, or you can sit there and have me to look at for the rest of the day, because I'm not leaving until you tell me what I need to know."

I looked around for a seat, and when I found none, I leaned against the wall behind me, crossing my arms over my chest and getting comfortable.

The cop glared at me, but when I refused to wilt under his fury, he stood abruptly. "I could just have you thrown out. That's option three."

My palms were sweating. I clenched my fingers together and willed myself to calm.

"If you were going to do that, you would've done it already."

He sighed, flopping back down into his chair. "Why you're hellbent on irritating me, I don't know. If I give you the information you want, you'll leave?"

I placed the palm of my hand against my heart. "Scout's honour."

"Fine." He yanked his top drawer open and rummaged in it, coming up with a business card. He held it out, but as I moved to take it, he withdrew his hand. "One thing, before you go. Reach isn't someone who takes kindly to strangers banging on his door." His gaze slid over me again, taking his time. When his eyes met mine again, he raised his eyebrows suggestively. "I, on the other hand, am known to be very helpful when it comes to lovely young ladies."

I leaned forward, dropping my right shoulder ever so slightly, making my loose t-shirt gape open just enough to give him an eyeful of my cleavage. His grip on the business card slackened as he took in the sight. I snatched it from his fingers, tucking it into the pocket of my jeans. "Yeah, I'll keep that in mind."

I stepped outside again, glad to be out from under the cop's gaze. I pulled out my phone, brought up my map app, and input the address, waiting for the results. The heat of the sun on my face was relentless. It rose from the pavements and the asphalt, the smell of exhaust fumes full in my nose. People surged around me, like water moving around a rock, and I found myself longing for the open spaces of The Sands, for its clear air, for the family I'd left there.

Directions to the address the cop had given me appeared on my screen. I'd have to drive. It was twenty-five minutes away, according to the map. I would have to drive deeper into the city, navigating what looked like a massive network of highway, back roads, and narrow streets. I retraced my steps back to my car, and sat there for a long moment, the engine running and the aircon blasting. I could turn around now. I could go home. I'd be welcomed with open arms. *And Pop? What about him?* I thought of Chloe. She'd be home by now, back at The Sands. Was she with Josiah and Rachel? Or had she gone home to Brad? I clutched my phone a little harder, the urge to call her so strong my fingers had already dialled the first three digits of her number before I was able to still them.

Instead, I put my phone in one of the car's cup holders. I pulled out into the traffic, following the robotic voice as it directed me deeper into the heart of the city.

***

I stood outside the door, staring at it in confusion. I looked down at the address on the business card I held. This couldn't be it. It was a nondescript brown door. There was no sign hanging above it; nothing at all to indicate there was a business operating beyond it.

I took the one step leading up to the door and knocked gently. When there was no answer, I knocked more forcefully. Footsteps sounded from the other side, before the door was wrenched open, and a man stood in the doorway, glaring at me. "What?" he snapped.

"Carter Reach? PI Reach?"

He gave me a long once-over before answering. "Yes."

He was enormous. His arms were the size of my thighs, and his shaven head gleamed in the sunlight, as if he had shined it just that morning. His thick eyebrows shaded large, dark eyes, and the long reach of his eyelashes gave his otherwise masculine face an edge of femininity that was as unsettling as if he'd been wearing lipstick.

My assessment must've gone on too long for his liking because he stepped back and made as if to close the door, but I took advantage of the small gap he'd given me and I stepped into what I assumed was his office, forcing him back into its interior.

We now stood uncomfortably close together in the confines of a small dusty room that wasn't much bigger than a closet. It looked all the smaller for the size of the crammed furniture, which took up so much space it was as if every molecule of air had been forced out, making it hard to breathe.

Carter took another step back and one step to his left, which took him around to the chair, and with difficulty, he extracted it from beneath the desk and sat heavily, still glaring at me with mute hostility.

"What do you want?"

"Are you always this rude to potential clients?"

That gave him pause, and for a moment the silence hung between us.

"Sit."

He motioned to a chair I hadn't seen upon entry, because it was heaped with a mound of papers and notebooks. I reached to move them, but Carter beat me to it and gathered them with one sweep of his meaty hands, dumping them on the already overcrowded desk.

"Coffee?" he asked.

I stared at him. He smiled humourlessly. "Do you want some or not?"

I nodded, clamping my hands together in my lap. I wasn't sure what I had expected, but it hadn't been this.

He moved around the cramped space with surprising dexterity and grace, and within minutes a steaming cup of coffee was placed in front of me, with no offer of milk or sugar. No matter. Probably not something easily procured in this place, anyway.

I peered into my cup. "The real stuff?" He sank into the chair opposite me. "What do you think?"

I took a tentative sip and tried not to grimace. Definitely not the genuine article.

He looked at me expectantly.

I pushed some of the towering paperwork on his desk aside to make room for my mug, setting it down carefully. I sat in the chair. It didn't feel stable enough to hold my weight. I planted my feet on the floor, just in case. "I need your help."

"Upfront fee is 500 coin. After that, I work on an hourly basis, at 250 coin an hour."

"What?"

He looked at me, faintly amused. "You don't think I work for free, do you?"

"Well no, but—" I paused to breathe. "You knew my parents. Frank and Lena."

He stared at me. His eyes were moving over my face in a way that felt calculating, as if he were trying to uncover something beyond what the naked eye could see. I grew uncomfortable beneath his scrutiny, unable to endure the silence one second longer.

"Novac. Frank and Lena Novac."

"You're Harlow." Out of all the things I'd expected him to say, this hadn't been it. It hadn't even occurred to me that he might recognise me. I tried to recall ever meeting him, but even though Ma had said he'd been there when Pop had rescued me from Matt, I couldn't recall a single detail between being taken from Matt's house and arriving home.

"Yes. You know me?"

He stared at me as if I'd asked him a particularly complicated question, one that needed careful consideration.

"I mean I know you were there when... when I was rescued, but—" I couldn't go on. The growing fury on his face was so intense I rose and took a step back, my chair bumping into a pile of precariously stacked files behind me. They crashed to the floor. Carter still said nothing, and not being able to bear it a second longer, I started babbling.

"I need help finding mercenary work. You're the only contact in Gloam my mother could give me."

"There's good reason for that."

"What? What do you mean?"

"I can't help you."

He motioned to the door, as if the subject were closed. As if we'd naturally concluded our conversation and I was overstaying my welcome.

"Is this about money? Because I can pay you, if you help me find work."

He stiffened, rising slowly, every movement deliberate.

"Money?"

"Do you want to be paid to help me? I understand I shouldn't just assume that your ties with my family automatically means–"

Carter rose. "Frank and I haven't spoken since the day you were returned home. And now you just turn up here, and ask for my help?"

"Look, I understand it's unexpected and out of the blue, but what exactly is the problem?"

His mouth twisted. He seemed to be struggling for control. "You don't remember me?"

Was that what this was about? That didn't make sense.

"I know you were there. That you helped. But I can't recall a lot of what happened over that time. And I can't recall you, at all."

Confusion was replacing his anger, and it occurred to me that neither of us really knew what the other was talking about.

I stared down at my hands. What else would I do here, if not mercenary work? Be a barmaid, or even worse, a dancer, hauling my body at all hours up and down a greasy pole for the pleasure of strange men? How long before I could afford to put Pop in the ground, on those salaries? Weeks? Months? Nausea clawed my throat, and I stared at a dark stain on the wall behind Carter's desk, forcing air into my lungs.

"My father is dead. My family doesn't have any money to bury or cremate him. I need to find work, fast, and I'm willing to do whatever jobs you could help me find."

Carter had gone deathly still. So much so, that I had to stop myself from reaching out to touch him, just to see if he was still breathing.

"Frank is dead?" He seemed to say this more to himself than me, as if he'd forgotten I was there at all.

Carter sank back into his chair, the anger going out of him without warning.

"That's why I'm here. I need money. You're the only contact we still have in Gloam." I knew I was repeating myself, but my words hadn't penetrated at all. He seemed dazed, uncomprehending.

"What happened?"

"He was murdered. It may have been someone from a gang. The Natives. Or so the cops say." I said all of this on a single rush of air, just wanting to get it out, as if letting the words linger in my mouth would leave an aftertaste on my tongue.

"Ah shit." Carter ran a massive palm over his head. "I'm sorry." He looked as if he meant it, and I wondered why they'd lost touch. Was it to cut all ties from our previous life?

"Will you help me?"

"No. I'm sorry for your loss, but I can't involve myself in this." He rose and crossed to the door, wrenching it open, the door squealing in protest against the violence of the gesture. "You need to go. Now."

"I already said I'd pay you—"

"This isn't about money!" he roared. "Do you know what it's like thinking you know someone, and then it turns out everything you believed about them was wrong? To trust someone, and realise that they've lied to you about everything that mattered?"

"I don't understand. What do you mean?"

"Your father was a corrupt cop. He did business with the Natives. Cut deals with them. Destroyed evidence in cases against them. Did their bidding. That scumbag who kidnapped you? He was their leader. When Frank finally found his conscience, they took you. And helping him get you back cost me my place on the force."

"You lie." I breathed the words, unable to draw enough air to scream them. My thoughts swooped and circled around his accusation, and in the medley of it all, two words stood out – *the Natives*.

Instead of angering, he softened. "He wasn't who you believed him to be. I wish I could help. I would if I could, but I can't forget that."

He let go of the door handle and reached over his desk, pulling out a drawer and rummaging around. When he withdrew his hand, he had a fistful of coin, which he tried to hand to me. When I refused to accept it, he forced my fingers open and then closed. "Take it. It isn't much, but it should get you home again. You should go be with your family."

I leaned close so he wouldn't miss one word of my next sentence. "If you think this is the last you're going to see of me then you better etch every detail of my face in your memory, because you're going to need to remember me when I come back with a fistful of your fucking coin!"

I'd shouted the last word straight into this face, and the anger that flared there for just a moment was enough. I turned and strode out of his office, his words of protest cut off as I slammed his door behind me.

Chapter Seven

Markham

HE STOOD OUTSIDE THE house. How was it that it looked exactly the same? She hadn't changed the curtains in years and that same blue front door, the paint cracked and peeling. The same paved walkway. There used to be flower beds flanking each side of the paving, and the beds had bloomed with pansies and geraniums, their bright faces turned upwards as if in welcome. They were empty now, the ground muddy and churned, as if turned recently, in preparation for new planting. His pulse throbbed. His palms were slick. Walk. It's just a few steps to the door. Walk! He made his feet move. One step. Two. Just a few more. And then he was in front of it, the dusty white doorbell eyeing him ominously. The key was in his pocket, rusted with disuse, but how could he use it? He pressed the doorbell instead and waited for its high chime, but it was dead. He raised his fist to knock. His hand was shaking. He rapped hard. Black dots moved in his field of vision, and he released the breath he'd been holding in a harsh exhale. Footsteps.

He waited, making his breath slow and ease, the way Dr Black had taught him. Inhale. Hold. Exhale. Release. The footsteps slowed on the other side of the door and then there was silence. Was she looking at him through the peephole?

"What do you want?" Her voice sounded gravelly, as if she'd just woken up, even though it was early afternoon. He imagined her smell – a mix of sweat and booze, the whisky she favoured seeping from her pores in an invisible mist.

"Mom, it's me."

"I know it's you, Mark. Do you think I wouldn't recognise my own son? I'm not senile just yet."

She opened the door a crack, keeping the doorknob within her grasp.

"What is it?"

No tearful greeting. No words of welcome. Not even an inkling of surprise.

The years that had passed clung to her face without mercy. Her skin sagged in great pouches of misplaced gravity, her pallor ashen and grey. Her once ocean-blue eyes had dulled to a rheumy grey, and her hair had lost every strand of the strawberry blonde of her youth. A whiff of stale cigarette smoke and body odour came off her, and he forced his face into what he hoped was an expression of neutrality.

"Can I come in?" he asked.

She regarded him for a long moment and then looked over her shoulder stiffly, seeming to quiet and listen.

"Matt is here."

Matt. Still here, after all this time. A fixture in his mother's life as he himself had never been.

"Great. I'm sure we can have a great family reunion now that we're all here, huh Ma? Yeah yeah yeah – a family reunion after all this time!" His body was flushed with heat, his blood at a high boil within his veins.

As if feeling the intensity coming off him, she took a step back, eyeing him warily. And then, as if choosing to ignore his anger, she opened the door wider, and smiled. "Matt will be pleased to see you. It's been so long."

Of course. What else had he expected from her? A confession? A breakdown? An apology? No. She could no more see her part in everything that had happened than she could grow wings and fly. She was as much a victim as he was, if not more so, although, if asked, she would not paint herself that way.

Footsteps sounded behind her, and before he could step over the threshold and into his childhood home, Matt appeared at her shoulder, looking at him through old and bleary eyes. Matt's pallor was shockingly pale, and the bruises underneath his eyes were so dark he looked like he'd been in a bar fight just the night before. His cheeks were sunken, and the scruff of a beard which had been left untended for several days added years to his face.

He considered Markham for a long moment, silent and hostile, and then, comprehension filled his face. Astonishingly, he held out a hand, and Markham was so taken aback that at first he couldn't understand what Matt wanted, and then, breaking from his paralysis, he grudgingly took Matt's hand and shook it. *A fist thudding into flesh. Her scream and breaking glass. The wail of a police siren far off, its warble as inconsequential as the song of a bird.*

"Markham! I didn't know you were coming today. Angie didn't mention anything about visitors." Visitors. Could you be a visitor in your own home? A home that Markham himself had lived in long before Matt had ever arrived, a home that Matt had joined, and not the other way around. *Prick.*

Matt's new and jovial attitude towards Markham was profoundly unsettling, but even more unsettling was the way he referred to Markham's mother, as if their marriage had never been one of extreme violence and fear, as if their being together, standing on the step of his childhood, was a logical conclusion to a sequence of happy events leading to just this moment.

Matt's hand settled on Angie's shoulder and drew her back, allowing Markham the room to step across the threshold. Now that he was here, he realised he'd stupidly expected to find Angie alone. A waft came at him through the open door, as if the house had exhaled, and Markham breathed in that old scent which held so many bad memories – booze, onions and cigarette smoke.

"Come on in, kid. We just made a pot of coffee – how about a cup?" *Solicitous bastard. Who did he think he was fooling?*

Markham looked at his mother's face, tight and pinched, her eyes searching his, filled with that familiar plea. He fought against the urge to hit her, a compulsion shocking in both its suggestion and strength. Hit her and then him, and then stand over their sprawled bodies and eject all the hate and fear he'd felt as a small, helpless kid, as if he could permanently eradicate all the violence that moved in him like another being, as if by righting the wrong he'd had done to him, he could emerge a different person, newly minted and unblemished. He caught himself. He mustn't blame her. It wasn't her fault.

All men are beasts, love, they can't help themselves. Her voice from long ago, as she'd stroked his face, her free hand holding an icepack against his cheek.

"Well?" Matt was staring at him with ill-concealed impatience, and his mother's eyes were still locked on him, entreating him to make a decision, to stop lingering on the step. He moved through the doorway, fighting the instinct to turn and run, inhaling the scent of the house as if he had never left.

***

The house looked the same inside. The one he remembered from his childhood – cream walls, which always looked like they needed to be cleaned, the old rug beneath the dining room table, the pots and pans which hung above the oven. Matt walked ahead of him, as if trying to show him around his own home, while his mother puttered in the kitchen. She took down three mugs, although he couldn't remember having accepted the offer of coffee in the first place.

"So what brings you here, Mark?"

Matt leaned against the kitchen counter, drawing Markham's eyes to it. It was the same one Matt had slammed Angie against, knocking her out cold. She'd been hospitalised for three days with a concussion after that particular incident.

"How long do you think it's been, Matt?" Markham asked.

Matt looked confused for a moment, then shrugged. "How would I know?"

"The last time you saw me was on my eighteenth birthday. The day I became a legitimate adult. Do you remember what you gave me?"

Matt had straightened now, his shoulders tensing. Angie had paused with a teaspoon in her hand, mid-stir.

"No recollection, huh? This." Markham pointed to a small scar just below his right eye. "You came after me with a blade. You also gave me a blue eye, but fortunately bruises fade, don't they? And wounds close."

"Same old Mark," Matt smirked. "Always causing trouble. And here I thought you were just dropping by for a nice visit, coming to say hello to your old lady and old man."

"My old man? My father is dead. He was a drunk, same as you. My mother is incapable of choosing any other kind of man, and men like you attract women like my mother. Weak, pliable, easily manipulated. You like your women malleable, don't you? So you can be the man of the house, the one who calls all the shots?"

Matt was closing the distance between them. He was still muscled, and quick, but Markham was no longer a frightened child, or a gangly teenager. He stood his ground, waiting for Matt to swing, to rush at him, but Matt stopped but a stride away, looking at Markham with contempt. He laughed, the sound reverberating off the walls. "You've grown some balls, I'll give you that. Sit down. Have your coffee."

Markham waited a beat longer, mistrustful of Matt attempting to get in a surprise blow, but he took a seat at the kitchen table and motioned for Markham and Angie to do the same.

His mother carried two mugs to them, placing one in front of Markham and the other in front of Matt, slopping coffee over the rims. Matt took her hand, squeezing it. She flinched just a little, only relaxing when Matt smiled up at her without a hint of malice. She then retrieved her own and sat next to Matt, the two of them facing Markham across the table.

In every instance of imagining how this moment would unfold, this scene of domesticity was the last thing Markham had expected. He sipped his coffee and studied his mother's face, searching for the bruises, cuts and scrapes that she'd sported all through his childhood. There was nothing. Could things have changed? The way Angie had just flinched at Matt's touch, that was more in line with what he remembered. But there had also seldom been a time when Angie's body hadn't been marked in some way by Matt's random violence.

Sensing his scrutiny, and perhaps wanting to distract him from it, Angie spoke. "Why are you here, Mark?"

Markham considered his answers. Why was he here? What had he hoped to find? Domestic bliss? The answers to his childhood? Why he'd turned out this way?

"I thought it was time." Time for what exactly, he himself wasn't sure. To bury the hatchet? He took a scalding gulp of coffee to disguise his snort.

"Where are you living now, anyhow?" Angie asked.

"The city."

"As in, Gloam?" Matt asked, a smirk growing on his face.

Markham knew he shouldn't rise to the bait. It was a deeply entrenched habit.

"What?" He snapped.

"Ah nothing. I just can't imagine you out there, in Gloam. You're not exactly the type, are you?"

The old anger stirred, awakening a fire in his belly. It spread its fingers, bringing heat to every part of his body. Sweat formed at his hairline and beneath his arms. His palms became slick.

He fought to keep his voice even. "What's that supposed to mean?"

"Ah come on Mark. You were this little scaredy cat as a kid and then this wimpy, stringy teenager who shat his pants every time I said boo to him."

He glanced at his mother. Her hands were tight around her mug, holding onto it as if it were the only thing keeping her grounded. She stared hard into its contents, refusing to look up, avoiding looking at him. Her usual reluctance to participate. She'd never seemed to realise that her very presence here, her very refusal to say anything, or intervene, made her a participant just as much as him or Matt.

Matt had risen from his seat, towering over them. "Don't you look at her! Look at me. Don't look at her for help." He snorted and shook his head with disgust. "Still a Mama's boy. Always was, always will be."

Markham found himself on his feet, although he couldn't remember rising. A terrible heat exploded within him, and the room swam in front of his eyes. He could vaguely hear his mother's voice, placating and then pleading, but the words made no sense to him. Maybe this was why he'd come. Not to check on Angie, because he had known Matt would still be here. His mother was incapable of leaving him. Why shouldn't he do it? He could hang all his childhood problems on Matt, because blaming his mother was like taking a match to his own skin.

He lunged across the table, grabbing the front of Matt's shirt, bunching it in his fist. He pulled hard, and caught by surprise, Matt fell forward. Markham released him and Matt fell against the table, his hands shooting out just in time to break his fall. Matt's mug had fallen over, spilling coffee over the table and splattering the floor with drops of brown liquid, the mug rolling ominously close to the edge and then falling, shattering into shards of ceramic.

Angie rose without a word, as if the broken mug had been caused by an accidental sweep of the arm, a careless swipe of the hand. She retrieved a cloth from the sink, wetting it and lowering herself to her knees to wipe up the spill.

Markham's breath felt caught in his throat. He couldn't get enough air. There wasn't enough of it in the room. Black dots swirled in front of his eyes, and beyond them, he could still make out Matt, straightening and gathering himself, and he knew there was no going back from this, no backing down, no more apologies or trying to smooth things over. He was tired. So tired. The other voice crowded his mind, gibbering and then building to a crescendo of screaming, his skull filling with the noise until he was convinced his brain would burst like an overripe peach.

Matt rushed around the table at Markham, adding his voice to those of the others. Markham drew back his fist and hit him, connecting with Matt's nose, feeling the bone give beneath his knuckles, the satisfying crunch and the blood which followed. Angie was screaming now, but her voice was muted and far away, and seemed of little consequence.

Matt stumbled back, both hands trying to stem the flow of blood from his nose, outrage stamped on his face. He drew his hands away from his face, staring at the blood on his palms and trickling between his fingers. The sight of it seemed to enrage him further, and he charged at Markham, head down and arms reaching. Markham neatly sidestepped him, sticking a foot out, and sent Matt sprawling to the floor, his arms and legs flailing comically, his shout of pain and surprise making a giggle rise in Markham's throat. The voices gibbered, loud and gleeful, and Markham felt all the memories in this place, at the hands of this man, come together in one clear, cohesive thought.

He stepped over Matt's body, his legs on either side of Matt's torso, and sat on the small of his back with all the full force of his weight, straddling him. He locked his hands around Matt's throat, squeezing.

Pain flared across the length of his shoulders and he released Matt, his hands opening of their own volition. He turned to find his mother standing over him, one of her heavier pans in her hands, and only then could he hear her screams again. "Get off him! Get off!"

It took Markham a second to realise she was screaming at him. At him. Not at Matt. Nothing had changed. All the years of him beating her, for burned food or spilled milk or other imagined slights, and she still protected Matt. Still treated Markham like he was the problem. Like he was the one who caused it all – the drama, the violence, the beatings. He pushed her away without much effort, but his momentary lapse of concentration had given Matt the moment he needed. He bucked violently beneath Markham and managed to unseat him. He fell sideways and saw the blow coming too late.

He turned his face, and Markham's fist glanced off his cheekbone, leaving a trail of fire along his cheek. Matt tried to pin him to the ground, but Markham managed to throw him off and stagger to his feet. Small frantic hands encircled his arms, and there his mother was again, her face wet with tears, her screams diminished to whimpers. Markham heard Matt behind him and swung around to face him. Matt threw himself at Markham but he stepped out of the way just in time, and Angie, standing right behind him, took the full blow of Matt's weight. The two of them crashed against the kitchen table, Angie's head slamming into the wooden surface. Her body went boneless, and she slid to the floor, her head connecting with the floor with a dull thud. Markham rushed to her and knelt beside her, his hands slipping in the blood that was rapidly pooling around her head.

"Mom?" He touched her face, leaving behind a smear of blood on her cheek. Her skin was warm, her eyes wide and staring. "Mom?" He closed his hands around her arms, shaking her gently. "Hey." He shook her harder, her body flopping like a fish out of water. "Wake up. Mom. Mom. Wake up!" He screamed those last words, and felt like that little boy again, standing over his mother's prone form, yelling at her to wake up, to get up. How every time he'd been convinced this was the time she wouldn't rise, because she couldn't.

Matt had lowered himself to his knees on Angie's other side, taking her head into his lap and cradling it. He began to howl, loud and long, the sound so guttural that it seemed impossible any human could make that kind of noise.

"Shut up,' Markham muttered, then shouted. "Shut up!"

The voices rose in Markham's head, whispering and muttering, their voices rising into a single, screaming chorus.

Markham threw himself at Matt over Angie's body, his hands locking around Matt's throat. The force of his weight knocked Matt over and he sprawled on his back. Markham locked Matt's torso between his knees and squeezed harder. Matt's feet kicked out behind him, slipping in the blood, and he gurgled, his hands scrabbling at Markham's hands, his eyes bulging grotesquely.

"This is what you deserve. You killed her. You killed her! I always knew you would. You would. And you did. You did."

Harder. His thumbs dug into the vulnerable spot between Matt's collarbones, pressing until he was convinced his thumbs would go straight through Matt's throat and to the other side of his spine. Matt stopped struggling, his feet going still, his hands dropping to the floor. But still Markham squeezed. He had to be sure. He had to make sure the bastard was dead, dead for sure this time, and when he was finally satisfied that Matt was gone, the voices went silent, and the only sound in the room was the ticking of the kitchen clock.

Chapter Eight

Harlow

I wandered the street in a fog of despair. I still wasn't used to the labyrinth of streets, how they crisscrossed and double-backed. Some streets in different parts of the city had the same names, and businesses which seemed innocuous on the outside could be anything on the inside – black market workshops, sex bars, or weapon stores.

The only familiar thing in this city was the heat, but even the quality of it was different somehow. Heavy, and laced with pollutants from the passing cars and bikes, it seemed to coat my skin, weighing me down and sinking my shoes into the gluey surface of the asphalt. I had no idea where I was, but it didn't matter, because where was I going to go? I had nowhere to stay. My only thought had been to get here, to enlist Carter's help, and with that done, everything else would somehow fall into place. Several people brushed against me as they passed, some forcefully enough to push me back, but no one apologised or looked me in the eye. I wanted to get off the street, out of the heat that felt familiar and foreign at the same time, and to get away from the depressing anonymity of the crowds.

I studied the street I was on, and then turned my attention to the people passing me. Many of them looked like street bums, dirty and unkempt, but one or two walked in tailored suits and stiletto heels, and I made a beeline for one particularly well-groomed woman. She eyed me as I approached her, her arm visibly tightening around the bag she had slung around her shoulder.

"Excuse me. I'm so sorry to bother you." I knew one place in this city, and it was the only place I could think to go to. The Dive.

"What?" She snapped.

"Do you know where The Dive is?"

She relaxed a little, her hostility gone. "Sure. You're not too far from it actually." She paused. "You seem too young for a place like that. It's not the only work to be found in Gloam."

It took me a while to understand what she meant. "Oh." I laughed. "No. I'm just looking for a place to drink, and it's the only one I know."

She pointed back the way I'd come. "Two blocks down, take a right, the next left, and then you're basically there. Did you come in a car?" I nodded. "Word of advice – don't leave it on this street. Park it as close to The Dive as you can."

I glanced at my watch, a gift from Pop for my second birthday spent in The Sands. Ma had frowned at its extravagance, but I'd sensed, even at fourteen, that it was a kind of apology, one I hadn't understood.

To my surprise, it was nearing late afternoon, and only then did I notice that the sun was starting its descent. I had meant to be ensconced somewhere before this happened, before dusk darkened the streets and hidden corners became means of opportunity. It was pointless now to wander around looking for a place. I had nothing to lose. I followed the woman's advice and drove my car the short distance, lucking out when I found a parking spot just across from The Dive. I got out of my car and examined the unlit sign. It looked so different in daylight. Without the glitz of its lights and the surrounding forgiving dark, it looked more like what it was – a seedy place for people to go who preferred to conduct their business in dark corners.

I moved towards the doorway, noticing a bouncer for the first time. Tall and sinewy, he eyed me for a long moment. "ID," he barked. I almost laughed. Was he kidding? I didn't move, but when he held his hand out, I sighed and dug through my pocket, feeling for the slim wallet I always kept inside my jacket. The bouncer's gaze followed the movement of my hand, and when his gaze sharpened, I realised he must've caught sight of my handgun. I handed him my ID, which he gave a cursory glance before returning. "No weapons," he said and gestured inside towards a garishly lit booth where a petite redhead sat. "Scarlet will write you up a receipt and keep it until you're done inside." With that, he dismissed me, looking over my shoulder at the next customer waiting in line.

I approached Scarlet and held out the Sauer, and she took it as blithely as if I'd offered her a cigarette. "Twenty-five coin," she barked, and for a moment I considered retracing my steps back onto the street. She extended her hand towards me, waiting for the fee. I extracted the amount and handed it to her, feeling it leave my hand and stifling the urge to snatch it back. She smiled her thanks, stiff and insincere, motioning towards a musty red curtain ahead. It kept the interior of the bar hidden from view but did nothing to muffle the roar of voices and music beyond.

I pushed through and found myself at the top of a short flight of stairs, which opened into a huge bar area. The bar top stretched almost the entire length of the place, the glittering bottles of booze catching the light above. Tall bar stools ran along its length, and almost every one of them was occupied already, despite the early hour. Dancers gyrated on three raised platforms, a collection of barely clothed men and women. The left side of the bar led to a small staircase which wound to the second floor. It was cordoned off, manned by another buff bouncer. Funnily enough, these weren't details I'd taken particular note of when I'd been here with Chloe.

I looked for a place to sit, and watched as a slim brunette vacated her seat at the bar. I crossed the room quickly and claimed it, and for the first time, the day's events came crashing down on me. I propped my chin against my upturned palms and tried not to cry. I must be insane. What was I doing here? What had I been thinking?

I took my phone out of my jacket pocket and laid it on the bar, staring at its screen. Five missed calls. Three from Ma, and one from each of my brothers. I hadn't even heard it ring or felt it buzzing. My hand remained on it for a long moment as I considered the ramifications of calling home now. I imagined their voices down the line, clear and crisp, as if they were standing right next to me. The thought was comforting. I picked it up, but then thought about Rich's anger when I'd left, of how sad Charlie was, how Ma had supported me, despite her fear. I returned it to the bar, my feeling of solitude growing until I felt it in every pulse of my blood.

"New to town?" The barman stood before me, smiling.

"Huh?"

He motioned to my phone. "You'll soon learn that anything you put down will be picked up again, but not necessarily by you."

I reached for my phone abruptly, as if he'd made a move to take it, and he smiled lightly at me, unoffended.

He looked familiar. He returned my stare and then grinned. "Hey. It's you. Weren't you here a few nights back with Chloe?"

The sound of her name, dropped so casually, sent a bolt of pain through me.

He must've seen something in my face because he paused, hesitating before laying a quick and warm hand on my shoulder. "Everything okay?"

The club felt stiflingly hot, as if someone had turned up the heat. My head swam, and the features of the barman blurred before my eyes. His hand on my shoulder squeezed, giving me a gentle shake.

"Hey. Do you need a doctor?"

I managed to shake my head. "I just need a minute." I dragged the stale, hot air into my lungs, and slowly the cobweb of my thoughts cleared.

"Chloe was attacked. That same night." His name came to me then. Denny.

"I'm so sorry. Is she okay?"

I massaged my temples. "She's fine. Got off lightly, compared to what–" I caught myself just in time. What was I doing, offloading on a stranger?

"Compared to?"

I shook my head. "Nothing. Ignore me. Rough day."

He reached beneath the bar for a glass. "In that case - something to drink?"

I considered the long expanse of bottles and thought about the comfort of losing myself to oblivion, even if for only a few hours. The temptation was almost too much, but the slimness of my wallet, as I fingered it, reminded me I had more pressing concerns.

"Do you know where I can go to spend the night?"

He raised an eyebrow. "It's forward of you, but I'll consider it."

It took me a moment to digest what he'd said, and then I barked a harsh laugh, shaking my head.

Before I could clarify, he set a glass of something colourless in front of me, a slice of vivid lemon nestling among the ice. I tried to push it back towards him, but he shook his head.

"On the house. You look like you could use it."

I was so taken aback by this gesture that I spoke before thinking. "I'm not going to sleep with you, if that's what you're after." To my surprise, he laughed.

"I wasn't expecting you to." He seemed about to say something else, but then another customer took the barstool beside me and his attention shifted. For some time I sat there, just watching the ice melt in my glass, the music thudding around me, a wave of people coming and going.

I picked up my drink and sniffed it cautiously. Sharp and tangy. I brought it to my lips and took a tiny sip. The booze trailed down my throat in a fiery blaze, warming me instantly, and this time I took a longer swallow, the blaze building. What was I drinking? It wasn't something I'd ever tasted before. A cross between vodka and gin, perhaps, and before I knew it, my glass was empty, punctuated by the slight rattle of the remaining ice.

Denny reappeared and smiled as he swept away my empty glass. Feeling grateful, and guilty for my earlier comment, I returned it. "Can I ask you something?" I had to lean across the bar and shout above the noise, and as he leaned into me, I caught the scent of soap and something else which was distinctly male.

"Sure," he roared back at me.

"I need a place to stay tonight. And for a few more nights. Know of any places?"

He paused for a moment, thinking, and then he reached behind the bar for something and came up with a scrap of paper and a pen. He scribbled something and handed it to me, the unexpected brush of his fingers against mine making me jump. I looked down at the note and read the five options he'd listed there. He noticed my helpless look and took it back, flipped it over and started sketching. A little while later, he pushed the scrap back at me, and I saw that he'd drawn a map, complete with landmarks and small notes on where each place he'd listed would be.

Motioning for his pen, I scribbled, "How much?" He answered with a scribble of his own, and I sat calculating. A week at most, if I was careful. And if I ate as little as possible. I needed a plan, but for now I would find the nearest place on the map and get some sleep. I would figure the rest out tomorrow. I nodded my thanks.

"Feel free to come by again once you're settled. There may be another drink in it for you." He grinned, boyish and eager. I waved and left my seat to another impatient patron and pushed out of the bar into the balmy night air. Tomorrow I would regroup, but for now, I needed a shower and a bed.

***

The first two apartment blocks I tried were full, a possibility which hadn't even crossed my mind. Their sheer bulk and the number of apartments made it seem impossible, but the digitised system I was consulting remained stubbornly insistent – *No Vacancies.* The third was impossibly expensive, and the next two were nothing but hollowed out shells – buildings that looked like they'd had their guts ripped out. Shit. I sat down on the pavement outside the last one, wishing suddenly for a cigarette, even though I didn't smoke. I needed something to soothe my frayed nerves. I pressed my hands together, trying to quell the wave of panic which threatened to drown me.

The flickering light of the streetlight above me did little to dispel the press of night. I rose. I had two choices – sit here and wait to be butchered by some crazed city dweller, or return to The Dive to figure out Plan B. I got back in my car. Already, the smells of Gloam had buried themselves in the seats – grease, pollution, humanity. I retraced my path back to The Dive, arriving to find a queue of more than twenty people. I stifled a groan, wondering what the odds were of starting a fight if I tried to jump the line.

"Hey. You again." I turned towards the voice, and found Denny leaning against a wall nearby, his phone in his hands. He lowered it, smiling, and then caught sight of my expression.

"Uh-oh. Didn't come right with the places I gave you?"

I shook my head, wondering why I was suddenly on the brink of sobbing.

Denny slipped his phone into his pocket and moved towards me. "Come on. There's a few motels downtown that you could stay at for a few days. Is your car nearby?"

I hesitated. He seemed nice enough, and Chloe had liked him, but he was still a stranger. His smile felt calculated, and I wondered how many women he'd bedded with that smile.

"I get it. You don't know me, and in Gloam it seems crazy to just get in a car with a stranger. But if you like, you can wait for Hannah to get off work, and then we can drive together."

I considered this, and then shook my head. "Are you done with your shift?"

"Not yet, but it won't take long. Downtown is a few minutes away, and I'll just catch a Uber back."

I led him to my car, and he slipped into the passenger seat, pulling the seatbelt across his chest.

I turned to him. "Okay. Where to?"

He directed me with ease, and as promised, we arrived outside a squat brick building. Its name was lit with garish red lights. *Sleep With Me.* I regarded the sign, wondering what a building with a name like that hid behind its walls. It would have to do. In the morning, I could start my hunt for a short-term apartment.

We walked in side by side, into a small open space which contained nothing but a desk with a biometric hand scanner and a touchscreen beneath a pane of glass. Denny motioned for me to put my hand on the scanner. It beeped and then several options appeared on the screen, with pricing beside each one. I considered, then chose the cheapest. I had probably just enough to see me through the next few days if I was careful.

The screen showed me my room number then went blank.

"That's it?"

Denny nodded. "All the rooms are linked with this system, so you just need to scan the same hand again, and you're in."

I felt limp with relief and exhaustion.

"Thanks Denny. I owe you one. Really."

He smiled and lightly touched my shoulder. "No problem. And welcome to Gloam!"

Chapter Nine

Harlow

I WALKED THE STREETS of Gloam the following day for so long that when I returned, my feet ached. I hadn't made a single contact in my hunt for mercenary work. I'd been shoved out of apartments and offices, large and small, told the same thing over and over. *You need a mentor. No mentor, no work. We have our reputations.* I'd found an apartment, sure, and with my meagre coin too. No rats so far, but the stench of discarded trash both in and outside of the building crept in under my door, carried in on the hot wind through my open windows. But it was either die of heat or live with the smell. The apartment looked out over the mass of other high-rise buildings. The blare and blatt of cars and bikes below was still audible even fifteen floors up. Below, the streets were already teeming with activity, as people streamed out of apartments exactly like mine to destinations I could only guess at.

The sun was high and the window I pressed my hand against was warm with its heat already, but despite the warmth and the cheer of the day, I felt flat and demotivated. I missed the familiarity of The Sands. I missed its birdsong, and the feeling of waking up in the same bed for the past fifteen years. I missed the sound of Ma's quick step outside my door, as she made coffee and spoke to Pop, their quiet laughter drifting beneath my door. Rich's slow drag of feet, and Charlie's complaints about all the noise.

Carter's words had played over and over in my head. The temptation to call home had only grown with all the questions I had. If what Carter had said about Pop was true, how much of it did Ma know about? My head ached with all the unknowns, with the questions that circled and cawed like a murder of crows.

My plan had been to call them as soon as I'd gotten Carter to agree to help, but of course that's not what had happened, and now as I considered things, I realised I had limited options. If I returned to Carter, what would I even say? Was I ready to hear more of what he had to say about Pop? And why would he agree to help me now, when I still didn't have a job or a way to pay him, and when he'd already refused me once?

I could go back to The Dive, get that free drink, and maybe Denny would know someone else I could get in touch with that would be able to help me find work. There was a third option too, one which meant going home with even less money I'd left with. One which meant Pop wouldn't be buried or cremated, but... I couldn't finish the thought.

I shoved my phone back into my jean pocket and stood. No matter how I looked at it, I needed Carter's help. Another part of me also wanted details. An explanation of the things he'd said. Maybe it wasn't what I thought. Maybe I'd misunderstood the whole thing.

I retraced my steps back to his office, keeping my eyes on my path to avoid the stream of humanity flowing my way. A small girl made a beeline for me, followed by a shuffling, mumbling old woman, and I knew before she spoke a word what she would ask for.

"Please ma'am, just a bit of coin?" Her small hand was grubby, coated with such a thick layer of grime that it was a stark contrast against the milk of her wrist.

I considered what I had left. Not near enough. In fact, if I didn't land a job today, or tomorrow at the latest, I was royally screwed, and would have to leave my apartment and go god only knew where.

I shook my head, feeling guilty, but she persisted, her hand still outstretched. I stepped around her, muttering an apology. She followed me, her voice becoming higher and reedier with every step I took, and when I increased my pace, she shouted at my back, her words a garble of fury. A man just passing us stopped abruptly, and I glanced over my shoulder. He grabbed the little girl, shook her hard, and shouted straight into her face, spittle flying. I stopped, turning to intervene, but the girl simply went limp and unresponsive, and when the man released her, looking shocked and afraid, the girl went rigid again, kicked at the man's shin, and took off running. The old woman who had been following in her wake did a surprisingly agile about-turn and headed in the opposite direction.

The man muttered a string of obscenities and then strode away, his hands shoved into the pockets of his filthy coat.

I shook my head. *This fucking city.* Chloe had been right. I hated this place and worse, feared it, too.

I glanced up at the lopsided street sign just ahead and kept heading straight on. A few blocks later, the neighbourhood changed. The buildings grew ever seedier, with broken windows and faded signs, dingy shops and filthy laundry flapping in the hot breeze.

Ah, there it was. I was about to take the two short steps to the door when it sprang open, and Carter stood there, trying to shove a notebook and pen to join the handgun in the pocket of his oversized coat.

"You again. What now? Here to scream at me some more?"

I stood my ground, blocking his path. "The same thing I wanted before."

"I already told you—"

"I know what you told me. My request is the same."

He considered me for a long moment.

I reached into my pocket and withdrew my wallet, which contained little else but the coin he'd tossed at me the last time we'd met.

I removed it and held it out to him.

"Yours, I believe."

He shook his head. "By the looks of it, you need it far more than I do."

I continued to hold it out, unwavering. "It's not mine. And I told you I don't want it. Take it and help me with the investigation and then we're even. I told you the next time you saw me I'd have a fistful of coin. I'm a woman of my word, wouldn't you say?"

The corner of his mouth twitched, but he made no move to take it. I stepped forward, grabbed his hand, and shoved the coin into it. He closed his fist reflexively around it and I smiled, triumphant.

"Cute. Barely enough to cover even a tenth of my initial fee. I told you, no coin, no investigation. Also, I told you that money wasn't the main reason. Or have you conveniently forgotten that detail?"

"No. I wanted to ask you more about it."

He looked surprised at this. "You called me a liar."

"Thanks for the recap."

"Why would you want to hear more if you don't believe anything I've already told you?"

I fell silent, not knowing what to say to that.

"You're hoping I'm going to tell you it's all a mistake. A misunderstanding?"

When I looked up at him, his face looked tired, but his eyes were kind.

He sighed. "Come on in."

He turned back into the open doorway and invited me in with a sweep of his arm.

I took the same chair as before, but he chose to stand, his agitation clear.

"Frank and I were partners for years. He was paired up with me when he first joined the force. We got on right from the start. He became my closest friend, both on and off the force."

"But there were things that happened on cases, things that I overlooked for a long time. Evidence which went missing or turned up contaminated. Misplaced files. Lost witness statements. I didn't want to believe what my gut was telling me, but it became undeniable. When I eventually confronted him, he denied it. Until you were taken."

He'd directed his words to a spot on the wall beyond my shoulder, but now he finally met my gaze. "I was fired. Frank disappeared. All these years—I assumed he was either dead or in hiding. Turns out, you were all only a short drive away."

"Why would he do that? Why would he help people like gangsters?"

Carter's face sagged a little, and he hesitated, as if reluctant to voice his thoughts. "For the coin."

That rage I'd felt before swept through me again, and I clutched the armrests of my chair with all my strength, knowing that losing my temper now could mean his final refusal to help.

Before I could say anything, Carter went on. "Plenty of cops got kickbacks from gangs. Some were for smaller jobs like drug-running or the exchange of other illegal goods. Firearms, black market liquor – that kind of thing. But I always found that those who had long-standing relationships with the gangs were then expected to do things that even a lot of corrupt cops were unwilling to do."

Carter finally sank into the chair opposite me, as if he were too tired to remain on his feet. "You caught me on the backfoot when you arrived here. You were the last person I was expecting, and seeing you brought back so much."

I met his gaze. I sensed this was my chance.

"I really do need your help. I know you don't owe my family anything. But you're all I have in the way of contacts. I need to make enough money so we can send Pop off properly. I just need you to steer me in the right direction, and I'll pay you when I get paid."

"And how exactly are you going to get paid? With what job?"

"That's where you come in."

"I'm not going to help until you have a means to pay me." I started to say something, but he flapped a hand, cutting me off.

"There's a bar in town. The Dive."

"I know it."

"Good. There's a mentor that goes there most days, and if he isn't there when you are, you can leave a message with one of the bar staff. He's more into charity than I am, and your best bet at making some coin. His name is Jesse. Just ask one of the bartenders to point him out. They all know him."

His gaze left my face and travelled down, and for a moment I thought he was staring at my breasts, but it was too quick a glance for that, and when he gestured, I realised he'd been looking at my gun. "That's a good handgun. Solid, dependable. You know how to use it, I'm assuming?"

"Yes," I muttered.

"Good." he said again before pushing past me and onto the street, swallowed by the maw of humanity a moment later.

★★★

The midday sun was beating down on my unprotected face, and I thought about one of the many things Pop had said over and over again, until its repetition became a sort of lullaby in the background of my childhood. Always wear a hat. That's what I'd done through all the years of living in The Sands but in my hurry to leave home, I'd left it behind. I couldn't believe how long the queue was to get through the front doors of The Dive at this time of the day—didn't people work in this place? —and I kicked at the broiled pavement impatiently, feeling like the queue had grown rather than diminished since I'd joined its ranks.

Finally, after standing for another fifteen minutes and feeling like I'd been boiled alive by the time my turn came, I glared at the bouncer without meaning to. He took in my expression, and instead of being affronted, he laughed. "You look like you could use a drink, girlie." I prickled at the ridiculous nickname, but then laughed too, and felt the irritation slide off me.

"In you go," he said, waving me through. Gratefully, I checked my gun in at the reception and then stepped into the heart of the bar, hesitating at the top of the small flight of stairs, craning my neck for a glimpse of Denny. A young woman with a mass of blonde curls was manning the right side of the bar, and an older, tattooed man was serving customers on the opposite side. No Denny. I sighed. Just my luck. There were no seats available either. I hesitated. Both the blonde and Tattoo Guy were swamped with requests from patrons, and I couldn't afford to pay for a drink. I supposed I could ask one of them of Denny's whereabouts. As I moved towards the blonde, a set of swing doors behind the bar flew open, followed by Denny carting in a crate of beer. I pushed through the crowd and waded in through the press of bodies to the front of the bar, not bothering to wait my turn and ignoring the obscenities that followed in my wake.

I stood next to a huge and tattooed man who was overflowing from the barstool he occupied. I brushed his shoulder, and he turned to me, looking annoyed, and then his expression changed into one of sickening lasciviousness. He leaned in and spoke in my ear.

"Hi there, little lady. You can have this seat here." I was about to thank him, willing to overlook his perversion in favour of his seat, but instead of rising, he patted his knees, leering at me. My skin crawled. I forced a smile, hoping the disgust I felt wasn't written all over my face.

"Hey Jimmy." Denny had appeared, smiling genteelly, but with just an edge of steel. "You want to be a gentleman and give this lady here your seat?"

Jimmy grinned, displaying weirdly perfect teeth. "That's what I was just saying to this sweet girl," he replied as he patted his knees again.

Denny grinned back. "Come now Jimmy. This girl and I have some business to discuss, nothing for your ears, and you can take your drink there"—he nodded towards Jimmy's beer—"and go watch the show. Ginger's up next, and I know she's your favourite." He winked, and Jimmy nodded, suddenly obliging. He grabbed his beer and slid off the stool, meandering towards the stage. The current dancer finished up her routine with a final toss of her thong into the crowd, to roars of approval.

I slipped onto the vacated stool and smiled gratefully at Denny. "Thank you."

He nodded and returned my smile. "More for Jimmy's safety than yours. You looked ready to pummel him." I laughed, surprised he'd read me so well.

"So, you're back. Did you find an apartment, or are you still staying in that hotel we found?"

"I found an apartment." *For now.*

"That's great. Where's it at?"

I hesitated, then smiled and shrugged my shoulders.

He nodded. "Smart girl. I could be an axe-murderer, for all you know."

I pointed my index finger at him. "Exactly."

"Fair enough."

"So I was hoping for that drink you offered."

"I haven't forgotten. Same as last time or something else?"

"Something else, I think. I may as well take advantage of your generosity while I can."

He laughed and made his way down the bar, plucking at bottles, and soon a murky pink drink sat in front of me, its little umbrella bobbing.

I regarded it suspiciously. "This looks like cough medicine."

"Kind of tastes like it too." He winked and before I could respond, he turned to the next customer, and I took a tentative sip. The flavours mixed in my mouth in an explosion of contradictions. Sweet and sour. Salt. Something heavy and creamy, and then a smack of fruit and sweet again. *Good god. If this man fucks the way he makes drinks, then bedding him must be* – What? Where had that come from? I shook my head, bemused.

He was back in front of me, and I seized my chance, grateful that the stage was empty for now, and the music had been lowered to allow conversation between the patrons.

"Do you know someone called Jesse?" Even as the words left my mouth, I felt ridiculous. Hundreds of people must pass through here every day. Could I really expect him to know who I was asking for?

The music suddenly blared, the noise of the crowd rising with the arrival of who I assumed was Ginger on the stage, and I had to lean halfway across the bar to be heard.

To my surprise, Denny nodded. He pointed to his right, further down the bar. "As luck would have it, there's your man now." I looked in the direction he was pointing. A short but stocky man was standing a few metres away, his gaze concentrated on his drink. His leather jacket was black and battered, and as I watched, the crowd around him seemed to take special note of his presence and moved around him accordingly, as if he were a lazy but dangerous predator, unpredictable and likely to bite.

I considered the man doubtfully. His blonde hair looked unwashed. My gaze fell on his shoes, which were filthy white sneakers with no laces. "Are you sure?" I yelled over the din.

"Oh yeah, I'm sure. He's in here a lot of nights, and he's always asking questions about something or another. Mostly alone, and not the friendliest of dudes I've ever met, so maybe approach with caution. Obviously not a friend of yours, so why are you looking for him?"

I spoke without thinking. "I need work. And he's going to be my meal ticket."

Denny raised an eyebrow. "Ah. Well, good luck."

I nodded, already sliding off my stool. I downed the rest of my drink. A little liquid courage couldn't hurt.

I approached Jesse and then stood behind him, indecisive. After a moment he turned slowly, looking directly at me, eyebrows raised.

"Yeah?"

"Jesse?"

"Indeed."

I held my hand out and then withdrew it when he didn't offer his own in return, feeling ridiculous. "I'm Harlow. Carter sent me." Not entirely true, but what the hell, he wasn't to know that.

His expression changed somewhat, and hope flared in me, hot and bright. He tipped his bottle of beer to his mouth, taking a long swallow.

"What do you want?"

"I need a mentor."

He sized me up slowly and gave a small laugh.

"What?" I snapped, affronted.

"You know how to use a gun?"

"Short range, long range. Pistols, rifles, revolvers, you name it."

"No." He turned away and directed his attention to the stage, dismissing me without another glance.

Enraged, I stepped in front of him, attempting to block his view. "Why not?"

He glared at me. "Why? Because you obviously have no experience as a merc, or else you wouldn't need a mentor. You're a nobody, and my reputation hinges on the mercs I supply to fixers. I don't just take on anyone who asks." He motioned to me. "You're obviously new to Gloam. Your hair is its natural colour, you don't have any ink, and if you were native to this place, you would know better than to come into The Dive unarmed."

I opened my mouth to protest, but he cut me off. "You're wasting your time, kid. I came here for drinks and the show." He gave me a gentle shove, so he could see the stage again. "Good to meet you."

As he raised his bottle to his lips again, my hand shot out of its own volition and knocked it from his hand. The bottle shattered on the tiled floor. I felt, rather than saw, the patrons around us step away, sensing trouble. Jesse sat immobile; his hand still raised to his mouth as if he hadn't quite realised what had happened. Before he could speak, I stepped into his space, until we were nearly nose-to-nose.

"You may not know me, but I can promise you I'm not the kind of person who takes no for an answer. You've got your reputation—I get that—so let me prove myself. I came here to get something and you'll have no peace until I get it." I waited, feeling faint from the adrenalin flooding my body. I fully expected him to punch me, but instead, he laughed, his gaze falling to the broken bottle at our feet.

"You owe me a drink."

I blinked.

He motioned upstairs, behind the roped-off section where a burly bouncer stood, looking bored and threatening at the same time.

"Let's talk upstairs. Much quieter."

I followed him, wondering how we were going to get into an area that was clearly for more monied and well-known patrons, but the bouncer flicked a glance our way and then stepped aside wordlessly, and I followed Jesse up the grubby carpeted stairs. A long hallway opened up in front of us, with multiple closed doors on each side. Another bouncer stood at the head of the hall, and when he saw Jesse his face split into a huge grin. "Jesse! My man!" He slapped Jesse on the back with such force a smaller man would've gone sprawling, but Jesse returned the grin and smacked the bouncer on his shoulder with a slap that could be heard above the muted roar of the music.

"Mind if we grab a booth? Any free ones available?"

The bouncer frowned. "You know I can't let you in there for free, man. House rules. Boss lady will have my hide."

"Not a live one. Static will do fine."

The bouncer thought this over before nodding. "Okay okay but it's a full night tonight and if a paying patron comes up with some actual coin then you'll need to beat it."

The bouncer gestured to the third door on the left. "You can grab that one. And don't be long. Even if no one comes along, boss lady doesn't like me doing favours. Even for you."

We stepped through a door into a booth. It had a curved seating area which was covered in red faux leather, wall to floor mirrors, and a small raised platform in the middle, with a pole dead centre. A woman danced around the pole, and I stopped, confused. Jesse caught my expression. "It's a projection." He waved his hand at the woman. It passed straight through the image.

I shook my head, amazed. "It looks so real. The way she moves, and how solid she looks."

I watched the image gyrate for a moment longer, then joined Jesse on the curved couch.

Jesse leaned back into the booth, assessing me. I felt a prickle of irritation.

"I've been shooting since I was old enough to hold a gun. I can handle a blade too," I blurted.

"That remains to be seen."

He dug in his pocket and pulled out a pack of cigarettes. He dug one out, holding it between his fingers. "That's the first time in years anyone has caught me by surprise. You're fast."

He tilted the pack towards me.

"No thanks. I don't smoke."

He smiled a little and lit one, inhaling deeply. "In this line of work, you've got to have some vices."

"Mine is men."

He barked a laugh, surprised. "Well, I better watch out then."

I smiled, feeling myself relax a little. "You're not exactly my type."

"No? That barman more your speed?"

I willed myself not to blush, even as I felt the heat rise to my cheeks.

"Denny is a good one. Rare in this city. He's still the same kid he was when he arrived, and he's worked at The Dive for years now. You could do with worse friends, that's for sure."

I was tiring of this chitchat. "Are you going to mentor me, or are we just going to sit here shooting the shit?"

He took his time lighting his cigarette and taking a drag, expelling a cloud of smoke towards the ceiling. "Carter sent you, huh?"

I sighed. "Not exactly. I'm starting to think he sent me to you just so you could turn me down, so I'd give up and go home."

"Doesn't seem your style." He stretched his arms over his head, his jacket creaking with the movement. "But I must tell you—Carter never sends me potential talent, because he's a PI, not a mentor. So clearly, there's something else at play here, which you're choosing not to mention."

I'd hoped to avoid bringing this up. "Carter knew my father."

"Your father?"

"Frank Novac."

Jesse stiffened, lowering his arms, his cigarette dangerously close to the pleather of the booth.

"You're Frank's daughter?"

"Yes."

Jesse nearly dropped his cigarette as he gawped at me. "As in the one—"

"Yes." I couldn't bear to go over the details again. I stared at my hands, too afraid to look up.

The silence between us stretched until I couldn't bear it any longer.

"Does it really matter who I am? Carter chose to help me by sending me to you."

It occurred to me then that perhaps Jesse had known my father, too. "Did you know him?"

"Carter and I have been friends for a long time. I don't know him personally. But I know of him." Jesse paused. "Wait, why are you referring to him in the past tense?"

Talking about Pop was making my head ache. I avoided the question, asking one of my own instead.

"Do I at least get an audition, to prove myself?"

"An audition? Are you trying out for a part then?" He guffawed, but stopped when I didn't join in.

"Christ on a unicorn. You're serious?"

"As a heart attack."

A knock sounded loudly on the other side of the door, and the bouncer's voice came through. "Time's up, Jesse. Boss lady makes her rounds about this time. You two need to beat it."

Jesse rose, still smoking. I remained where I was, staring up at him, refusing to move. He was almost to the door when he turned back and realised I was still where he'd left me, and he sighed heavily. "Fine fine. Geez kid you're persistent, I'll give you that. Let's go."

I jumped to my feet instantly, resisting the urge to hug him. "Now?"

"Why? You got a hot date? Maybe with Denny?"

I glared at him, which only made him laugh harder, and he shooed me out in front of him, opening the door and giving the bouncer one more hearty clap before following me down the stairs and back into the heaving din below.

Outside, the city air greeted us with a humid slap to the cheek. Jesse led the way a bit further down the street, and then motioned to an immaculate Kawasaki parked at the curb, its sleek black and green lines gleaming.

I gasped. "Yours?" Jesse nodded, grinning. "A beaut, huh? It's a—"

"ZX-10R," I finished.

He gaped. "You know your bikes."

I nodded, running a quick hand along the seat. "Merc work must pay well."

Jesse shrugged. "As a mentor, I make more. But I've also been in this game for more than a decade, and she's restored. I bought her off the junk heap a year ago and did the work myself."

"Amazing. She looks brand new." I looked up from my inspection to find Jesse's gaze on me. "What?"

"Nothing." He handed me a black helmet. "You may just grow on me, kid."

Chapter Ten

Harlow

Traffic was a snarl of metal, exhaust fumes and blaring horns, but Jesse navigated the network of streets and congestion with ease, and soon we were approaching the outskirts, the road opening ahead, and the high-rise buildings diminishing until I could see the open sky and its endless blue. To my right, the mass of the landfills rolled so far out I couldn't see the end of them, but to my left I could see the start of the Dust Bowl, and unexpectedly, my eyes stung. What were they doing right now? It was late afternoon, so Pop was probably sitting under one of the shade-cloths, assessing the slow dip of the sun and probably yelling at Charlie and Rich to stop horsing around. Ma would be inside, making her usual batch of what she referred to as her "brew" which was simply water mixed with the aromatic herbs that grew in abundance in the area. And then I remembered – Pop wouldn't be there. How could you forget someone had died? I swallowed against the fist in my throat, and concentrated on the low thrumming of the bike, and its roar when Jesse changed gears, the scenery started to blend into a blur I was grateful for.

Half an hour later, Jesse turned right, and soon after that he slowed and stopped. We were in the middle of nowhere. I swung off and stood looking around, my hands on my hips. Jesse parked the bike and cut the engine, coming to stand beside me.

"It's just over that hill there." As he said it, the pop of a gunshot reverberated around us, and Jesse motioned for me to follow him. We crested the small hill and found a small mixed group of men and women standing in a neat line, all of them in some stage of shooting or reload, aiming at a haphazard assortment of targets, all set at various distances from where the shooters stood.

A few people called greetings to Jesse, which he acknowledged with a wave and a grin, but he didn't stop to speak to any of them or introduce me. We walked the length of the line until we reached the end, and what I assumed was a free spot, although there were no demarcations or separations of any kind indicating where to stand.

"Right," Jesse murmured. "See those?" He pointed ahead at four targets clustered together twenty metres away.

"Seriously? I can shoot those with my eyes closed."

He shrugged. "At this range? You'd need to be really accurate. Show me."

Exasperated, I reached into my side holster and removed the Sauer. I checked the ammunition chamber and took my stance, my eyes trained on the first target.

Pop pop pop pop. I hit each one in quick succession, right in the middle. I turned to Jesse, expecting him to be impressed, but he simply nodded.

"This way." He led me back the way we had come and stepped up to a small and compact woman. "Marian! Good to see you." He smiled warmly and I stepped forward, expecting to be introduced.

Instead, he motioned me back, exchanged a few more words with Marian that I couldn't catch, and made his way back to me, holding a precision rifle I didn't recognise. He handed it to me, and before Marian appeared at his side again, handing him a Smith and Wesson revolver.

"Your handgun accuracy on the Sauer is great. But I'm guessing it's a gun you've had for a while, so you're familiar with all its intricacies. But to be a decent marksman, you have to be able to handle all kinds of guns, because opportunity in this city can mean the difference between keeping your brains in your skull or losing them to the pavement."

Marian stepped aside, making room for us. The targets ahead were much further away. I lifted the rifle to my shoulder, testing its weight and looking down its barrel at the two targets ahead. I fired and hit the target somewhat left of the centre.

Laughter rose behind me. I glanced over my shoulder, and it was only then that I realised a small cluster of people were gathered around, watching. The rifle felt heavier in my hands as I turned back to the target, trying to ignore the drone of voices behind me. I steadied the gun and took my second shot, but as I squeezed the trigger someone shouted something incomprehensible, and my shot went wide, missing the target altogether. More laughter.

The gun was slick in my hands. I lowered it, drawing a deep breath of the hot desert air into my lungs. I waited for my palms to dry, then raised the gun again, only to be interrupted by a loud male voice from the crowd.

"Ah come on princess! Having trouble? Need a lesson?" His comments were met with guffaws and cheers, and when I swung around to face the mob, I didn't bother lowering the rifle. A few people took a step back, as if separating themselves from my tormentor. A clear division formed around him. He stood at the centre, his arms crossed over his barrel chest, his smile sweetly condescending.

Jesse touched my arm, drawing my attention to him. "Ignore him. Concentrate on the target."

Refusing to be placated, I shifted my gaze back to the commentator. "What's his problem?"

Before Jesse could say anything more, the man shouted again "Hey honey. You talking to me? Want me to come a little closer and show you how it's done?"

I stood for a long moment, staring at the man without blinking, the rifle still pointing into the crowd. Out of the corner of my eye, I saw two men move from the outer perimeter, detaching themselves from the rest. Were they moving to circle around me?

I handed the gun to Jesse without looking at him. He put a restraining hand on my shoulder, but I shrugged it off, striding towards the man. He opened his mouth, but before he could utter a word I'd stepped right into his face, close enough to make out the tiny gold stud in his left ear.

"Did you say something?" My words were low and sweet. I smiled, watching his eyes. My hand moved to my Sauer beneath my jacket, slow and purposeful, drawing his gaze to it. The air between us stilled. He reached behind him, presumably searching for his own piece. I drew my knee up and hit him squarely in the crotch. He dropped with a grunt. I knelt beside him, pressing the barrel of my pistol to his temple.

"Want to repeat anything you said? Hmm?" The man's hands were at his crotch, clutching the area as if in fear of detachment. A low groan was my only answer.

"Got anything else to say to me?"

"Kid. Hey." Jesse's hand was on my shoulder, drawing me away. Two men stepped forward, helping the man up.

One of them turned to Jesse as he hauled the man to his feet. "Jesse, man, that was uncool. Jace was just playing."

Jesse ignored him, his eyes on me. A small smile was growing at the corners of his mouth, but his eyes remained cool, assessing.

"There's a job I need to get done. You're coming."

***

The night had turned windless and sultry. When we pulled up on the street where I assumed the job was, I realised it looked familiar.

Jesse pointed directly opposite to where we'd parked.

"There."

I squinted. "The police station?"

Jesse nodded and shooed me off his bike, leaning it on its kickstand and pulling off his helmet, settling it on the seat I'd just vacated.

"Our job is for the cops?"

"Actually, I don't know who hired me. It was done through a fixer. The client wanted to stay anonymous."

"So what exactly are we supposed to do?"

"Steal intel."

I gaped at him. "From the police?" My voice had risen with incredulity and Jesse shot me a look when several people passing by on the street glanced at us.

"You may know how to use a gun but you definitely need a few lessons in discretion," Jesse muttered.

I closed my mouth, abashed. When I spoke again, I was careful to keep my voice down. "I can't show my face in there. The cop at the front desk and I had a little...exchange. And he's a perv."

Jesse laughed. "All the better. Because you're the bait."

"Wait, what?"

Jesse waved towards the front door. "How many female cops do you think there are in Gloam? Those cops in there don't want to see my ugly mug. They'd rather feast their eyes on your lovely female form." Jesse did a mock leer, and I laughed, despite myself.

"The intel is apparently in the evidence room, which is not only at the centre of the building, but it's also just above the morgue, which means it's on the second-lowest floor. Getting there will mean negotiating my way past a lot of cops. So when I say you're bait, I mean you need to create a diversion. One big enough to hold their attention for say... ten minutes?"

The enormity of this task was making my stomach clench. It seemed impossible. Ten minutes? And more than one of them? How was I going to do that? Jesse was watching me.

"Problem?"

"No." I pushed my doubt away. "How will I know when you're done?"

"I'll come to the front desk. If I've got the layout of this place right, then there's a door which will lead back to the street and I'll just walk in again and pretend that you're my crazy sister who forgot to take her medication."

Crazy. Great.

I walked into the police station and saw that the same cop who'd given me Carter's details was on duty again.

I glanced briefly into the room behind him, beyond the plexiglass, and saw it was occupied by one other cop, who seemed to be dozing at his desk.

I moved to the duty desk. What were the chances he wouldn't recognise me? After all, he must see hundreds of people on a weekly basis.

When he looked up, the gleam in his eye was unmistakable. "So I see you took me at my word, huh? Seems I was right about PI Reach, after all. Not a helpful sort of fella, am I right?"

I hated using my looks the way I'd seen so many women do. It had always been a bone of contention between Chloe and I, but years of watching her meant I had some idea of how it was done. I forced my lips into a smile, and leaned over his desk, drawing his eyes to my chest.

Like the good dog that he was, his gaze went there immediately, and I felt a rush of sudden confidence. I couldn't be sure when Jesse would use his moment to slip past, so I had to make sure I kept the cop's full attention.

I flopped into the chair across from him, heaving my best damsel-in-distress sigh. "You were so right. He was of absolutely no help."

I reached across the desk and gripped his hand tightly, widening my eyes until they felt fit to drop out of their sockets.

"I need to report a crime. I've been in this city for three damn days and do you know what happened to me?" My voice was rising, and the cop beyond the plexiglass looked up. Good. Now that I had his attention, too, it was time to raise the volume even more.

"I was robbed! First on the street, and then my rat-infested apartment was ransacked for whatever I had left." When the cop just stared at me wordlessly, the earlier gleam gone from his eyes, I smacked the palms of my hands against the desk, hard enough to make him jump.

"What are the cops in this city doing about the crime? Huh?"

"Ma'am." A beefy hand was on my shoulder, squeezing painfully. "You're causing a scene and you're being disruptive."

"Causing a scene?" I screamed. "Your colleague here has done nothing but stare at me since I got here. He hasn't written down one word. Not one!" I gestured dramatically to his empty hand and the absence of a notepad in front of him.

I was vaguely aware of more cops appearing from behind closed doors and hopefully from other floors, the racket I was making drawing them to crowd around me.

More hands were closing around me – my arms, my other shoulder. This was the moment where I could either make sure I kept them centred on me or the moment I got my behind thrown in a holding cell.

Somehow, I willed myself to cry, and miraculously, the tears appeared, rolling down my cheeks. I dropped my voice to a near-whisper, so they all had to close in around me, leaning in to catch my words.

"I just need some help. Just some help. I'm alone in this place."

It was, at least, partly true.

My tears seemed to have the desired effect. The hands pulling at me eased away, and someone had tucked a tissue into my hand, which I balled and dabbed at my face, thinking how this had been all too easy.

A shout shattered the quiet, and when the door behind us was thrown open so violently it hit the wall, the attention moved from me to the new arrival. A man stood in the doorway, a shotgun in his hands. The noise and confusion which followed provided me with the perfect escape. When the cops around me turned towards the gunman, I slipped out of my seat, my Sauer already in hand. I ran for the cover of the plexiglass, wondering even as I did whether it would provide any cover from a shotgun slug. Gunshots reverberated in the enclosed space. I ducked behind the half-wall, peering over just enough to see what was happening. Three other men had joined the first, while the cops had dived behind desks and ducked behind doorways. *What the hell was going on? And where the hell was Jesse?*

I needed to get out of here but the only entrance I knew of was blocked by the three gunmen. I thought of the exit door Jesse was supposed to have used. The only other accessible doorway to me, without trying to fight my way through the gunfire, was behind me. I ran for it, crouching as low as I could, my thighs burning.

I yanked the door open and rushed inside. The room was empty, save for six desks and chairs, but it held the air of a recently vacated space, as if only moments before the desks had been occupied. There was only one other door and as I pulled it open, I wondered if I was going to be met with another empty room and nowhere else to go.

Instead, it led into an open space and then a staircase, and when more gunshots sounded behind me, slightly muffled but still clearly audible, I took the stairs down two at a time, knowing that if I tripped and fell that it was likely I'd break a leg.

Four flights of stairs led to what I hoped was the door that led outside. As I reached for the handle a hand fell on my shoulder. Without thinking I turned and raised the Sauer, pointing it straight into Jesse's face.

"Whoa! Easy now." He grinned, looking completely unruffled by the pandemonium we could still hear going on four floors up.

"Please tell me you got what we needed."

He grinned and held up a memory stick. "Let's get out of here."

Jesse grabbed the door handle, but when he pushed it down and pressed his weight against the door, nothing happened.

"It's locked."

The door splintered with the force of a shot that sounded behind us. The shot had been so close that my ears were ringing with the retort. I swung around, forcing back the rush of panic coursing through me. I steadied my stance and fired. A bloom of red darkened the sleeve of the man's denim jacket, his face white with shock. He grabbed at the wound and lost his balance, tripping down the final two stairs, landing face-first at our feet. Jesse kicked at the vestiges of the door still clinging to its frame, and as he grabbed my arm and dragged me out, I caught sight of the insignia on the man's jacket. An eagle, wings outstretched, talons extended.

We ran out the door and found ourselves in a small side street. The wails of sirens blotted out every other sound, and when we came around the corner, melting in with the rest of the crowd of spectators, we could still hear the pops and roars of exchanged gunfire.

Jesse pulled me through the crowd and led me to his bike. My throat felt narrowed to a pinprick as I laboured for air, my skin slick with cold sweat.

I bent over, resting my hands on my knees, forcing slower, deeper breaths into my lungs until finally the pound of my pulse slowed.

"Did you see the insignia of that guy's jacket?"

Jesse nodded.

"Why would the Natives be mixed up in this?" I asked.

"Fucked if I know. But this is bigger than we thought – a lot bigger. If the Natives were after the same intel then there's more to this than meets the eye."

"You think that's why they were here?"

"There could be other reasons, sure. But in my experience gang members don't walk into a police station and shoot it up unless they're after something."

As we watched, more cops spilled from newly arrived vehicles, and only minutes later, the gunfire ceased.

Jesse lit a cigarette and inhaled deeply, looking up at the sky. There were no stars, or if there were, they were completely blanked out by the smog and lights of the city.

Neither of us said anything for a few minutes. Finally, Jesse stubbed out his cigarette and turned back to me.

"Go home. This may be nothing, but I'll let you know if I find anything out."

"What about the intel?"

"I'm going to hold onto it for now. Want to do some digging."

He pulled out his wallet and held out some bills. "Here. You earned this."

I nodded my thanks and turned, about to make my way back to my apartment.

"Harlow." I turned back to face Jesse. "Thanks kid. You did good. Consider your audition successful."

Chapter Eleven

Harlow

THE AFTERNOON LIGHT WOKE me. I lifted my phone to my face, groggy. 4pm. Shit. I'd been asleep for close to twelve hours. I'd meant to set my alarm and call Jesse for an update. I scrubbed my hands over my face, then dialled his number.

It rang three times. "Hey kid," he said.

"Any news on the intel?"

"Not yet."

I drummed my fingers on the scarred wood of the bedside table.

"Got anything else for me?" I glanced at my wallet, which contained only the few bills Jesse had given me the night before. It felt like a reproachful eye glaring up at me. I waited. If Jesse had nothing for me, then going home was my only option. Going home with nothing but the money Jesse had given me. I closed my eyes against the wave of defeat which threatened to swamp me. On the other side of the phone, I realised Jesse was quiet, as if waiting for me to say something.

"Sorry. What was that?"

"I said, nothing right now."

I paused. Who else was I going to ask? I had no one else to turn to. I forced the words to my lips.

"Can we meet? There's something I need to ask you." There. No taking it back now.

"Sure."

"Around eight? At The Dive?"

"See you then."

The line went dead and I sat for a few moments longer, trying to shake off the odd dread that clung to me from the dreams I'd had that I couldn't quite recall.

I thought about the insignia on the man's jacket. The second appearance of the Natives since Pop had died, when just days before I hadn't even known of their existence. I thought about how I had to go home, whether I had the money to bury Pop or not. What was I going to say to Ma and my brothers? Could I really keep this from them? Pretend I'd come to the city and then home again, with nothing in between?

I dragged myself from my bed to the grimy window of the hotel. It looked like a change of weather was rolling in, the horizon dark with approaching clouds. The streets below teamed with activity. People, cars and bikes streamed past, the city smog hanging heavy in the air. Even through the thick windows and fifteen floors up I could hear the faint buzz, the muted blare of horns, the occasional shouted greeting or warning.

It was a city that seemed to attract a very specific kind of persona. Drifters. Criminals. Gangs. Corrupt cops. This city held a weird promise, the possibilities of total reinvention, of disappearing into its mass of humanity and emerging changed, like a butterfly emerging from its chrysalis. It was a promise I already sensed as false, and I was wary of being pulled into it and finding myself unable to escape.

★★★

I scanned The Dive, searching for Jesse. At this time of night, the place was only starting to gear for the night-time rush. There were plenty of open seats at the bar, and so Jesse was easy to spot as he sat as far left of the bar as he could go, the same place I'd found him in two nights ago. He spotted me and waved me over, grinning.

He patted the bar stool next to him. I slid into it, scanning the bar for Denny. "Looking for your boy, huh?" Jesse waggled his eyebrows suggestively. I willed myself not to flush, hoping the heat I felt rising in my cheeks wasn't obvious.

"Do you always sit here? Is your name on that particular seat?"

He shrugged. "What can I say? I'm a man of habit."

He motioned to the beer in front of him. "Want a drink?"

I sighed. I wasn't someone who easily asked for help. And yet it seemed that was all I'd done since arriving in this city, and I was about to do it again. "My funds are really low. I need to go home."

Jesse looked puzzled. "Home? But I thought you needed merc work?"

"I do. That's why I'm in the city in the first place, but things haven't exactly gone to plan." I willed myself to look at him but could only manage to direct my gaze beyond his shoulder.

"My father was murdered."

Jesse slowly lowered his beer to the bar top. "You didn't tell me that."

I sniffed, closing my lids against the sting of tears.

"I know. I came here because I needed to make some money, fast. We can't bury him out where we live. At least not the way we want to. My throat felt tight as a fist, a wad of grief impossible to swallow. "That's why I asked to see you."

Jesse's meaty hand came briefly to my shoulder. He squeezed gently, his eyes sympathetic.

A sudden shriek of feedback from the speakers made me jump, music blaring from them, and the tears shot from my throat to my eyes. I swiped a hand across them, feeling humiliation blossom in my chest until it felt like a boulder was sitting there. Jesse gave my shoulder another squeeze. I concentrated on the stage, where the first dancer of the night had appeared, dressed in a skimpy sparkling dress that caught the lights overhead.

I gave a shaky laugh. "You must think I'm a complete idiot. The truth is, I didn't really think this through. I came to Gloam not knowing any of the rules. And now I have no money to take back to my family."

I crossed my arms on the bar, not caring that it felt sticky against my skin. I laid my head down, wondering if I could just lay here forever, an unmoving, unthinking form, no more remarkable than a barstool.

"You took a chance, Harlow. You wanted to help your family."

I raised my head. It felt like it weighed a thousand pounds. "Yeah. Look how well that worked out. I'm some country hick who thought she could make it in the real world. Joke's on me, right?"

"You're hard on yourself. What you did took guts."

He leaned closer to be heard over the din. "Why didn't you say anything before?"

"You're a stranger, Jesse. Going to Carter and begging for his help was bad enough. And I had to do that twice."

An unfamiliar barman appeared in front of us, smiling. Short and dark, he had pleasing brown eyes, his smile warm. "Get you anything?"

Jesse turned to me. "Let me get it. Consider it a small token."

I nodded, too embarrassed to argue. "Surprise me," I said to the barman, and he smiled knowingly and picked up a tall glass, adding ice and a couple of splashes of alcohol from two unidentifiable bottles.

Jesse turned back to me. "Let me help you. To be clear, this isn't a favour. And it's not a gift. It's an advance on whatever you make on your first few jobs."

The tears threatened again. I bit down harder on my lower lip, digging my teeth in trying to keep them at bay. I'd always known that asking him for a loan was disingenuous. I was repaying his kindness with dishonesty because I had no intention of coming back.

He misinterpreted my silence.

He smiled. "I've plenty of savings, kid. An old guy like me, the only shit I have to spend my money on is booze and girls. You can start paying me back as soon as you earn on the next job."

The barman reappeared with something that was bright pink and garnished with a slice of pineapple. I took a sip, weighing my options. If I took the money now, I could leave for home first thing in the morning. We could then bury Pop the same day, even if we had to dig the grave ourselves. I shuddered at the thought.

What happened after this? Did I slip back into my old life, the one which no longer felt like the right fit? Did we all arrange ourselves around the loss, careful to mind the gap, to never look directly at it?

The alcohol swirled on my tongue and then slid down my throat in an explosion of sweet warmth, and for the first time since I'd arrived in this city, I felt my shoulders lower a little, and the clenched fist in my stomach unfurl, one finger at a time.

I held out my hand for Jesse to shake. "Deal. And…thank you."

He waved my words away. "No biggie, kid." He picked up his beer and took a long swallow, turning in his seat to face me fully, his eyes leaving me to roam the room with a practised sweep, as if taking note of every patron.

"How was he killed?"

I liked the way he asked it – no apology or asking for permission. I liked that he already felt familiar to me. The only person I could say that about in this place, the only person I felt I could call a friend. The thought made my stomach curl. If I really thought of him as a friend, then how could I treat him this way? Take his money and lie to his face?

"I came home from a night out with a friend. I was in the kitchen when I heard my father shout. It took me less than a minute to get outside but… I was too late."

I stopped, the reality of Pop's death washing over me again. He was really gone. My father, my friend. One moment he'd been with us, and we'd been going about our routine as a family, and the next he was being rolled into a blank white sheet by strangers, another body to bag. The finality of it was staggering. I was no longer a child, but I still needed him. I still wanted the assuredness of his presence, the solidity of his existence. Without him, I felt like a leaf caught in the heart of a storm, tossed about and then dropped to the ground, vulnerable to the brutality of the world. I felt unsteady without him, and unsure of how we were supposed to go on.

If I was really honest, my motives for coming here weren't as simple as I'd made out. I'd wanted to escape, to run from the smothering familiarity of my home and my family. I'd wanted to avoid facing it all, to avert my eyes from the hole in our lives which had opened like the maw of a monster.

"What happens after?"

I blinked. "After?"

"Once your father has been taken care of. What's your plan?"

"I can't really think that far. Right now, I can only concentrate on what needs to be done next." It was only a partial lie.

"If it were me, I'd want to know who did it. You won't get any answers through the cops. The ones here aren't exactly known for solving murders or even giving much of a shit about their jobs."

I stared at him.

"Carter is considered the best in his field. He knew your father really well. He could help you find the killer, if that's what you wanted."

Had Carter really known my father? Had any of us?

I thought of what Jesse had said. Of course, it wasn't the first time the thought had occurred to me – the idea of investigating Pop's death myself, of finding his killer. It had seemed absurd in the confines of my own thoughts, but hearing someone else say it, someone like Jesse, suddenly made it seem possible.

Jesse drained the remainder of his beer, the thud of his glass against the bar audible.

"I'd want justice. Waiting on the cops to do something won't get you justice, but there's the other kind. The one you get at the end of a pistol."

Chapter Twelve

Harlow

THE CITY FELL BEHIND me with every kilometre I drove. The sky was still lit by its lights, while the horizon ahead lightened, going from orange to pink to grey. I'd woken before dawn, the money Jesse had loaned me burning a hole in my pocket, and without making a call to my family, I packed my few belongings and made my way to my rickety old car, parked outside on the street.

I slipped behind the wheel, tossing my bag onto the back seat. With any luck, I'd arrive before my brothers left for work, so we could discuss the arrangements for Pop.

The roads were quiet, with only the occasional car passing by, and I twisted the radio knob, fiddling with it until I found a station from home. I drove on autopilot, without really seeing the road or making any of the turns consciously, making my way home by memory.

The Sands loomed ahead, the red sandy peaks coming into view. I navigated a few more twists and turns and pulled up to the front of the house at seven am. As I parked, my gaze moved to the kitchen window that overlooked our driveway, unsurprised to see Ma already there, her eyes cast down as she washed dishes in the sink. She looked up and caught sight of me, and her pleasure was visible before her worry overshadowed it.

She disappeared from view and reappeared at the front door, her hand still lingering on the door handle, a dish cloth clutched in her free hand. She called over her shoulder, her words muffled, but I could hear enough to know she was calling for my brothers. I wasn't sure what kind of reception to expect.

I stepped into my mother's embrace, breathing her in. Soap, heat and bacon. A smell that immediately took me back to my childhood, to countless breakfasts and the moments we'd always had as a family before everyone left for the day. Her arms closed around my whole body, her softness against my slighter frame a balm to my anxiety. She stroked my hair, running her hand from the crown of my head to the tips of my hair, rocking me slightly as if I were still a child.

Rich stood behind her, his arms crossed over his chest, and Charlie beside him, his eyes sad and dull, the deep purple of the circles beneath them making his face look bruised.

Ma hustled me in and closed the door. "I'm so glad you're back, my love." Her face looked pinched and grey and old, the strain of recent events evident in the new lines around her eyes, and the hollows beneath her cheeks.

Unexpectedly, Rich pulled me to him, my cheek pressed to the rough fabric of his shirt. When I stepped away from him, Charlie squeezed my arm in greeting, the darkness in his eyes brightening briefly.

I set my bag on the floor at their feet and fished around until my hand found the bundle of notes. I pulled them out and handed them to Ma.

"I found merc work. It's an advance."

"An advance?" Rich asked. I wanted to kick myself.

I'd avoided thinking too hard about this. Money was going to be an issue for our family. The fact that Ma didn't work, and hadn't since our move to The Sands, meant that we only had the meagre incomes my brothers and I earned doing odd jobs. Employment out here meant employing yourself, and our community was only so big and filled with people like us with limited resources.

I'd hoped to sidestep this particular conversation until much later, until we'd figured out the details of today and actually knew the answer to Rich's question, but there it was now, laid out between us, undeniable and glaring, demanding an answer.

"I'm not sure if I'm going back."

"What about the person who loaned you the money?"

"I'll find another way to pay him back."

I crossed to the kitchen and poured myself a cup of coffee, sinking into a chair at the old dining room table. "We have other, more pressing things to talk about right now."

My family joined me at the table. "We need to take care of Pop. That's what's got to take precedence now. Tomorrow is the last day they'll keep his body, so whatever you had planned for today, cancel it. We need to discuss where we're going to take him, and how."

Rich looked ready to explode. "We have to plan a funeral. We can't do that in one day!"

"Rich, there's no more time. We're his family – we're the most important people anyway. We meant the most..." I couldn't finish. My throat locked and my eyes stung, and I stared hard at the tabletop, my hands clenching the cup, burning my palms.

I looked at Rich, knowing his opinion had the potential to sway both Charlie and Ma. I waited, drumming my fingers on the mug before forcing myself to stop. Pop wouldn't have wanted a big funeral anyway.

Rich finally nodded, letting out a huge exhale. "She's right. We don't have much time. Where are we going to take him?"

We all turned to Ma. She considered for a long moment, her gaze trained past my shoulder and out the kitchen window. "I don't think it would've mattered to Pop where he was buried. Especially if it cost us more than we could manage."

She laid the bills down on the table, motioning to Rich.

He counted them out, and we all came to the same conclusion. We couldn't afford a legal cremation, but it was still more affordable than burying him.

"Who's going to make the deal?" Charlie asked. Rich rose as if volunteering, but I put a hand on his arm. "I'd like to do it." Rich looked as if he was about to protest, but something passed between him and Ma, and he nodded, handing me the money. The bills were already slightly damp from being handled so much.

I left the house and walked the short distance to the mortuary, the sun already a blazing disc in the sky.

When I arrived, the man who'd helped us previously stood behind the reception desk, his head bent towards a pile of papers. At the sound of my footsteps he looked up, his expression brightening when he recognized me.

"Good news, I hope?"

I held out the coin. "Will this be enough to cover your costs, as well as…" I trailed off, my tongue locking around the word cremation.

He took it from me and counted it, and a look passed over his face, his hands stilling. A knot of dread formed in my stomach, threating to eject my morning coffee.

His gaze met mine, and I could feel him considering me. For the first time I felt he was really seeing me, taking in my bedraggled appearance, my unbrushed hair and unwashed face. He took most of the coin, and then handed the rest back to me.

"When you've spoken to Neville and settled with him come back here. He will take your father. It will be your last chance for a goodbye, so make sure everyone is here."

He closed the door before I had a chance to reply. I stared at the notes in my hands, doubtful. It didn't seem like enough. When I'd asked Jesse for the money, I'd known the cost of the cremation, but not once had I thought to ask the cost of the morgue.

★★★

I wove my way through the dirt roads for another five minutes before coming to Neville's home. His was right on the border, only a few steps from the sandy roads which then connected to the highways. I reached his door and knocked loudly since Neville was not known for his sobriety or early morning habits. Silence. I knocked again, louder, and this time was rewarded with the stumbling footsteps and muttered curses of activity inside.

The door was yanked open, and Neville swayed in the doorway, his clothes dotted with something brown and chunky, his eyes bloodshot and narrowed.

I reeled back from the smell of him – vomit, smoke and booze.

"Whad da ya want?"

My stomach roiled. This was the man who was going to handle my father? This was the last person who was going to touch him, to see him, to help him to the other side?

The injustice of it all came at me all at once. Breathing through my mouth, I braced myself against the other side of the doorway, reminding myself that this was the only way. The other alternative would be to take his body to the cliffs of The Sands and leave him to the elements. The thought was unbearable.

"Neville?"

"Nah. The Pope. Who else?"

Despite his appearance he seemed sober enough, or at least enough to make a deal, and that would simply have to be good enough.

"My father. I need you to go to the mortuary. We need his body…taken care of."

He nodded, suddenly sombre.

I held the remaining notes out to him. "How much?"

He flicked a cursory glance at the coin. He held out a hand for it, and I gave it to him. A long silence ensued. Finally, he spoke. His tone was gruff but apologetic.

"It's not enough."

"What? But…"

He pushed the coin back into my hand, gently. "I'm sorry, but it's not enough. I wish I could help." He looked as if he really meant this, which only made it harder for me not to break into raging sobs, right there on his doorstep, in plain view of anyone who cared to look out their window.

"My next shift is tonight." He shifted, and a waft of his body odour washed over me. I resisted the urge to cover my nose. "I'm sorry but I have things to do."

He started to close the door but I braced a hand against it, forcing his attention back to me. "What am I supposed to do now?"

He considered me, his expression impatient now. "There are other ways of disposing of a body."

I wanted to scream in his face. To claw at his skin until he bled, to eject all my fury into him, so I wouldn't have to stand there feeling like everything I'd done up until this point had been for nothing.

"I can't just dump him somewhere. He's not an animal. He's..." I couldn't go on. The day suddenly felt close and stifling, and despite my savage breathing, I still couldn't get enough air. Neville regarded me impassively, neither closing the door nor offering any help. He simply waited me out, until finally the air I managed to drag into my lungs calmed me, and the feeling of receding into a tunnel faded.

Neville's hand landed on my shoulder unexpectantly, and I tried not to shudder. "Your family needs you now. Go. You'll figure it out."

***

I stepped back through the door into our kitchen. All three of them rose, expectant.

"It's not enough. Neville won't cremate him."

Ma sank back into her seat, her legs giving out beneath her. I couldn't bear the look on her face. I looked from Rich to Charlie, but both of them started mutely back at me, and I knew I would have to be the one to say it.

"We'll have to deal with it ourselves."

Rich was already shaking his head. "No. We can't do that. We can't do that to Pop."

He looked ready to cry. My heart felt leaden in my chest. I'd given them just a scrap of hope that we could do this one last thing for Pop, and then I'd taken it away.

Ma began to keen, the sound high and unbearable, rising to a crescendo until I wanted to clamp my hands over my ears and run from the room. Charlie went to her, taking her into his arms. He held her the same way she'd held each of us when we were little. Tenderly. Gently. As if we could break.

"Ma." I said the word sharply, more so than I'd intended. She went silent, turning to me, still within the circle of Charlie's arms.

"There's no time for that. Not now. We're expected. We need to go fetch him."

Rich held his hand out for the remaining bills, which I handed to him. "We'll do what we can," he said.

He moved towards the door. "I'll get the car." He glanced meaningfully at me. Wordlessly, I went to my parents' bedroom, opening the cupboard and reaching for two blankets on the top shelf. My father's shirts hung in the space below, as if waiting for his return. The blankets slipped from my hands as I reached for one, bunching it in my fist and pressing it to my nose, inhaling. Memories of a lifetime contained in that scent of heat, smoke and desert air. I clutched the sleeve of that shirt I'd seen him wear a dozen times, held onto it like I could drown in the sea of despair which crashed over me.

I clung just a little bit longer, then forced myself away, picking up the fallen blankets, and taking them to Rich. He motioned to Charlie. "Let's go."

"I'm coming too," I said. Rich looked at me and then his gaze passed over my shoulder, to where Ma sat sunken in Pop's favourite armchair, her shoulders hunched as if she were trying to disappear into herself.

"I want to say goodbye."

Rich's gaze returned to me. "Low, he'll look…different now. Maybe it's better you don't."

I had no strength left in me to fight, and when my brothers turned wordlessly to leave, I let them.

I sat next to Ma, holding her damp hand. Her tears had dried, and she sat silently and perfectly still, as if the slightest movement would shatter her. I sat, feeling my failure so keenly it was like a blade between the ribs. All I'd wanted was to help. Instead, I'd made things worse.

Chapter Thirteen

Harlow

THEY RETURNED HOURS LATER, sweaty and filthy.

It was obvious what the outcome had been, but I still had to ask. "No one could help?"

Rich shook his head, pressing the money back into my hands. "It wasn't enough."

I closed my eyes against the imagery of my brothers digging a grave for our father. How Rich would've used his rage to dig harder, faster, and how Charlie would've dug through a film of tears, the widening grave wavering before his eyes.

We sat at the dinner table to a meal Ma had insisted on cooking, but none of us were hungry. We made every pretence of eating, of going through the motions, but the food remained untouched, and finally, Ma gave up and cleared everything away.

I knew that if I was going to say anything about what I'd learned in Gloam, now was the time.

"Ma."

She stopped clattering the dishes in the sink and turned to me. "Come sit, please."

She returned to her seat.

"I need to ask you something."

She nodded, and I continued. "I went to see PI Reach. He told me some things about Pop..." I trailed off, watching her face. Watching for a tic, something to give away the fact that she'd known all along. But her expression was expectant, and open.

"He said Pop was a corrupt cop. That he was working with some gang called the Natives. That Matt was his gang contact, and their leader." The words rushed out of me so quickly I wasn't sure she'd really heard me or taken in what I'd said. A loaded silence followed.

Rich had half-risen, as if torn between leaving the table to escape my next words or staying to hear the truth. Charlie was staring at me open-mouthed. When I finally dared look at Ma again, her face was a mask of denial.

"That's a lie."

She spat the words. I wanted to believe in her vehemence. Wanted to believe that Carter was lying, that his reasons for doing so didn't matter.

"Why would he lie, Ma?"

Rich slammed his palms against the table, leaning so close I could feel his breath on my face. "That's enough Low! Ma can't take anymore—can't you see that?"

Was he right? Was my need for answers blinding me to how much I was hurting her?

Ma reached for Rich, laying her hand on his arm. "Let her speak."

Rich stiffened against her hold, and then, defeated, sank back into his chair.

"Carter said it was the reason I was taken. Pop was trying to leave the Natives, and Matt wouldn't let him. That taking me was his punishment."

"Wait." Charlie spoke so quietly I almost didn't hear him. "You're saying Matt was a part of this gang, too? And their leader, to boot?"

"Yes."

The weighted silence broke under the assault of Ma's wails.

Rich glared at me, but I met his gaze square-on. Charlie rose and crouched in front of her, looking scared and unsure, taking her hands and gripping them, as if for stability.

My chair felt like it was sinking, as if I'd sat in quicksand. Would the ground ever feel safe beneath my feet again?

Watching my brothers close around Ma, their hands reaching for her, I understood something I'd circled but not yet faced—with Pop dead, I was an outsider in my own family. I'd always been the closet to him; he was the one I confided in, the one who I'd orbited around. I also knew that while they would eventually resign themselves to never knowing who killed Pop, or all the events that had led to his death, I would never be able to do the same.

"I'm going back to Gloam." As the words left my mouth, fear washed over me. I willed it away. There was no time for that now. It was now, or never.

"We can't lose you too." Rich said.

The anger had gone out of him, leaving him deflated. I preferred his anger, because it meant there was fight left in him, but now, looking at him, he seemed hopeless. His huge hands, so much like Pop's, hung at his sides, his fingers clenching and releasing—open, shut, open, shut. I thought of the history of those hands. The way he'd lifted me over things when we'd explored The Sands, when my shorter legs couldn't bound and climb as effortlessly as theirs. How he would carry me when I tired, even if we were far from home. The way those hands had doctored me through the years; scrapes, cuts, burns. How he would come to me when I had my nightmares, my screams cutting through the quiet of the night, and how he'd held my hands in his, singing quietly until my eyes would drift closed again. He'd taken care of me that same way Pop had. The way Ma had. As if I needed three caretakers. My throat closed, the edges of the room blurring. I swallowed and closed my eyes, willing myself to keep it together just a little longer.

I crossed the room and took those hands, making him look at me. "Rich. I have to do this. Pop can't have died for nothing. We need to catch this bastard. For Pop. For Chloe. For anyone else he might hurt or kill."

"Revenge isn't justice."

"Revenge is the only justice I know." I thought of Jesse's words then—*justice at the end of my pistol*. That was how I would finish this.

I kissed Rich's cheek and he clasped me to his chest, his arms tightening around me briefly, and then releasing me, resigned. "Go. Be careful. Call us."

He turned and disappeared into his room, the door closing behind him.

I hugged Ma, holding her to me for as long as I could. Her tears fell, dampening the cotton of my shirt. I kissed her, then held her at arms-length so I could see her face.

"I'm sorry Ma. I thought you may have known. I didn't..." The rest of the words lodged in my throat, tight as a fist.

She pressed her palm against my cheek. "You have your Sauer?"

"Yes."

"Good. Don't be afraid to use it."

***

Charlie stepped out the front door with me. He took my bag from me, placing it in the boot of my car. His movements were slow, deliberate. I could feel him thinking, stalling, wanting to find a way to make me stay and coming up empty.

I moved to open my door, but he stepped between me and the car, leaning against it. "Are you sure you want to do this?"

I sighed. "Charlie. We've been over this."

"Do you have to go right now? Can't you stay the night?"

The thought was tempting. One more night in my childhood bed. But I couldn't. I was afraid that if I did, I wouldn't find the strength to leave when morning came. He saw the refusal in my expression and sighed.

He looked up at the sky, scratching his chin. "Is Pop still the same person to you? Now that you know?"

The question had been niggling at me. I'd ignored it. I didn't want to look at it, because it felt like a tin of meat gone bad, a tin I knew was crawling with maggots. I didn't want to open it, knowing what I'd find.

"I don't know. I always thought of Pop as an honourable man. But there's no honour in gangs."

"Do you think he killed people?"

I took a step back, as if Charlie had raised his hand to me. There it was. The maggots. Crawling over my hand. Let out of their prison. Undeniable now.

"I don't want to think about it. I don't want to think about Pop differently. He's dead. It's not like we can demand answers. Or ask him why."

A gust of hot wind blew the sand in small whirlwinds around our feet. The sun had lowered, and I was reminded of the time. Of how the roads leading back to the city were wrought with opportunists – criminals and cops alike.

"He can't be honourable and an ex-gang member, Low. The two can't exist together."

I reached out a hand and squeezed his arm, a code of love between us. Charlie wasn't easily embraced, and was generally uncomfortable with affection, but an arm squeeze between us had always been a communication of affection, one he could comfortably bear. The only person he'd ever freely given affection to was Ma.

"Sometimes it is possible for two, seemingly contradictory, things to be true at once. He's still our father. He was, to us, an honourable, honest, decent man. A good father. Don't let what you know now change that. He was all those things to us, if not to other people." Even as I spoke the words I wondered if I believed them.

Charlie grabbed me in a hug, taking me by surprise, but before I could even get my arms around him, he stepped back out of reach.

"Be safe, Low. Come back to us."

Chapter Fourteen

Markham

IT WAS ONLY WHEN she screamed out the boy's name that he realised his mistake.

"Run, Johnny! Hide! Ruuunnnn!" The last word was a prolonged shriek of anguish. His head rang with it, turning his mind feverish. She had to stop. Someone would hear.

He grabbed her and slammed her against the wall. She'd braced herself for the impact, so it was only her torso that took the hit. He'd intended on dazing her, just so she'd stop screaming. It had all unravelled too fast. He'd intended on baiting her, on seeing the recognition, and then the understanding dawn in her eyes, but now she was thinking only of surviving, all thought of their previous interplay forgotten.

He tightened his grip on her shoulders, shaking her hard enough for her teeth to chatter. "Skylar! Hey!" He wanted her to look at him. He wanted to reassure her. He needed her calm, at least for just a little while longer. He needed her lucid. She would see the end coming all the more clearly, and it was that, more than anything else, that he craved. The fear. The helplessness.

He tried not to think about the boy. Crammed into some small, dark space, his small heart racing. His ear at the door, listening. Hoping with all the childish optimism of the young that the stranger would leave, leave him and his mommy alone. The thought was so close to a memory. A memory of pressing himself against his bedroom door, listening to the screams on the other side, the crash of furniture, and then, silence. The quiet so much worse than the noise. There were possibilities in silence.

His momentary lapse of focus seemed to give Skylar hope. She latched onto his arms, digging her nails into his skin, raising a knee meant for his groin. He sidestepped her kick, ignoring the pain as she dug deeper into his skin. He crushed her to him, her arms caught between them, her hands losing their grip on his arms in the impact. Heat washed through him at the feel of her against him, at the sound of her whimpers, her pleas for mercy.

He brought his mouth to her ear. "Skylar. Do you remember me?"

She quieted. He pulled back just enough to observe her expression, waiting for the moment she'd realise who she'd really brought home.

Harlow

I arrived back in the city after dark. I parked my car, finding a parking spot close to my building for a change, and made my way to the fifteenth floor, my eyes gritty and heavy, my limbs feeling like they were filled with lead. Driving away, I'd watched Charlie grow smaller in the rearview mirror. I'd torn my eyes from him, knowing that if I looked for much longer I would end up turning the car around, and then I would never return to the city. I had to find the killer. For me, for Pop, for my family. If the Natives were behind this, who was to say they wouldn't come back for Ma, for Rich or Charlie? The idea of the rest of my family being in danger gnawed at me like a relentless rodent.

Tomorrow I would contact Jesse and find out what he knew about the Natives. If there was a link between Pop's past, and his murder. As I lay down on my bed, not bothering to shower or even undress, I wondered if all of this was for nothing. If maybe, Pop's death had simply been the result of finding Chloe before the killer could escape. Convinced I would never sleep despite my exhaustion, I drifted off, the toll of the day sinking my body into oblivion.

***

When I woke nearly ten hours later, bleary and still exhausted, the sun was streaming in through the windows where I'd forgotten to close the blinds the night before. I groaned, rolling away from the light and trying to burrow further under the covers, despite the heat.

I knew I should be getting up and facing the day. I willed my body to move, but I felt cemented to the bed. Despite my convictions yesterday, my determination to leave home and come back here, I felt out of my depth. I didn't have a single friend here, no one to turn to. I wouldn't burden my family with how I felt, because they would simply try to reel me back, and I couldn't let them. My grief filled every pore, every fibre of my body. It clung to every bone and muscle. How could this have happened? How could he just be gone?

My phone came to life beside me, trilling with the notification of a message. It was from Rich, but I couldn't bring myself to read it. Not now.

I forced myself out of bed, and to the shower, dropping my clothes to the floor.

I slipped beneath the spray of hot water, scrubbing until my skin glowed pink, wondering if guilt was something you could slough off, like a snake shedding its skin.

When I finally felt more human, I grabbed my phone and messaged Jesse. It was late morning, but I still didn't want to impose. I knew next to nothing of his personal life. Maybe he had a wife I would piss off by calling too early?

I barely had time to put my phone down before he answered. He suggested a diner I hadn't heard of, and I fired off a reply before bundling my sheets and stripping off the pillowcases and duvet cover, stuffing them into a trash bag for lack of a better alternative. I hadn't washed them since arriving here. They smelled strongly of body odour.

Throwing the bag over my shoulder, I searched for the nearest laundromat to my place. Turned out that the closest one was six blocks away, in the opposite direction to the diner. I sighed, and tapped a quick message to let Jesse know I would be later than we had originally planned.

I trudged through the streets with my dirty laundry, my feet feeling heavy and my head full of thoughts of Pop. I wasn't really paying much attention to where I was going, and it was only when my phone beeped in agitation that I realised I'd taken a wrong turn. I considered my surroundings, and realised I was completely lost. Nothing looked familiar.

I glanced at my phone's screen. It was directing me back the way I'd come. I turned, catching a glimpse of movement out of the corner of my eye. A flash of black, as if someone had just turned the corner ahead of me in a hurry. I quickened my step, aware of the passing of time and not wanting to keep Jesse waiting too long. *Tap tap tap.* It was strange. The city was as crowded as ever, the streets teeming with people, and yet, I'd heard it, loud and clear. I froze. Whoever, or whatever, was making that noise, had to be close for me to have heard it so clearly. I spun around, searching the street behind me. No one stood out. No one was staring at me or acting strange.

I picked up my pace, wondering if I should run, and then felt ridiculous. Paranoid. And yet. I was sure that someone was watching me, someone very close, the heat of their stare prickling up my back. *Tap tap tap tap tap.* Faster now. Like whoever was following me was increasing their efforts to keep up with me. If I turned now, would I come face to face with them?

I ran, turning a corner blindly, no longer caring about seeming ridiculous. Finally. The faded blue and white sign of the laundromat appeared like an oasis. I crossed the street, glancing briefly over my shoulder. No one was pursuing me.

I pushed the door open. It was thankfully empty, and choosing a washing machine in the furthest corner, I dumped my bag of laundry on the floor and began sorting through them. It probably wasn't advisable to leave the machine unsupervised, but I was already late. Hoping for the best, I dumped the whole lot in the machine, added detergent from the bottle above my machine, and turned it to its longest setting.

As I straightened and turned to leave, I caught the briefest glimpse of a retreating back, clothed in a jacket with the Natives insignia.

***

I followed Jesse's directions and soon enough came upon the diner he'd described. I joined him in a bright yellow booth, the fake leather faded and torn, the steel table scratched and well-used. I glanced around as I sat down, taking in the neon colours of the interior – yellow and orange booths, bright blue counters, hot-pink bar stools.

"You look like hell."

My hand went to my hair, clean but pulled back into a hurried ponytail, my clothes grubby and my face without a trace of makeup.

"Thanks. Nice to see you too."

His eyes searched my face. Unexpectedly, he reached out and gave my hand a squeeze. The contact made me squirm, and my eyes burned with tears. I hated myself for being so easily undone these days. I pulled my hand away gently, and stared at the table, willing myself to get a grip.

A waitress appeared, her long hair piled on her head in a messy bun, tendrils already escaping and brushing her shoulders. Her electric-blue eyeshadow paired with her pink blush and orange lipstick made it difficult not to stare. I averted my eyes to my menu, pressing my lips together to stop myself from laughing, grateful for the distraction.

I scanned the menu and looked up at Jesse.

"What's good here?"

Jesse turned to the waitress and ordered for both of us, which I found sweet and condescending simultaneously. I tried not to look at the prices, and mentally tallied what I had left of Jesse's money. Maybe enough to cover breakfast. After that...

"There was a recording on the intel we recovered. It's a murder scene."

I stared at him, the dread from last night rushing back.

"A murder? You mean a gang-related one?"

"It seems that way. The X mark of the Natives was carved into the palm of the victims' hands."

My head felt crammed with too much information which didn't make sense.

"Victims? As in plural?"

"Yeah. A couple. The woman died from a blow to the head. The man was strangled." He considered me for a long moment. "There's something you're not telling me. What is it?"

Batting his question aside for the moment, I asked "What do you mean by an X mark?"

He gave a short laugh. "Oh. Right. You're not familiar with all this gang stuff. Every gang has a mark they leave on their victims' bodies, to showcase their work. The Natives specialise in blades. They pride themselves on killing quietly, and up close. They carve the letter X into their victim's palms. Always the left one."

I drummed my fingers on the tabletop, my agitation growing. "The Natives seem to be cropping up a lot lately. I assume since you and Carter are such bosom buddies that you know my father's history with them?"

The waitress arrived then, her tray laden with our coffee and drinks for another table. She balanced it expertly on one hand while handing us our drinks with the other. "Food will be up soon. Enjoy your coffee!"

Jesse leaned over the table, pushing his mug aside. "I only know the basics. That he had dealings with them that weren't exactly above board." Jesse's face momentarily darkened. "And how that involvement cost Carter his place on the force."

"How do you know Carter wasn't involved in the dealings, too?" I felt defensive of Pop. It was still difficult for me to believe what Carter had told me. It was a ridiculous accusation when I tried to align it with the man I thought I'd known.

Jesse shook his head vehemently. "I know Carter. He would never involve himself in something like that. He has…history with the Natives that he's never got past. And not the kind of history your father had."

"I thought I knew my father too."

Jesse went quiet, as if mulling over my words. I took a sip from my mug, surprised by the richness of it. Not like that dishwater Carter served and called coffee.

"We lived in Gloam when I was young. And then…" *Drip drip drip.* I shook my head hard, trying to dislodge the memory.

I was grateful when Jesse interrupted. "I know the story. Of how you were taken by Matthew Cummings. And how you and your family disappeared afterwards." He leaned forward, the coffee at his elbow momentarily forgotten and no doubt growing cold. "And here is where it gets interesting. The victims in the recording are none other than Matthew Cummings and his wife, Angela."

My mug slipped from my fingers and hit the table with such force it shattered, splashing both of us with scalding coffee, shards of ceramic flying in every direction.

The waitress reappeared as if by magic, mopping at the spilled liquid and the glass. I stammered an apology and she waved it away, the table clean again in less than a minute.

When she left again, I stared across the table at Jesse. "Do you think this is a coincidence? The death of my father, and then Matt? And all immediate clues pointing to the Natives?"

"No. I don't think it's a coincidence. What feels even less of a coincidence is how I was hired to do the job that just happened to be the pickup of this intel. And how you happened to be with me at the time."

Our food arrived, and Jesse motioned for me to eat. I regarded my plate, the smell of the omelette rising to my nose and making my mouth water. I hadn't eaten since the morning before, and I was suddenly ravenous.

I ate quickly, cutting into the egg, bacon and mushrooms, the cheese rich and oozing onto my plate. I was done before Jesse, and waited impatiently for him to finish, staring out the window of the café and contemplating the city streets beyond.

Jesse finished up, wiping his mouth with a paper serviette. "The other thing I've been thinking about is who actually hired me. Like I said, I dealt with a fixer, and the client remained anonymous, which leaves me to think there's two possibilities—that the Natives hired me, or someone somehow knew what was on the intel and wanted it for themselves."

I nodded. It was so much information all at once. I'd need time to process it all. To sift through it.

"Did you know your kidnapping made the news? Your father's disgrace and fall from the police force was extremely public. The news hounds loved it."

I wasn't sure why he was telling me this. It felt like salt in the wound.

"No wonder Carter didn't want to help me initially. He must've hated my father after what he did."

Jesse shook his head. "Carter and your father were closer than any two men I've ever seen. They worked many cases together. The only bone of contention between them was when Carter found out about Frank's gang ties. I think Carter felt betrayed. He never hated your father. It shook him to the core that he never actually knew the person he spent so much time with, the person he considered his closest friend."

He signalled to the waitress for the bill. "But right now the priority is to get you a few gigs so you have the coin to get Carter going on your father's case. It just so happens that the owner of The Dive called me last night. One of her girls hasn't come to work for three days, and no one has heard from her. In her line of work, it isn't exactly unusual for girls to flake but Evans is adamant that Skylar isn't one of them."

Jesse paid the bill without looking up, as if we'd agreed earlier that it was his treat. My face burned with the humiliation, but I said nothing. I was in no position to refuse.

Chapter Fifteen

Harlow

WE SLIPPED OUT OF the booth and out into the street, the sun a burning disc overhead. A man, his gait dragging and uneven, brushed too close to me, and the smell that came off him made me think of burning rubber. His eyes were sunken and his skin grey, stark red and peeling patches of skin marking his cheeks. Jesse pulled me away from him, watching the man shuffle on without so much as a mumbled apology or a backwards glance.

I brushed at my arm, as if the man had left a residue on my skin. "What was wrong with him?"

Jesse shook his head. "Drugs. Skeet, specifically. Choice drug of the streets. Cheap and widely available. This city. Even after more than a decade of living here I still can't get used to how depraved it is."

"So as I was saying. Evans needs us to stop by The Dive. She has keys to Skylar's apartment, which she wants us to check out for clues. Maybe get an idea of her whereabouts and if there's anything to be alarmed about."

"Why would she have keys to Skylar's apartment?"

Jesse chuckled dryly. "The Dive, and Evans specifically, makes her own rules. Having keys to her employees' places is one of them."

Before I could ask anything more, he pointed me down the street. "Can you find your way?"

"You're sending me alone?"

"Ah honey... you need me to hold your hand?" I glared at him. He laughed, unfazed, and nudged me in the right direction. "The sooner you get on your feet on your own doing these jobs, the better. But don't worry, once you've got the keys I'll meet you there. Here's the address." He handed me a slip of paper. "I'm assuming you can use your phone for directions?"

I huffed. "I'm not a complete moron, you know."

He grinned. "Never said you were." He glanced at his watch. "Meet there in forty-five minutes?"

I grunted assent.

As he turned to go, I remembered my laundry. I glanced at my watch. The wash cycle would've finished fifteen minutes ago. I could only hope it would still be there. I detoured back to the laundromat, and to my relief, I found my laundry in the machine where I'd left them. There was a folded note stuck to the door of the machine. I stared at it. It hadn't been there earlier. I was sure of it. I plucked it off and opened it.

Harlow. Welcome back to Gloam.

My guts clenched, and I wondered if I was going to eject every bite of food I'd just eaten. I looked out at the street, searching for someone who might be watching me or loitering near the laundromat, but I didn't see anyone suspicious. I crumpled the note and shoved it into the pocket of my jeans. No one knew me in this city. Who could've left this note? I thought of the feeling of being followed earlier, of the glimpse I'd caught of someone hurrying away. Someone wearing a jacket with the same insignia as Pop's attacker.

I grabbed the damp laundry from the bowels of the machine and stuffed it into a tumble dryer, twisting the knob to the right setting and feeding it the coins it needed. I wanted to get out of here. I felt safer on the street, where I could blend with the crowds, than standing here alone in this laundromat. Funny how fast things could change. When I'd first arrived in Gloam, I'd seen a threat in every strange face on the street. Now I drew comfort from it, knowing I could simply step outside and become one with the scenery.

I punched the address Jesse had given me into my phone, rejoining the throning crowds on the streets, and feeling my breath ease in my chest. I followed my phone's directions, turning down one incomprehensible street after another until a few minutes later, I recognised the street I was on. I turned towards the entrance, and the bouncer standing outside gave me the once-over before letting me through.

"You know the drill," he muttered, and I realised he'd recognised me from the last time I was here. I smiled, feeling a little less strange in this city.

It was mid-afternoon, and there was a steady stream of people leaving, and a trickle of them arriving. The Dive was always open and always doing business, it seemed, to some extent. The stage was empty, but the music loud and braying, the bar occupied with a line of people who seemed in no hurry, and entirely unconcerned by the time of day.

I realised I had no idea who to ask about Evans. My eyes searched the bar, and there he was, resplendent in clean, faded jeans and a button-up blue shirt. I pushed my way to the front, smiling sweetly and unapologetically at the other patrons as I elbowed them out of my way. I rested my arms on the bar, watching Denny pour a beer and then mix a cocktail, his movements confident and quick, his manner with the patrons warm and efficient. He caught me staring, and I smiled, fluttering my fingers at him in a small wave. He exchanged a word with the pretty blonde who was working beside him, and she glanced in my direction slyly, her smile knowing.

"Back again so soon?"

"Can't stay away, it seems."

"Well, I don't like to brag, but I tend to serve my drinks with a side of banter."

I considered him. For the first time I noticed details I'd missed. His dark hair, which was slightly too long, and made him look younger than what I estimated his true age to be. His eyes, which I'd previously mistaken as brown, were flecked with green. He put his hands on the bar, palms down, leaning towards me. Big, with long tapered fingers. Big enough to span a small waistline.

"Get you a drink, or have you just come to admire me?"

I wasn't sure whether to laugh or take offense. Caught between the two, I let out a kind of guffaw, and hoped he'd missed it over the sudden bray of feedback from a nearby speaker.

I leaned over the bar to be heard, and this close up, I could make out the stubble on his chin and cheeks.

"Neither, actually. Do you know where I can find Evans?"

"Ah. Yeah. Her office is on the second floor, first door on the left." He cocked his head curiously. "Business with Evans, huh? Landed a gig?"

For some reason, I hesitated. It was just a job, and I was probably one of a dozen mercs who came and went in this bar. Nothing new. But Denny made me nervous. It wasn't something I was used to.

"Something like that." He nodded and motioned to the curving staircase to my left, the same one Jesse and I had taken on the first night we'd met.

I waved my thanks and shouldered my way out of the crowd, which had grown dense in the past few minutes.

At the foot of the stairs, a bouncer assessed me. "Spread your arms and legs."

"What?" I stepped back, shocked.

A female bouncer, the only one I'd seen work The Dive so far, stepped forward. "We need to search you for weapons."

"I already checked my weapons in at the front desk."

She popped her gum loudly, assessing me with a glint of amusement in her eyes. "You expect me to take your word for it? You're here to see Evans, right? No weapons."

"Evans is expecting me."

"And Evans expects me to bodily search everyone before they enter her office. You let me search you, or your meeting with her doesn't happen. You choose."

Heat rose in me until I could feel it behind my eyes, beneath my arms, and in the small of my back.

I hated being touched by strangers. I wanted to turn and go back the way I'd come. I'd tell Jesse that if we were going to do this job, then he'd have to come and deal with Evans. I imagined the look on his face, and how, even before Evans had met me, she would've formed an opinion of me.

I bit back the retort that was rising to my lips and submitted to the search. The bouncer's hands roamed my body – down my arms, underneath my arms, down the length of my legs. She lifted the hair off the nape of my neck and stuck her hand down the back of my shirt, feeling underneath for a concealed weapon. My skin felt itchy beneath her touch, and I willed myself not to slap her hand away.

"Satisfied?" I asked when she came up empty.

She grunted something and waved me through.

I followed the spine of the stairs and was waved through by a third bouncer, this one heavily armed. I stood outside the closed door and rapped briefly.

"Come," a voice answered from inside.

I opened the door and stepped through. Evans sat behind her solid wooden desk, her leather chair the same red as the barstools downstairs. The wall behind her was all glass and overlooked the entire bar, dancefloor, and stage area. She motioned to the chair across from her, watching me as I lowered myself into it, the leather creaking beneath my weight.

"So," she said, as she reached for a package of cigarettes, extracted one, and lit it between her scarlet lips. "You're the new recruit."

"Yes. Harlow."

She opened a drawer and extracted an envelope, pushing it across the expanse of her desk. "Information on Skylar."

I opened the envelope and extracted a single sheet of paper and a photograph, which showed a smiling woman, her gaze directed straight into the lens of the camera. Her dark hair was cut in a sleek bob, shiny and perfect.

I scanned the sheet of paper, which contained a few lines on Skylar's address, age, contact numbers and other background information.

"Jesse gave you the details, I assume?"

"Just the basics."

Evans nodded and rose, turning her back to me briefly, scanning the bar below. "You know why I replaced the wall here with a window?"

"To keep an eye on things?"

She turned back to me. "Precisely. I miss very little of what goes on here. I clock every single patron and staff member who walks in here, and I know just about everyone by name. When a stranger walks into my bar, I know it." She took a deep drag on her cigarette, exhaling towards the ceiling.

"Skylar hasn't shown up for work three days in a row. Girls who work here do it all the time – they sleep through their alarm or have a run-in with their drug-pusher boyfriends and show up with a shiner, if at all."

Something must've shown on my face. The corner of her mouth curled. "You look shocked."

"I'm new to Gloam and its many charms."

She raised an eyebrow. "A newbie. Jesse must really have faith in you." There was something in the arch of her eyebrow which insinuated more than faith.

When I held her gaze and said nothing, she went on, unperturbed.

"She isn't the type to have cut and run."

"You seem very sure of that."

"She has a son. Six years old. She would never leave him. If she's taken off, she would've taken him with her. Something's amiss. I need you to find out what it is."

I nodded, rising. I knew when I was dismissed.

I turned back, something occurring to me. "What about a partner? Does she have one?"

Evans nodded. "If something has happened to her, it's likely he's involved. They're separated, but he still shows up unannounced, and drunk, whenever the urge takes him."

I turned to go.

"Oh, and Harlow?" I turned back to her. "Do this right, and you'll have more jobs than what you'll know what to do with. Fuck it up, and we'll never do business again. I'm at the pulse of nearly every fixer in this city. If I put the word out, your reputation as a merc, such as it is, will be dead in the water. Understood?"

That urge to say exactly what I thought rose to my tongue again, burning with its urgency to leave my mouth. I nodded and left the room without a word.

★★★

Jesse was outside the apartment block when I arrived, his bulk propped up against the doorway of its front entrance. "What took you so long?"

I thought of my detour to the laundromat. The note in my pocket felt illicit, something to keep hidden away. Should I show him? Express my fear about what it could mean?

I opened my mouth, then closed it. Whatever relationship Jesse and I had, I needed to measure how much I shared with him. With any of the people I'd met here. They weren't my friends – they were my contacts, and for the moment, I needed to keep things close to my chest.

My silence went on too long.

"All good?"

I nodded and handed him the envelope. He slid the paper out, gave it a cursory glance, then turned his attention to the photograph. He let out a long whistle. "Fuck. I know her. Seen her perform a few times. She's got a little kid."

Jesse slid the photograph back into its envelope. "Let's get going."

The front door of the building was unlocked. We made our way up the stairs to the third floor, the stairway littered with beer cans and broken glass, the shards winking dully beneath the bare bulb hanging above us.

Her apartment was numbered 301. The numbers, once gold, were tarnished. The number three hung slightly askew, one of its nails missing.

Jesse unholstered his gun and loaded it, motioning for me to do the same. "We can't be too careful." He slotted the key into the door and unlocked it, pushing the door wide and stepping through slowly, his arms outstretched and his gun aimed into the bowels of the room.

Silence. The apartment was tiny. The kitchen, lounge and dining room were one with a closed interleading door to the left, which I could only assume was the bedroom. We advanced slowly, one step at a time, listening for any noise beyond the closed door, but there was nothing beyond the sound of our own breathing. A lone coffee cup sat on the small dining table, a ring of pink lipstick at its rim. A pack of open cigarettes was laid beside it, atop an empty astray. In a corner of the lounge was an open toy box, its contents neatly packed, but missing its lid.

Jesse crossed the apartment and pushed open the closed door. The stench greeted us first, cloying and sweet. A woman lay on the bed, her hands crossed peacefully over her chest, her eyes closed. There were no signs of violence bar the livid purple and blackening bruises around her throat. Her left hand was crossed over her right, displaying a small diamond engagement ring with a smaller connected band. It sparkled beneath the room lights, winking mockingly up at us.

"Shit," Jesse muttered. He moved to the bed and pressed his fingers against her neck, feeling for a pulse. Even as he did, we both knew she was dead.

"Check her hand," I said. A feeling was forming in my gut, an idea crystallising in my mind.

"What?"

"Check her hand, Jesse."

He shook his head. "We shouldn't be touching the body without gloves. We should be calling the cops."

I pushed past him, brushing off his hand as he reached for my arm. I lifted her left hand, titling her palm towards me. There it was. A livid red X carved into the pale skin of her hand.

I stumbled back, my hand at my mouth. Jesse was standing at my shoulder, and I heard his sharp intake of breath, as he too, saw it.

"Jesus. Another one."

He reached for his phone, starting to dial.

I put a hand out, stopping him. "Where's the kid?"

Jesse lowered his phone. I moved to the closed door on the other side of the bedroom which had been hidden from sight when we first entered the apartment. I opened the door, praying the little boy would be there, unharmed and safe.

But the only things which greeted me were a toilet, a shower and a basin, and nothing more.

Jesse's footsteps were loud as he searched the rest of the apartment, opening kitchen cupboards and banging them shut again, all thought of contaminating the crime scene gone.

I stepped back out into the living area, dread building in my chest. Three murders in the space of two days. The same killer. It had to be. But what connected all of this? Pop? But why? There was an obvious connection between him and Uncle Matt and Aunt Angie, but I didn't recognise this woman, so what was her connection to all this? Was there a connection? Could it all be random?

Jesse was dialling again. "Carter? Yeah. You need to get here." He rattled off the address. Then he hung up and dialled a second time. He spoke into his phone, but I couldn't hear a thing over the buzzing in my ears.

***

Hours later, after Carter and the cops had arrived at the scene, dusted for prints, taken their photographs, and removed Skylar's body, the three of us stood in Evans's office. Our appearance together brought the news home to her before we could say a word, and she sank into her office chair, her face tightening.

"She's dead, isn't she?"

I stepped forward, feeling somehow responsible for delivering the news she'd already guessed at.

"Yes."

I outlined the facts, leaving my father and Chloe out of it. The three of us had discussed it on the way here, and Jesse and Carter had agreed that we had to keep this under wraps for now. There could be no link at all between the murders. Right now they had two things in common—strangulation and the mark of the Natives. There was the connection between Pop and Uncle Matt, but beyond that, there were no other connections between the victims and one of the three had taken place in a different location. Something niggled at the recesses of my mind, but it wouldn't come into focus, and so I batted it away.

Evans chain-smoked through it all, stoic except for the almost imperceptible tremble in her hands. When I was finished, she rose, stubbing out her final cigarette, and smoothing her hair. "Thank you for letting me know. If you'll excuse me, I need to break the news to the other staff."

She handed Jesse an envelope. "Your pay." She nodded in my direction. "Make sure she gets her cut."

She looked directly at me, assessing. "I'll have several jobs lined up for you in the coming weeks."

Chapter Sixteen

Denny

HE LEANED AGAINST THE ebbing warmth of the brick building, waiting. He'd caught a glimpse of her earlier, but that had been a half hour ago, and she still hadn't reappeared. He shoved his hands in his pockets, wishing he could light a cigarette, just so he'd have something to do.

The passage of time felt like it had slowed to a trickle. Finally, just as he'd decided to give up and head home, she appeared, stepping out of the front door, pushing against the crowd clamouring to get in.

She paused, seeming to consider her next move. Her long, dark hair fell past her shoulders and caught the final glimmers of the sun as it sank towards the horizon. She wore jeans and a plain white blouse, with impossibly white sneakers. She looked impeccable, as if she'd gone through her day in a protective bubble, a barrier against dirt and grime. She started to move off, and he knew if he didn't move quickly he'd lose her in the gathering dark and the crowds that seemed to only appear as the sun gave way to night.

He needed to correct his mistake. He pictured that dark hair twisted in his fingers, the strands like black silk. He imagined the feel of her skin beneath his hands, the soft slip of it as he ran them over her body.

The distance between them was growing, but he still hesitated. He felt stuck to the wall he was leaning against, like a fly in a spider's web. His gut was so tightly clenched he felt sick.

She rounded the corner and he lost sight of her. That seemed to do it. He pushed away from the wall and broke into a jog to catch up to her, making sure to make plenty of noise so he wouldn't startle her. He touched her arm and she swung towards him abruptly, her face taut and her eyes suspicious. Recognising him, she let out a ragged laugh, running her hand quickly through her hair.

"Sorry," he said, his hand still on her arm. "I didn't mean to scare you."

"No, that's okay." She let out a huge breath of air. Her face looked pale, and she looked tired.

"Long day?"

"The longest in human history, I'm pretty sure. Look, I don't mean to be rude, but—"

"I was hoping you'd grab a drink with me. You look like you've had a rough day and could use one. And maybe some company?" He grinned boyishly, hoping to charm her into agreeing. For a long moment she considered him, her eyes studying his face, and he was sure she was going to refuse.

Then her shoulders released a little, lowering, and she smiled. "Okay. But one drink. And a quiet one. Know a place?"

★★★

He led them along the streets, turning corners with ease and confidence. She was forced to follow behind, the streets still teeming with people as they streamed in and out of restaurants, clubs and sex bars.

After a few minutes the buzz of the crowd faded and they turned into a quiet street, lit only by the lights spilling from the few diners nearby. He turned right again and led her into a bar which had only a few drinkers installed in high booths or sitting at the counters.

They chose a booth which overlooked the street right at the back, where the music was quieter, and they were as far from the other patrons as they could get.

He waited for Harlow to sit and then motioned to the bar. "What will it be?"

She smiled. "Surprise me." He smiled back. Their catch phrase.

He walked to the bar and ordered himself a beer, ordering a flavoured one for Harlow. The barmaid handed him the ice-cold bottles, along with two glasses. "Start a tab for us, will you?"

He returned to Harlow. Her face was turned towards the window, her eyes trained on the street. Her fingers tapped restlessly against the surface of the table.

He placed the beer in front of her. "Glass or bottle?"

She answered by taking a swig straight from the bottle, wiping her mouth with the back of her hand and then turning the label of the bottle towards her, inspecting it.

"How is it that you always seem to know what kind of drinks I like, even when I don't?"

He smiled and slid in across from her. "Occupational hazard, I guess." She didn't respond. She seemed distracted, her attention only partly on their conversation.

"So I'm guessing the job you did for Evans didn't end well?"

He watched her as she watched the street, her relentless tapping on the table distracting.

"Did you know Skylar?"

The question caught him off guard. Half a dozen weekly shifts at The Dive gave him plenty of opportunities to get to know the other staff, particularly the dancers. Between sets they would come to the bar, requesting the non-alcoholic drinks they were entitled to. Some would flirt and give him the eye, but Skylar had been the worst, openly eyeing him and making suggestive comments that would make Hannah howl with laughter as his skin pinkened.

"Why are you talking about her in the past tense?"

"She's dead." Harlow said this without meeting his eye, and studying her profile, he watched as her jaw clenched, as she struggled to keep a hold on her emotions. When she spoke again, her voice was steady. "She has a little boy. He wasn't at the apartment. We don't know where he is."

He felt winded, as if someone had punched him. All those nights spent talking to Skylar, and she'd never once mentioned her son.

He reached across the table, hesitant, and covered Harlow's hand with his. He didn't think he could bear it if she pulled away, but instead her fingers closed around his, squeezing.

She turned back to him. "How about we don't talk about it anymore? Honestly, after the day I've had, I could use a good time." Her fingers stroked the back of his hand lightly, just once, twice, and then she withdrew her hand and picked up her beer, her gaze on his, her body language unmistakable.

***

They'd found a dark street. Several beers in, and his head felt pleasantly fuzzy. Her hands were underneath his shirt and moving up his back, her fingers tracing light patterns on his skin, lighting every inch of him on fire.

He tipped her chin back and kissed her throat, baring his teeth just a touch, grazing them against her skin, and she let out a growl that he felt vibrate against his lips.

He grasped her chin with two fingers and moved her mouth to his, opening her lips with his tongue and exploring her hot, greedy mouth. Her hands moved out from under his shirt to his hair, tangling her fingers in it and pulling to the point of pain. He pressed her harder against the brick wall, his thigh pushing between hers. His hands pushed beneath her shirt and skirted her soft skin beneath, brushing against the promise of her breast. She gasped into his mouth and he felt himself hardening, the need to rip off her clothes growing with every second.

What am I doing? The thought stilled his hands as they spanned her waist. The desire drained from him, leaving him limp and weak. This was not the plan. Had never been the plan from the moment he'd laid eyes on her. He felt the heat of Harlow's gaze as she stared at him, and when he looked back at her, her expression had turned cold.

The top button of her blouse had come undone, revealing a hint of cleavage. Heat rushed through him, his fingers locking into fists, and without realising it he'd closed the distance between them. Something in his stance, and the way he'd moved, made her flinch from him, her hand instinctively going to the gun strapped at her side. He stopped, forcing air into his lungs and flexing his fingers until they relaxed.

Neither of them said anything, until the silence between them had dragged out so long he couldn't think of a single thing to say to break it.

Finally, Harlow reached for the button on her blouse, and stepped away from the wall, forcing him back. She straightened her clothes.

"What was that?"

He couldn't look at her. He examined the pavement at her feet, fighting for control, embarrassment flooding him with heat.

"Right. That's the way it's going to be?" She swept past him, the smell of her lingering. Her footsteps faded as she walked away from him, but still he could not get his feet to move, his mouth to open to call for her. Soon enough, there was nothing except the sound of his own panting, and the smell of his sweat.

Chapter Seventeen

Harlow

WHEN MY PHONE RANG, the last person I expected on the other end was Denny. I'd left him in that back alleyway feeling humiliated and ridiculous, like I'd misread all the signals and he'd simply allowed things to unfold between us until they threatened to go too far.

I watched his name flash on the screen and considered letting it go to voicemail. Considered never calling him back and never setting foot back in The Dive. I could delete his number and never speak to him again. My thumb hovered over the answer button. Finally, I swiped right, not understanding why I'd done it even as I brought the phone to my ear.

"Hello?"

"Harlow?"

"Yes. Who is this?" Let him think I hadn't programmed his number into my phone. Right now, I'd take any grab at dignity I could get.

"It's Denny."

I waited for a beat, not knowing what to say, and not wanting to make things any easier for him. Let him sweat.

"I'm calling to apologise. For the other night. I know I embarrassed you and—"

"What do you want, Denny?" It came out harsher than what I would've liked, but the memory of that night was like an imprint on my brain, and the humiliation was fresh, like a constantly weeping wound.

"Another date?"

"Another date? I think you need to have a date in order to have another one, wouldn't you say?"

What was I doing? Why was I even talking to him? My hand tightened around the phone. Something about last night had unsettled me. The way he'd gone from searing desire to nothing at all. How something had flared in him, bright and hot, something I hadn't recognised and couldn't name.

"I'm sorry. I froze." He paused, and I waited, standing at my window overlooking the city. The street below was a throng of people and vehicles. I watched as a man across the street drew up the shutter gate which protected his shop from would-be thieves, how a woman on a scooter narrowly missed a drunken man who had stepped out on the street in front of her. The sound of her blasting horn wafted up to me, and I closed the partially open window, even though it wouldn't be long before the temperature in here became stifling.

"I really like you and I want to make it up to you." Denny's voice was quiet, but insistent, and I felt my resolve weakening. "Harlow." The way he said my name sent a pleasurable shiver through me, and before I'd given my tongue the command to speak, I heard the words coming from my mouth.

"Okay. When?"

"Tonight? Got any plans?"

I was meeting Jesse and Carter this morning to discuss the intel and Carter's ongoing case, as well as where to start with investigating my father's death. It was going to be gruelling, emotional work, and having something to look forward to at the end of the day could get me through it. I paused. Last chance to back out. To refuse. I thought of who I knew in Gloam. Jesse. Carter. And Denny. Out of the three, it was only Jesse I could maybe call a friend. I thought of the distance between Gloam and The Sands, of my family in the home that suddenly felt as alien as this city.

"Yes. Tonight will work."

The line went dead, and I stood there for a long moment, still wearing my pyjamas, and wondering about the wisdom of involving myself with someone so soon after my father's death, so soon after arriving in a new and unwelcoming place.

***

When I arrived at Carter's office, Jesse was already there waiting for me. It seemed he'd been there for a while, with a half-drunk cup of coffee in front of him, and what appeared to be case notes in his hands, his feet propped up on a nearby chair.

Carter stood with his back to me, contemplating something outside his window.

"Good morning," I said, placing my handbag on the floor near the door and stepping across the threshold. Carter turned and eyed my bag. "Walking in Gloam with a visible bag is a great way to get robbed. What's in it? Not your piece, I hope?"

I rolled my eyes. "No. Wallet. Keys. Phone." I patted my hip. "I have a holster, you know."

"Good to know you have some common sense." I was about to snap back when I caught the barely perceptible gleam in his eye. When he didn't get the reaction he'd wanted, he grunted and gestured to an empty chair.

"Let's get started."

I slipped into the chair next to Jesse. He smiled at me, turning from the desk to face me. He looked tired and haggard, the dark rings beneath his eyes stark against the paleness of his skin. The t-shirt he was wearing was rumpled. There was a dark stain at the neckline.

"Jesse." Carter motioned towards a laptop perched on the edge of his overflowing desk. "Let's see what you have."

Jesse fished in the pocket of his jeans and came up with a removable disk. I was sure it was the one we'd klepped from the police station but said nothing as Jesse inserted it into the laptop and waited. Seconds later, the computer had installed it and Jesse clicked on the message which appeared. A video started playing. There was no sound. It showed the inside of a house. Either it was dusk or extremely poorly lit because the images of what looked like three people was murky at best.

We all leaned closer to the monitor, trying to make out the details. I caught the swirl of a skirt as the one figure moved about the kitchen. The other two, who I surmised were men from the way they moved and from their height, seemed to be having a discussion.

For a few minutes, nothing of interest happened. Then, the atmosphere between the two men seemed to shift, and I waited, tensing. My eyes were gradually adjusting to the gloom of the recording, and I could now make out that they were all drinking coffee. There was a lull where nothing happened, and then, all at once, a confrontation began. I couldn't make out what was happening as the two men, and then the woman, disappeared from the frame.

The perspective of the recording changed abruptly. All I could see was floorboards and feet, and then, the faces of both the woman, and one of the men filled the screen, slack with death.

I slapped a hand over my mouth to keep from screaming. Even though Jesse had told me about the intel, I still wasn't prepared for the shock of seeing him. *Matt.*

The recording shifted again, and this time there was a close-up of one hand, and then another, each bearing a X mark, blood seeping from the wounds.

The video ended, and for a long moment, none of us said anything.

I lowered my hand to my lap. "This is the intel we took from the cops?"

Jesse nodded. "It must've been recorded with a cell phone. It was definitely recorded on something light and movable."

"Why? Why would someone record this?"

Carter cleared his throat and handed me a slim stack of photographs. The top one was of a woman, face up, her blue eyes blank and staring. Her hand was beside her face, palm facing up, the skin marred by a crudely etched X. I shuddered. Her neck was mottled with bruises - tapered stretches of blue. The shape of fingers.

The next photo knocked the breath out of me. It was of two bodies, a man's and a woman's, their corpses next to each other, the man's throat displaying the same bruises, his eyes bulging.

163

A pool of blood formed a grisly halo around the woman's head. Despite what Uncle Matt had done to me as a young girl, I couldn't help but feel for both him and Angie. It was a gruesome way to die.

"Strangled. Like my father. Like the attempt on Chloe." I lowered the photographs, shaking my head. "What's the link? At face value, the murders all seem to have been committed by a member of the Natives, if the mark is anything to go by, but my father wasn't marked with it. Or Chloe. The inconsistencies mean something, don't they?"

"Hard to say. If we're talking a serial killer, then usually they follow the same patterns. But they also tend to escalate with each kill. There's a link between all the people you just mentioned in the fact that they all knew each other, right?"

I nodded, then reconsidered. "Actually, Uncle Matt and Aunt Angie didn't know Chloe or her family. Pop kept them…separate. We all wondered about it but never asked."

Carter pointed at the first photograph of the blue-eyed woman. "Do you recognise her?"

"No."

"She was killed ten years ago. She was found in a street gutter in a shady part of town." He picked up the photograph and tapped it. "Look at her ring finger." I had to force my eyes from her face to her hand. The starkness of the bruises against her milky skin was horrifically mesmerising, like being unable to look away from a bloody car wreck.

"There's nothing there."

"Precisely. She was married. Her husband said she never took her ring off because she was afraid of losing it. And yet, the ring wasn't found on her body."

"She could've taken it off at home. Or it could've fallen off."

"Her husband said she was wearing it the last time he saw her."

Jesse took the photograph from Carter and studied it. "It could've been a random gang killing. Sometimes the Natives exact their revenge by killing the loved ones of their enemies. She might have nothing to do with these other killings."

Carter pointed to the bottom corner of the photograph. "See there?"

Jesse squinted, then sighed. "Ah shit."

I leaned over Jesse's shoulder to see what they were looking at. I couldn't make it out at first. When I spotted it, I put a hand to my mouth. The angle of the photograph and how her hand was positioned made it impossible to be sure, but what looked very much like an X mark was carved into her palm.

"You're a merc, Jess. You've seen just as much as any cop who's been on the streets for years. You really think this is the work of the Natives?"

I watched them, my eyes moving from Carter's face to Jesse's, trying to hear what neither of them were saying. Something came back to me then, something Jesse had said to me at the diner. "Don't they usually work with blades?"

Jesse pointed a finger at me. "Exactly."

Carter stood and paced the tight space between his desk and the opposite wall, shaking his head. "No blades were found at any of the crime scenes. And yeah, strangulation isn't really their style. They like to work up close, get personal with their victims, but strangulation is so…"

"Intimate?" I supplied.

"Yes. Like the killer wanted the experience of seeing them die up close. Like it was personal."

"Could be issues around control. Exerting authority." Jesse picked up a pen and tapped it rapidly against Carter's desk for a moment, as if in time to the pace of his thoughts. "Or it could be sexual."

"Sexual?" My stomach heaved into my mouth at the thought. What else might the killer have done to either Pop or Chloe if he'd had more time?

Carter shook his head. "Unlikely. Especially considering..." He trailed off, glancing at me.

"Because he killed my father?"

Carter's hand on my shoulder and the gentle squeeze which followed was so light and unexpected that for a moment I was sure I'd imagined it.

Jesse tossed the pen on the desk, shaking his head. "We still don't know if it's the same killer or what the link is between the victims and the Natives. So far, only two of them have ties with the gang. Or at least, strong enough ties to assume motive."

Carter slid another photograph towards me across the desk. "Recognise her?" It took me a minute but then I nodded slowly. "Skylar. The woman Evans had us check on."

"Four bodies in just over a week. The easiest assumption would be that these are the Natives' killings, but it doesn't add up. They don't kill just anyone—they have a weirdly strict code for killings. Hits are reserved for traitors, informants and as a revenge tactic." Carter turned to me, and before he'd said a word, I knew what was coming. "Do you remember much around the time you were kidnapped?"

Drip drip drip.

The office felt too warm. The walls felt close, as if the room had suddenly grown smaller. I went to the only window which looked out on the street. It looked immovable, but I was desperate for air – even if it was the air laced with the stink of the city.

"It doesn't open," Carter said from behind me. My fingers itched to try anyway, to manoeuvre my fingers beneath the wooden frame, to struggle against its weight just to distract myself from the memories.

I shoved my fingers into my armpits, my back to the room, my gaze on the streets outside, unable to take a single detail in, fighting the instinct to run from the room.

Maybe it would be easier to recount if I didn't have to look at them, if I wasn't able to see their reactions.

"I don't remember that much. What I do remember is strange and disjointed. I know there was a dripping tap somewhere in the room where they kept me, but I never found it. I remember feeling confused as to why they were keeping me downstairs, instead of in the main part of the house, with them. When I figured that part out, I was so…afraid. Uncle Matt was an old family friend. Up until then he'd treated me like a daughter. We didn't know anything about him being the leader of the Natives or my father's involvement with the gang."

I forced myself to turn and look at them. "I remember their son, too. He would sometimes bring me food. It was the most I'd ever seen of him, even though our families spent a lot of time together. But they rarely brought him. He always seemed to be sick or away. He always seemed to be watching me while I was there, as if Uncle Matt had asked him to, but I got the feeling he hated it. That he was being forced to do it."

Carter was frowning, and Jesse, too, looked puzzled.

"What?"

"Matthew was a highly publicised figure in the press and on the street. Everyone knew who he was. There was never any mention of a son. Do you remember his name?"

Nausea clawed at my throat. I spoke through my teeth, trying to ignore the surge of acid which was threatening to rise to my mouth.

"No. He never told me his name."

I turned back to the window, trying to concentrate only on my breathing, on the sight of the fading sunlight, how the shadows of the buildings grew longer as the day waned.

I glanced at my watch and startled out of my stupor. Shit. Later than I'd thought. If I didn't get moving, I would be late for my date with Denny.

At the thought of getting ready and going out again, I felt the deep drag of exhaustion. I regretted accepting his invitation. I should be here, delving deeper into all this. I was in Gloam to find my father's killer, not to date. I hesitated.

Jesse was watching me keenly. "You okay?"

I nodded, moving towards the door. Whatever I decided, I wanted desperately to get out of this office and onto the street. Anything to not breathe the close air of this room any longer.

I gathered my things. "I need to go. Can we pick this up tomorrow?"

"Got somewhere to go?" There was a teasing lilt to Jesse's tone, and something about the warm familiarity of it eased the tension in my shoulders, unravelled the ball of anxiety in my gut.

"Yeah." I managed a smile. "A hot date."

Chapter Eighteen

Harlow

RIDICULOUS. I'D RUSHED TO get here only to be left standing outside waiting for him. The restaurant he'd suggested was a swanky affair – white linen tablecloths, with pressed royal blue serviettes and glinting silverware. I fidgeted, my fingers working at the strap of my dress, my foot tapping against the pavement. I glanced at my watch again. Only a minute had passed since I'd last checked.

I stood there, again wondering why I was here. The guilt that I'd managed to keep at bay gnawed at me. I should have been with Jesse and Carter, going over the case. Or I should have been combing the streets myself. I hadn't come here to make a life. I'd come to find my father's killer. *Focus on that. On what kind of information Denny can give you about Gloam, about the gangs. That's why you're here.* It was a lie, but one I was content to sit with for the moment.

A dark head bobbed above the rest as a crowd of people crossed the street at once, and a moment later he emerged, dressed in clean dark jeans and an olive-green buttoned shirt, his shoes old but polished. When he caught sight of me, he smiled, and I found myself unable to hold his gaze, unsettled by this warm reception compared to the last time I'd seen him. He'd apologised, sure, but that feeling when his body had stiffened against mine and he'd pushed me away, remained branded into my memory.

When he reached me, he paused, as if unsure how to greet me. Should we hug? Shake hands? Kiss on the cheek? We both stood there for a long and excruciating moment before he motioned to the door of the restaurant. "Shall we?"

I walked ahead of him. The light press of his hand against the small of my back electrified my senses, making me aware of every sensation of my body and every movement of his.

A man in a sharply cut suit came forward to greet us. He consulted a list in front of him, asking for Denny's reservation and then led us to a table at the back, tucked cosily into a corner and lit by subtle overhead lighting and the flickering flames of two tea candles set into crystal candle holders.

I took in the opulence of the place uneasily. The host pulled out a seat for me and then pushed my chair in, as if I were a toddler in need of assistance. He handed us two menus with a perfunctory smile and disappeared.

For the first time since I'd arrived, I looked directly at Denny. "This is too much. It's a first date." I wanted to kick myself for calling it a date. I needed to curb his expectations from the start.

I half-rose, not wanting to embarrass him but at the same time not wanting him to think that an expensive meal equalled sexual favours, but he laid a hand on my arm, gently drawing me back into my seat.

"Sit, please. The owner is a friend of mine, and he owed me a favour."

"So, I'm supposed to be impressed by this place? By your contacts?"

The turmoil of contradicting feelings within me was making my head ache. I wanted to make it clear I wasn't here for company or food, but information. At the same time, I wanted to know him better.

Denny reached for my hand, taking it carefully, giving me time to pull away. "I'm sorry for what happened the last time we saw each other. I just…froze, I suppose." He laughed. "You make me nervous."

Something about his confession, about the vulnerable way he said it, as if expecting me to laugh at him, made me soften. I let him hold my hand but said nothing.

"I'd really like to get to know you tonight, and I wanted to bring you somewhere nice so we could eat a decent meal and not scream at each other over the sound of music and the shouting of horny men."

I laughed despite myself. "Horny men?"

"The Dive. Don't get me wrong—I'm grateful for a job that pays half-decently and doesn't involve me having to sell my own body, but men are endlessly insatiable. I feel sorry for the dancers. They're better paid than the bartenders but at least we don't have to listen to the catcalls of drunk, overzealous men."

"How about the catcalls of drunk, overzealous women?"

My nerves had settled now, and I was starting to enjoy listening to him talk, to see him outside the environment of the bar, of his workplace, and to see him like this. Talking animatedly, his eyes on me, his knee brushing against mine underneath the table. I pushed away the rush of guilt. The night was young. I still had plenty of time to get the information I needed.

171

"Those too."

The waiter appeared then, asking for our orders. Denny glanced at me. "Mind if I order for you?" When I didn't protest, he rattled off an order of drinks and then food, using terms I was unfamiliar with. By the time he was done, I had no idea what we'd be eating.

When the waiter was gone, I leaned over the table. "So how long have you been in the city? And why are you here?"

"A few years. Since I was eighteen. I left home and never looked back."

"Hmm. Plenty of time to build up contacts. Still, it's pretty impressive to know someone like the owner of a place like this." I wasn't sure why, but it made me feel uneasy.

He shrugged. "I meet a lot of people as a barman. This city can be surprising. I find so many of the locals almost hostile and yet, when they're sitting on a barstool, talking to a lowly bartender like me, they tell me things they wouldn't tell their best friends or family. I suppose it's a kind of trade. I listen to them talk about things they need to get off their chest, and then, in exchange, they offer me things like a free meal, a discounted ride, or a sample of drugs."

I raised an eyebrow. "What about the offer of women?" It wasn't something I'd planned to say, but all the same, I watched his face carefully.

He laughed. "Sometimes." He ran a light finger along the back of my hand and then rested it beside mine. "Call me old-fashioned, but I like to date women who aren't gifted to me."

There was something odd about the way he said it. As if he wanted to mean it, but there was a dissonance between what he'd said and how he really felt.

"Interesting. And why you'd come here? You were so young, and this city is pretty hostile."

"The same reason as everyone else, I imagine. A fresh start. Anonymity. A different life."

He paused, breaking eye contact. He seemed hesitant to go on.

"What was wrong with your life before?"

He let go of my hand, withdrawing further. "Nothing, really. I just needed a change."

He seemed unwilling to say much more, but desperation was bubbling up in me. This might be my only chance to discover what he knew.

"This might sound odd. But I was wondering if you've ever head of Frank Novac?" It felt like my heartbeat had taken residence in my brain. The sound of the rush of my blood threatened to drown out his reply.

Denny seemed to grow pale beneath the muted glow of the lights overhead. He straightened in his seat, his gaze leaving my face and moving to a point beyond my shoulder.

"No. Why?"

Was he lying? I pressed my hands into my lap, squeezing my thighs beneath the table in an effort to stop myself from grabbing the front of his shirt, and rattling him until the information I wanted fell out of him, like salt from a shaker.

"What about the gangs in the city? Met any of the members? I'm especially interested in the Natives." I was gabbling but didn't know how to stop.

Denny reared back in his seat, the scrape of its feet on the wooden floor loud in the muted pitch of the restaurant. "Why are you asking me this?"

I tried for nonchalant, even as sweat formed in my armpits and threatened to drip down my arms. "Because I'm new to the city. And I'm doing merc work. Some inside info would be useful, don't you think?"

He seemed to sense my discomfort. The tense line of his shoulders eased, and when he spoke, his words were measured. "Look, it feels like you're grilling me. I wanted us to get to know each other tonight. Can we talk about something else?"

He looked hurt. Heat rose to my cheeks.

"Of course. I was just…curious."

"Who is this Frank Novac anyway?"

I wanted to tell him the truth, but something made me hesitate. He was a stranger, after all, no matter how oddly familiar he felt to me. Already, Jesse and Carter knew my story, and that felt like plenty enough.

"No one. I just heard he was killed recently. A suspected gang killing in a small town."

His eyes roamed my face in a way that made me look away. I tried not to squirm in my seat. Looking him straight in the eye felt impossible, as if he'd be able to read my thoughts.

The waiter arrived then with a tall glass bottle, and I was so grateful for his appearance at that moment I had the urge to jump out of my seat and hug him.

God. Get a grip. What the hell is wrong with you?

Drops of condensation rolled along the glass as the waiter removed the cork and then poured out something light green and cold, disappearing again wordlessly.

For lack of anything else to say, I blurted, "I'm from The Sands."

For an excruciating moment, I thought he was going to keep asking me about my interest in Frank and the Natives, but then he relaxed again, and the guarded look in his eyes disappeared.

"The Sands? I've never heard of it."

"I'm not surprised. Not many people have. Tiny place outside the city. Old school. Everyone knows each other, and the houses are built so close together you can hear your neighbour snoring. But it was a good place to grow up. Safe. Sheltered." Even as I said it, I could see Pop's body in my mind's eye, the violence of his death in the lurid bruises around his throat. I closed my eyes, trying to shutter away the image.

Denny's hand covered my own, his palm warm, his fingers firm. "Are you okay?"

I opened my eyes and returned the squeeze, nodding. "I was just thinking about my father. I miss him." I wanted to tell Denny. The words formed on my lips, but before I could let them fall, they changed form, and instead I blurted out a lie. "He called me earlier, telling me how nuts I am to be here, going on about how dangerous it is. Parents, right? Even when you're an adult they still worry, still can't resist checking on you." The words felt like rocks I had to spit out, or risk choking on them. How I wished it were still true. How I wished I could still call him, hear his voice, hear him lecture me about being careful and the dangers of being away from home, from family. I would do anything now to hear the reproach in his voice, to hear him tell me how my place was with him, with my mother and brothers. How not everyone had a place where they belonged, and how I was one of the lucky ones.

I raised my eyes to Denny's face, and what I saw there surprised me. A kind of bleakness, his eyes so much darker than before, his

175

fingers tightening around the delicate stem of his glass, threatening to break it. He seemed to be having a kind of internal struggle, warring with himself, unaware of me or anything else around him, hearing something the rest of us couldn't. When I squeezed the hand which was still holding mine, he jumped, his eyes clearing and his other hand relaxing its grip on his glass. He gave a shaky laugh, as if I'd jumped out at him from behind a door, and he was embarrassed by his display of fear.

"Sorry. My mind wandered there for a second." He cleared his throat and withdrew his hand from mine, my fingers slightly damp from his grip.

He took a long swallow of his drink, the liquid sliding readily down his throat, visibly relaxing. He set his glass down, meeting my eyes again.

What had just happened?

I considered the liquid in my glass, a cool green, and raised it to my lips, taking a tentative sip. Light, crisp and fresh. A hint of sweetness. I swallowed, surprised and pleased, and took another sip, forgetting the oddness of the moment before, and savouring the surprising foreign flavour.

Denny watched me, waiting for my reaction.

I pressed my lips together, the taste of the drink lingering. "It's lovely. What is it?"

His eyes widened, and he stared at for so long I grew uncomfortable beneath his gaze. "What?"

"You've never had wine before?" The way he asked it, as if I was some country bumpkin who had never set foot outside her hometown, soured the taste of the drink in my mouth.

He must've caught my expression, because he hurried to finish his thought before I could take further offense.

"It's not uncommon, you know."

'What, my lack of worldliness?' I asked tartly.

"No. Not having tasted wine. It's scarce, and exorbitantly expensive, but it's part of the favour my contact owes me."

The food arrived, neat steaming parcels which I couldn't begin to identify.

As the waiter laid down several platters of different dishes, I watched Denny. He was good looking enough. Not a face you would necessarily remember, but one that was easy on the eyes all the same. There was something oddly forgettable about him, as if his easy charm and inviting warmth were a cover for something far more complex beneath. I'd hoped he'd be able to help me with my investigation – that maybe he'd be able to supply me with information. Names. A path to start down. But maybe it was better this way. I could keep him separate from all this. Someone for me to enjoy when my current life had so few other pleasures.

I took a bite of something warm and melting, and after that I was lost to the explosions of medleys of flavours I couldn't have imagined. I savoured every bite, every mouthful, unable to utter a single word until my plate was empty. I sat back, full and satiated, grinning.

I finally looked up to find Denny's eyes on me. "What did you think?"

I gestured to my empty plate. "This speaks for itself." I patted my stomach. "Thanks to you I might need a little post-dinner exercise." The innuendo had been unintentional, but as he looked across the table at me, the memory of his body pressed against mine, the heat of the brick wall against my back, flashed across my mind.

He raised his glass in a half-salute. "That can always be arranged." He was smiling wolfishly, fully aware of my reaction, as if the heat of my thoughts had warmed the air between us.

He leaned back, lacing his hands behind his head. The top two buttons of his shirt had been left undone, exposing the skin beneath, and I imagined the warmth of his skin beneath my hands, the grip of his fingers in my hair, his tongue inside my mouth.

I shifted, feeling uncomfortably warm. I wrenched my eyes away, looking around the restaurant instead, seeing nothing, willing myself to keep my cool.

"Space for dessert?"

I shook my head, taking another sip of my wine, surprised to find my glass nearly empty. "Never had much of a sweet tooth. Even as a kid."

"I feel like we've spent so much time talking about me tonight." He said it without rancour, but something unreadable remained in his eyes. "Your turn now." He leaned forward. The scent of him washed over me – warm and masculine.

"So why a merc?"

I considered this. I could tell him the truth. I eyed him over my wine glass. It was one thing to share my background with people like Jesse and Carter, who had a direct interest in the murders. But it was something else to share these details with Denny, who made me feel so many conflicting things at once.

"I'm good with guns. A skill highly valued in Gloam, apparently. It made sense."

"Been around guns long?"

A memory surfaced. Pop handing me my first gun on my thirteenth birthday—a family tradition. My brothers had received their own handguns on their respective birthdays. The Sauer had been mine. He'd taken me to the shooting range, despite Ma's mutterings about guns and children – the same protests she'd made on my brothers' birthdays. Pop had placed the gun in my hands, and I remember how the weapon had felt, how perfectly smooth and light it was, how the fit of it felt made for me.

"My father taught me to shoot. I held a gun for the first time when I was five. He bought me my own piece when I was thirteen, much to my mother's disapproval. We all got our guns at that age."

"We?"

"My brothers and I. Rich and Charlie. I'm the youngest. A fact they never let me forget." I forced a smile. Talking about my family was making my throat thicken. I felt dangerously close to tears. I looked down at my lap, pretending to fuss with my serviette, waiting for the feeling to pass.

"What about your family?" I asked, changing tact.

He shrugged, growing visibly uncomfortable. "What about them?"

"You haven't mentioned them. What are they like? Are you close?"

He looked away from me, searching the restaurant for the waiter. Catching his eye, he motioned for the bill, finally returning his attention to me.

The smile he wore when he turned back to me looked brittle.

"Not much to say, really. Your typical, white picket fence, run-of-the-mill family."

He seemed reticent to say more, which only made me more curious. "What about siblings?"

He shook his head briefly, his gaze leaving my face to roam the restaurant. "I'm an only child."

He sat rigidly in his chair, as if the subject of his family was causing him physical pain, despite his words. I knew I should leave it at that, but I felt a need to know him, to come away from tonight knowing something real about him, something that perhaps, he kept hidden from others.

I reached for Denny's hand, but we were interrupted by the arrival of the waiter with the bill. He proffered it like a gift.

The odd tension at our table broke as Denny reached for it. I got a glimpse of the total and forced myself to look away and pretend ignorance. How could food and one bottle of wine cost that much?

"Chef just needs you to sign. He'll take care of the rest." The waiter handed Denny a pen and he signed with a flourish and returned it to the waiter's eager hands.

He looked across the table at me, fixing me in place with his gaze, his smile growing into something else, something which made me squirm pleasantly, anticipation lighting in the pit of my stomach.

Once we were outside he reached for my hand. "Go to your place?"

Before I could answer he kissed me, his mouth warm and inviting, his free hand pressing into my back, drawing me to him until my body was pressed against his, and I could feel every outline of him through his clothes.

There it was. The truth I'd been hiding from myself the whole evening. The lie I'd told myself. I was here because I needed, so badly, to lose myself in something, someone. I'd thought the something would be this investigation, but now that I had Carter, and Jesse, I felt a kind of paralysis, as if getting closer to the truth scared me. I wasn't ready.

I drew back, breathless, and nodded wordlessly. We stepped out onto the curb and hailed a taxi, despite the restaurant's proximity to my place. I just couldn't think of walking now, of having him so close beside me, his body brushing mine, and not being able to do the things I wanted to do to him.

Once in the taxi he moved into me, but instead of kissing my mouth he kissed my forehead, my cheeks, my jawline, and then kissed just the corner of my mouth, his tongue teasing my lips, and every thought I'd had went silent.

We pulled up at my place and took the lift to my floor, not touching, the air between us electric. Stepping out of the lift, reaching my front door, I tried to insert the key into the lock, but my shaking hands only managed to rattle it against the doorjamb. He came in behind me, his front against my back, his hands enclosing my hips, pressing me against the door. The key fell from my hand, and his lips found my neck, trailing from just underneath my ear to my collarbone and then, lifting my hair, the back of my neck. I let out a moan I couldn't hold back, and then a nervous giggle. I turned in his embrace.

"We need to get inside. My neighbours will talk."

He slid down the length of my body, his eyes never leaving mine, over my breasts and stomach, between my thighs and to my feet, where he retrieved the key and rose, putting a space between us I couldn't bear. He unlocked the door and we fell inward in a tangle of limbs, our bodies pressed together as one. I kicked the door closed behind us, my hands pushing between us to get at his belt and then his jeans, and his breath grew laboured in my mouth, pitching my own excitement.

He tugged at my dress and I let go of the snap on his jeans so he could lift it over my head, tossing it to the floor and drawing back to drink me in, his eyes tracing my body in a trail that felt as physical as if it were his hands moving down the length of me. He moved behind me and unsnapped my bra with quick and sure fingers, his palms moving to cup my breasts, teasing the nipples, kissing my neck and then my mouth, his tongue probing and eager.

One hand dropped to my underwear, and he worked it over my ass until it dropped to the floor, his fingers finding me and touching, teasing, until the room swam around me, and all I could think about was the pressure of his fingers on me.

And then, as I was peaking, as I was turning to him, wanting him inside me, he pushed me away, forcefully enough that I stumbled back a step, clutching at my bare chest in shock. He buttoned his jeans, intent on dressing, his eyes avoiding mine. He dropped to the couch and pressed his forehead into his hands. The only sound in the room was of our laboured breathing, and then the rustle of material as I snatched my clothes from the floor, dressing with shaking hands.

"Really, Denny? Again? You do this to me again?"

My gut instinct had been right. I shouldn't have met him tonight. I'd told myself my intentions were to pump him for information, but I'd known from the moment I'd agreed to meet him tonight that I'd end up here.

He looked up at me, his eyes scared and vulnerable, and he seemed so young then, like a boy in a man's body, a kid who had started something he was too afraid to finish.

"I'm so sorry. It's not what you think."

"Really? It's not that you actually don't desire me?"

My voice was loud and I wished I could take back my words the moment I spoke them, my humiliation verbalised and now undeniable.

He rose, reaching to embrace me, but settling for taking my hands instead when I tried to step out of reach.

"You're the only person I've met in this city that I actually want to get to know. And things are moving so fast. Too fast."

I tried to pull away but he held onto me, his eyes pleading. "This city is all about the fast. About the immediate. About instant gratification. And I don't want that with you. With you, I want to take the time to know you. To see you. All of you."

He laughed quietly. "Trust me. It's not a lack of desire." He took a step closer, and tipped my chin up with one finger, so I was looking straight at him. The colour of his eyes had deepened, the brown in them disappearing almost completely, the green vivid and mesmerising.

I couldn't have said anything even if I'd wanted to. The way he was looking at me, I felt lost and tethered at the same time, like an anchor which was losing its grip on the bottom of the ocean, ready to drift into the unknown.

"Stick around, okay? I'll make it worth your while." He kissed me, carefully this time, politely, like a relative long since seen, but then his tongue touched mine; the taste of a promise.

"You're a complicated man," I said, smiling now.

"You have no idea."

Later that night, when I'd closed the door on his departure, leaning against the rough wood and thinking about the past few hours, I realised I felt happy for the first time since I'd left home. That the weight of everything which had happened felt lighter, and my grief was, for the moment, a little less suffocating.

Chapter Nineteen

Harlow

THE FOLLOWING MORNING, I showed up at Carter's office, juggling two cups of coffee and trying to knock at the same time. Sensing my presence, or hearing my struggle, Carter opened the door, taking one of the cups from me.

"Is this your way of saying you hate my coffee?"

I smiled. "You know your coffee is awful. Don't you make enough as a PI to buy the better stuff, and not that shit that passes as coffee?"

His smile turned to a scowl, and he waved me in, closing the door behind me. His office was more chaotic than ever today, stacks of papers and files taking up every available surface. It was stuffy inside, the heat of yesterday and the oncoming warmth of today caught between its walls. I considered the window I'd tried to open yesterday, and then reached for the spare chair shoved in the corner of the room, using it to as a prop to keep his office door open. "Make yourself at home," Carter muttered.

"How do you not die of heat in here? Don't you feel it?"

Carter grunted noncommittedly. I noticed that there was a mattress on the floor, shoved into the far corner, covered in rumpled bed sheets and a creased pillow.

"Did you stay here last night?"

He nodded, rubbing his palms over his face and then his bald head. "I couldn't sleep. Kept going over this case in my head and so I thought I'd go over everything again in case there was something I missed. Didn't want to go across town by the time I was done."

"Don't you have anything to go home to?"

The look he gave me made me wish I hadn't asked.

"You mean anyone?"

Immediately, I regretted my words. "Sorry, it's none of my business."

He took a sip of his coffee, watching me over the rim of his paper cup. "You're right, it's not. Also—" he held the cup away from him, looking at it with appreciation—"you're right about my coffee."

I hid my smile by turning my back and dumping my bag on the floor.

"Shall we get to work?"

He gestured to a file on my chair, bulging with paperwork. "I gathered everything for you last night. Every note, every report, every photograph of the victims so far." He hesitated. "I contacted Detective Madden for your father's and Chloe's case file. Everything on them is there too, including the photographs taken at the crime scene." A gnawing sensation started at the pit of my stomach and worked its way into my chest, making it ache.

"They don't have the X mark."

"I could've told you that."

185

Carter considered me. "Sometimes, in moments of severe trauma, we miss details."

I snorted. "You don't think we would've noticed an X mark in my father's palm? You don't think Chloe would've felt it when she came to?"

"All I'm saying, is the absence of the mark could mean the victims aren't connected. It could be a coincidence that they all knew each other. It also means we could be hunting more than one killer."

"You're a PI, Carter. Do you believe in coincidences?"

He shrugged. "When something can't be adequately explained, then what else is it but a coincidence?"

He sank into his chair opposite me, draining the last of his coffee and tossing the cup into a nearby dustbin. "Gangs have initiation rites. Killings, rapes. No new members can join without the initiation. No exceptions."

"What's your point?"

"Generally, they don't kill without permission from the top. Their system isn't that different from law enforcement. They have a tiered method of authority like ours. Nothing gets done without instruction from the head honchos."

I shuddered. What had Pop done to become a member? And why? That was the question that had taunted me since Pop died. Why would he join a gang?

"Did my father like being a cop?"

Carter turned to me, surprised. "He loved it. Aside from you kids and your mother, it was his first love."

"Then...why?"

"I wish I had an answer for you, Harlow. You deserve one. But I don't think I'm the right person to say. I didn't even know what he was doing until he was forced to tell me." He paused. "Every time I think I've seen every facet of human nature, something happens and I'm forced to reevaluate what I think I know. I thought I knew your Pop. Maybe I did. But maybe I only knew what he let me see."

My throat felt tight. I swallowed hard, dropping my gaze to the file in my lap, willing myself to open it. It wasn't so much the idea of looking at more corpses that I found repulsive. But this was my father. I knew there would be photos of Chloe's injuries as well, and I steeled myself for what was to come.

Taking a breath, I opened the file, folding the soft cardboard cover behind the stack of papers. I skipped past the handwritten notes and the typed reports, coming to the photographs. I cleared a space on Carter's desk and laid out each photograph without really looking at them, until they were all there, spread into four neat rows, a collage of violence.

I forced my gaze to the first row, which were all of Chloe. The bruises encircling her throat. The paleness of her skin beneath the harsh lighting of the hospital. The welt on her forehead from her fall when she'd lost consciousness. The look in her eyes as she faced the camera – fear and defiance and anger.

I drew a deep and shuddering breath and then directed my gaze at the next row of photographs, taking in the details. My father's beloved face devoid of all emotion, wiped clean like a dirty kitchen counter. The mottled skin of his throat, the blankness of his eyes.

I swallowed against the grief rising in my throat, giving way instead to the anger that seemed to always be there, just waiting for my acknowledgment. It rushed through my body and made my hand fist around the photograph, nearly tearing it. It was only when Carter's hand gently pried mine open, that I realised he was beside me.

I relaxed my grip and let him take it from me, placing it back in its row with the others, somewhat rumpled.

"You sure you want to do this? I'm a PI, Harlow. I can handle this on my own, if this is too much for you."

I glared up at him, my hands curled into such tight fists I could feel my nails digging into the palms of my hands.

"You think I'm too close to this to see clearly." It wasn't a question, because of course he thought that. It was written all over his face and in the way he was looking at me.

"I do. But I'm not going to bar you from being here, if that's what you want. But you can trust me to do this right. I want to catch this guy."

"Even if I wanted to, I can't stay away. This is my family. I promised them I'd find who did this. And I promised myself."

He regarded me, then nodded, stacking the photographs into a neat pile and placing them face down on the desk. "Okay. But no more crime scene photos for now. Read the notes and the reports. Then let me know your thoughts."

I started with the report on the murders of Matt and Angie. I examined the photograph of the front of the house, the blue door stark against the greying and flaking paint of the walls. I didn't know why, but I kept coming back to that detail – the blue door. Distinctive, and why blue? Why paint your door at all? The police had been called to the scene by a neighbour, who had noticed the open front door, gone inside, and discovered the bodies.

"Does the front door have any significance? The fact that it's blue, I mean."

Carter nodded. "Yes and no. I haven't been able to confirm this, but I found some information about the Natives from years ago, where a blue door signified the fall of a member. Whether by death, or because they betrayed the gang. The rumour goes that it was a way for the Natives to keep track of members. But like I said, not anything I would bank on. I found the info in a small article that came up, something written a long time ago."

Interesting.

I skimmed over the details of the report, not finding anything further of interest. Something occurred to me.

"Did Jesse hand the intel over to the cops?"

Carter looked up. "No. He and I agreed to keep it between us for now. We still don't know who hired him to get it, or why."

"Hasn't the client asked for it?"

Carter shook his head. "Jesse made a copy of the footage, so he could deliver on the job. But when he called the fixer who'd given Jesse the job, the fixer said the client was unreachable. The contact number the client gave no longer works, like it's been disconnected."

I mulled over this for a second. "So Jesse still has the original recording?"

"Yeah."

"Why would someone record it? Doesn't it seem deliberate? And it seems obvious it was the killer themselves who was recording it, because the angle changes during the attack."

"Unless there were two of them. That would fit with the likelihood of a gang killing more than a solo act. They often carry out jobs in pairs or trios, for safety reasons."

"Were there any signs of forced entry?" I asked.

"None. It seems they either never locked their doors, or they knew their attacker and let him in."

"So a friend, a neighbour, even a relative?"

"Sure, could be."

I shifted in my seat. A slick of sweat had formed beneath my legs, creating a sticky pool between my skin and the old leather. Despite the open door, the room felt suffocating in the heat. Outside the air was still and heavy, without even a whisper of a breeze.

"Have the cops traced anyone who knew the couple?"

"They're still working on it, as am I."

"What about the son I mentioned yesterday? Did he still live with them?"

"No. The neighbours maintain they haven't seen him in years. Not since he turned eighteen. Their closest neighbour, Mara Bishop, remembers that on the day he left, it was amid a heated argument. She says she hasn't seen the boy since, although by now of course he'd be a man."

"Did she give a name?"

"She can't recall the boy's name. She said she'd call if it came to her."

"What about the other neighbours? Could none of them recall his name?"

"Only Mara has lived there all this time. The other neighbours have moved since, and Mara's getting on in life. Hopefully it'll come to her."

I nodded, drumming my fingers against the tabletop, trying to remember if Pop or Uncle Matt had ever mentioned him by name during one of their visits but came up blank.

***

Hours later, a knock sounded at Carter's door. Without waiting for a reply, the door swung open to reveal Jesse. "You two look like you could use a drink. How about it?"

Carter's eyes were bloodshot, his head drooping slightly as he bent over his notes, squinting at the page. "I'm out." Carter rose and stretched, his back clicking audibly. "I need to go home and sleep in a real bed. And if I look at those case files any longer, I think I'm going to go blind."

He pointed at me. "You should go, though. You've had a hell of a day and I think you could benefit from blowing off some steam."

Jesse raised his eyebrows at me questioningly. "Coming?"

I rose, my legs cramping from sitting all day, my back stiff and unyielding.

"Sure. Can we go somewhere that's within walking distance, though? I'm so tired of sitting and a lungful of good old pollution and the opportunity to stretch my legs first would be great."

"Deal." He looked back at Carter. "Sure you won't join us?"

Carter waved us off. "This old man needs his sleep. You kids have fun."

Jesse laughed and followed me out the door. "I'm about as much of a kid as you are, but I'll take the compliment all the same."

Chapter Twenty

Harlow

WE WALKED ALONG THE sidewalk, the sun beginning to dip behind the buildings, a light breeze springing up and stirring a pile of trash on the sidewalk, pushing it along beside us. We dodged people as we walked, small children darting around us impatiently, their tired parents trailing behind. An old man shuffled past, reeking of unwashed skin and nights spent on the street, holding his left arm with his right hand, as if for support. A teen caught my eye, and immediately came towards me, her eyes sunken and bloodshot, her outstretched hands shaking. Her hair was matted against her cheek, her clothes filthy and one size too small.

"Coin? Just a bit of coin?" I wanted to reach into my pocket for the few notes I had there, but Jesse tugged at my arm, hurrying me away. "Don't give to her. She's strung out. You'll just add to her problem. She won't buy food with whatever you give her, she'll just get high."

The girl muttered an expletive underneath her breath as we turned away, just loud enough for it to reach us.

Ignoring her, Jesse propelled me forward, pointing down the street. "Ever been there?" I followed the direction of his finger, but instead of seeing what he was pointing at, my gaze fell on a group of loitering young men, their eyes fixed on us. One broke from the group and came towards us, sauntering, his hands in his pockets. Three more followed in his wake, and as I was about to say something to Jesse, they surrounded us, closing ranks so we were trapped between them.

"We got something to say, and we don't want to say it here." The leader directed his words at me. "So we have a little corner just around there, where I'd like to have my word." Sensing our reluctance, he took my arm, his other hand slipping beneath my shirt, easing my gun from its holster. "No funny business. Many more of us than you, so you answer our questions, and everyone gets to leave alive."

A second man came up beside Jesse, holding out a hand. "I know you're armed. Hand it over, nice and easy." Jesse unclipped his handgun from its belt and gave it over, catching my eye briefly. He carried a blade too, small but deadly, inside his boot, held in place with a specially made clip. Satisfied, the man took Jesse's gun and tucked it out of sight. The four of them closed around us and forced us to walk. The crowds mulling around us parted at the sight of us, and it was then that I noticed they all wore the same cut-off leather jacket. Black; an eagle with outstretched wings in flight, its talons extended. A jolt went through me. The Natives.

We were herded around a corner into a street which came to a dead-end. More Native members waited for us, the largest of them rising to meet us, his arms the width of my thighs, his shaven head a tapestry of ink.

"Ah. Good work boys." He motioned for us to come forward, his gaze passing briefly over Jesse before coming to rest on me. "I see you hooked two fish." He chuckled. "We don't need this one. Throw him back. I want to talk to this one alone."

Jesse stiffened. His fingers twitched, and I knew he was waiting for the moment to bend and reach for his hidden blade.

"If she stays, I stay. Whatever you have to say you'll say while I'm standing here."

The leader moved so fast I didn't even see him draw back his fist until it met with Jesse's face, his nose crunching beneath the blow, blood spurting and streaming on to the front of his shirt.

The leader grabbed Jesse, bunching his shirt in his fist, blood and all, pulling him closer until their noses were nearly touching, his words quiet but clear. "You leave now, or a broken nose will be the least of your problems."

"Jesse. It's okay. Go. I'll meet you where we planned," I said, willing him to cooperate.

The member who had taken Jesse's gun pressed it into the small of his back. "Move."

They disappeared around the corner, Jesse's hands laced above his head, the muzzle of his own gun snug against his back as the gang member moved him out of sight. I shut my eyes, taking a breath and then opening them again, looking at the leader. "You got me here. What do you want?"

He chuckled. "A firecracker. I like. I like my woman with a bit of fire, you know. Keeps things exciting."

He pulled a small blade from his belt, touching the tip lightly to my throat. "You know, us Natives love our blades. We're knife connoisseurs. You know why?"

I wanted to speak, but the blade was still there, and I was afraid any movement at all would pierce the skin, and so I said nothing.

"Precision, you see. Blades make a mess—aye—so much admin with the clean-up—but if your blade is sharp and perfectly made, it does the job cleanly." He removed the blade and held it up to the fading light, smiling. "You don't want to be hacking away, amiright?" Chuckles from the other members.

"A little bird told me you're looking into a few murders, and that we"—he waved his free arm in a circle to include the other men—"had something to do with it."

Before I could reply, the blade was at my back, the tip slicing smoothly through my t-shirt, pressing into the skin just enough for me to feel the pressure.

"Someone wants a word." He pointed upwards with a finger, indicating the building directly above us, its shadow growing longer as the sun sank closer to the horizon.

"Besides you?"

His expression darkened, and the tip of the blade pressed a little harder. I felt a pinch of pain and then the slow drip of blood, just a drop, but I refused to squirm, or scream, or show any emotion at all that would give this prick an ounce of satisfaction.

"Yeah, Spitfire. Besides me." He pushed me towards the doors of the building, the rest of the men forming a half circle at my back, blocking off the exit to the streets beyond.

The doors opened automatically at our approach. The coolness of its interior was a shock against my hot skin, and I paused for an instant, closing my eyes to the sensation. The touch of the blade urged me forward again, and I took in the foyer with an audible gasp. A high, vaulted ceiling, showcasing an enormous glittering chandelier. What appeared to be a reception desk to my left was occupied by a pert blonde. She smiled at the men, her lips curving a little more when she set eyes on me, as if she'd been expecting me.

The men directed me towards the elevator, it's door richly gold and ornate. It slid open silently as the leader touched the button, leading me and the other men inside. I watched the counter as we climbed higher, until it dinged merrily at floor thirty-five.

When I stepped out, my shoes sank into the plushness of the carpet. The corridor was silent, and even though it was brightly lit, it felt ominous. They led me to the last door at the end of the corridor, and for the first time I felt a prickle of fear. I was alone, and without my piece, being taken to a room I assumed would contain more Natives. I wondered if this had to do with Pop's death. Were they finally going to finish what they'd started all those years ago with Uncle Matt's kidnapping attempt?

The door was opened from the inside by a heavily pierced man. He leered at me, his teeth large and yellow, the smell of his vile breath washing over me. I suppressed a shudder, averting my eyes, hearing the conversation which had hummed a moment earlier around the room go quiet.

It was only when I could see the feet of an enormous desk that I looked up. The man across from me rose, his gaze intent on my face. He was smiling, his hand reaching out for mine. I hesitated, then took it, my fingers disappearing into his massive grip.

He shot a glance at my escort, and the pressure against my back was gone. The other men who had arrived with us left the room, until it was just me and the stranger, the room quiet and cool, the gentle hum of the air conditioner the only sound.

He gestured to a huge armchair. "Sit, please." The rich brown leather gave way beneath my weight, soft and yielding as I sank into it obediently.

He steepled his fingers beneath his chin, still smiling, the glint of his unnaturally white teeth unsettling beneath the lights.

"I apologise for the rude introduction of my men. They were street urchins before. You can dress them in finery and teach them to enunciate, but really they're still the same savages beneath."

I blinked. Was I supposed to agree with him? Laugh? Snigger?

I settled for silence, hoping to bury my discomfort beneath.

"Not much of a talker? No matter—I will speak for the both of us. You must be wondering why you're here, I'm sure."

I nodded, keeping my mouth shut. I needed to gauge him, get a feel of him before I said a word. Natural instinct wasn't something I'd needed in The Sands. That instinct which told you when you were in danger, even if it wasn't immediately apparent where the danger lay. That instinct which told you when to shut up, and when to speak.

"You're Harlow Novac."

I tried not to react, but my face must've given me away, because he let out a low chuckle.

"Not much escapes my notice in this city, Miss Novac."

He stood and walked to a small, spotless bar. He lifted a crystal decanter, tipping its amber contents into a glass. He held it up enquiringly. I spoke, keeping my voice low.

"No thank you."

He took a sip, staring out of the massive floor to ceiling window, watching as the city cloaked itself in darkness, the pinprick of lights erratic, leaving great swathes of blackness in between.

"I was sorry to hear the news of your father's death."

If he'd expected shock, I gave him no such satisfaction. I sat as still as I could, as if one wrong move would shatter the room and me along with it.

"Thank you." The restraint I'd shown until now broke. "Is that why I'm here? Because of my father?" I managed to keep the fear from my voice but was betrayed by my body as the sweat gathered beneath my thighs and arms. I sat straighter in my chair, clamping my arms against my sides to stop the sweat from trickling.

"No. You're here because in the short time you've been in the city, you've managed to amass some impressive friends. PI Carter. Jesse Haywood. Big names in Gloam. Long-timers."

He took a leisurely drink from the glass, his swallowing audible. I clasped my hands together, training my eyes to the gloom beyond the window, picturing Jesse waiting for me, maybe fearing the worst.

He turned back to me and returned to his desk. He sat, the chair creaking in protest as he settled his bulk.

"I don't like being blamed for something I didn't do. I would say that's a fairly common human trait. You see, when the Natives kill, they do it with reason. We are not a bunch of untamed animals running around with knives, killing anyone who displeases us. We have hierarchy, order."

He set his empty glass down on the desk with a muted thump. "Those murders that the three of you are trying to pin on us was not our handiwork."

"The evidence so far would suggest otherwise," I said mildly. I sensed that aggression wouldn't serve me here. He didn't seem like a man who responded to being antagonised.

He looked at me sharply. "I know some of the victims bore our mark. And I don't like the misuse of it. It's not something to be used lightly."

He paused, considering.

"However, there is a possibility, although a slight one, that one of my men have gone rogue. It happens from time to time."

He ran a hand down his face, his stubble rasping against his palm.

"If that's the case, I need to deal with it before any other members get the idea that this gang is based on democracy. So, I have a proposition for you."

The last thing I'd expected when I'd been brought here was this. "With respect, Mr..."

He waved a hand dismissively. "My name is unimportant. For now, you can call me Mr X." He smirked, and a snort escaped me. He laughed then, the sound rich and booming, so much like Pop's that I had to force back the sudden boulder in my throat.

"I don't think we'll make the best partners."

He raised an eyebrow. "No? We have the same objective."

I mulled this over. He could easily lead me astray, feed me false information and throw me off the trail. For all his protests, the Natives could still be behind this, even if none of the killings had been planned hits. I had my doubts that he knew what every single member of his gang did, every second of the day. It was impossible.

"How do I know I can trust you?"

He shrugged. "My dear girl, how do you know you can trust any of them? You think because Carter Reach is a PI, that he's on the right side of the law? And your mentor—being a mercenary yourself you should know that mercs are a law unto themselves.

They don't follow any of the rules." He smirked. "We have that in common."

"Why do you think it's possible one of your men went rogue?"

"I have a particular individual in mind who may have had motive to kill at least two of the victims. I'm unsure of the link with the others, but it's worth looking at." He paused, as if weighing his words. "I initially wanted to keep this part internal, and deal with it myself, but he's proving to be difficult to find."

He opened a desk drawer and produced a mugshot, sliding it across the desk towards me. "He was released from prison right before the killings began. Normally, members return to the fold, but he's gone dark since his release. No one has seen him or heard from him."

I examined the photograph. Shot in black and white, the man held up a placard against his sizeable chest, three lines of information displayed: *Tower Mason. The Natives. X1089.*

"Tower Mason?" I asked with an arched eyebrow. "Is that his real name?"

Mr X smiled condescendingly. "No. Members often change their names when they're accepted into our gang. His name is a play on words. His size, and his abilities with his hands."

"Why do you think he could be involved in these killings?"

"For now, you don't need to know my reasons. I need you to find him. You and your little helpers. They'll prove to be invaluable sources of information, I'm sure." He waved a hand towards the photograph. "Keep that."

The air in the office had become uncomfortably cold. I shivered, wrapping my arms around myself. The room was darkening as night fell. Only a single lamp on the desk lit the room, its light doing little to dispel the growing shadows. My discomfort grew. All I wanted was to leave this room. To get away from this strange man. The atmosphere felt planned. A deliberate attempt to unsettle me.

"I want to know who's performing these killings and using our mark. I will help you in your investigation. I will deal only with you." His expression soured, as if he'd caught an unpleasant scent. "I have a particular distaste for any kind of law enforcement, and your friend Jesse is of better use as an outsider. Only a trusted few have ever been in my office." He smiled again and winked, his broad face crinkling. He made me think of a snake I'd encountered in The Sands. It had blended perfectly with its environment. It had been content to allow me to approach until I almost stepped on it. Up until that moment, I'd been completely unaware of its presence. But once I was almost on it, it had reared up on its tail, fangs displayed and spitting.

"You will report your findings to me, and in return, whatever my men find, will be shared with you."

He rose, our conversation clearly over.

As I clasped his outstretched hand in farewell, trying not to show my reluctance to touch him, he tightened his grip briefly, long enough for me to feel the strength in his fingers. "Be warned, Miss Novac. I'm not someone you want as your enemy."

I turned to leave. As I had the doorknob in hand, he called to me again. "Failure in any regard will be seen as a breach of contract, Miss Novac. Be sure to find Tower. And be sure to report back to me."

I closed the door on his smiling face, the relief of escaping his presence flooding my body and leaving my legs weak.

***

I had no idea how I'd arrived at the bar, but suddenly I was in the doorway, the drone of conversations and the hum of background music bringing me back to the present.

I stumbled into the small bar, spotting Jesse at the far end, the worry melting from his face as he caught sight of me. "Thank god. I was on the verge of coming to your rescue. What the fuck was that? What did they want?"

I sank onto the barstool next to Jesse, snatching the beer he was drinking and taking a long swallow. Bitterness filled my mouth and my stomach clenched. For a horrifying moment I was sure it was all going to come up again and I was going to puke right there and then, right there on the counter in this tiny bar in front of all these strangers. I swallowed hard, forcing it down. I slid the glass back to Jesse. He watched me, his brow furrowed. "What is it? What happened?"

"I met the top dog of the Natives."

Jesse blinked, looking flummoxed. "What?"

I laughed, the sound close to a bark, and shook my head. "Yeah. He said he wants my—well, actually our—help with the investigation. And in return he'll help, too. He says they're not responsible for the murders, and he wants to find whoever is muddying their name. He thinks there's a possibility it could be one of his members who has gone rogue." I extracted the mugshot from my bag and laid it on the bar. "Former member. Released from jail recently and disappeared from the public eye."

Jesse took the photograph and let out a low whistle. "I'll be damned. This case gets weirder by the second."

I signalled the barman. "Gin. Clean. Just ice."

He reappeared with a glass of ice, holding the bottle of gin aloft, his eyebrows raised in question. "Double, please."

He obliged, and as soon as he slid the glass my way, I downed it, the heat of the alcohol burning a searing path down my throat, warming my body. I felt my shoulders lower, felt the slow release of the tension in my neck.

I gestured to the photograph. "Recognise him? Or heard of him?"

Jesse considered the image for a long time, shifting closer to examine the finer details. His face changed. Tension straightened his spine, his hands tightening around the mugshot.

"Shit. This goes further and deeper than I thought."

"You know him?"

"Oh yeah." Jesse paused, as if considering whether he should go on. He sighed deeply.

"It was years back. He was a real piece of shit. It was one of the biggest cases of that decade, which is saying a lot in this city. This guy raped and murdered his way through fifteen women before he was finally caught. There was a public outcry when he was only tried for two of them. No evidence on the others, they said. But in Gloam, that could mean a lot of things. Lost case files. Corrupt cops. Still, they nailed him and managed to put him away. It was a personal triumph, something the citizens of Gloam took to heart. That maybe their city was worth preserving, worth protecting. Worth *something*. That maybe there were at least two decent cops in this place."

Jesse looked up at me, and something about his expression tightened my gut into a fist.

"Your father was on that case. It was the last one he and Carter ever did together. The day Tower was put away, your dad and Carter were heroes." Jesse downed the rest of his drink. "If memory serves, it was less than a week later that you were taken."

I stared down at my hands splayed on the bar, my nails longer than they should be, the tiny scar on the back of my left hand. I felt like I was outside of myself somehow, that I was someone else and observing this scene from a distance, of interest for sure, but of no great importance.

Jesse drained his beer, placing the glass back on the bar. He dug in his wallet, coming up with a few bills, which he slid across to the barman who'd been hovering nearby. I knew he was talking, because I could see his lips moving, but I couldn't hear a word.

I felt like I was encased in a thick, growing fog. This was all too much. The information about Pop—a man I was convinced I knew—being described as if he were a stranger. The sense that I had enough of the puzzle pieces to form a picture, but I couldn't figure out how to fit them together. The feeling that the odds were stacked against me, that I was playing a game where I didn't know or understand any of the rules. The sense I'd had of being closer to unmasking the killer felt ridiculous now.

I was in over my head, even with Carter and Jesse's help. *Who am I kidding?*

I rose, wanting only my bed and time and space to think. My breath was coming too fast, making my head swim. I grabbed for the solidity of the bar, closing on air instead, and I felt myself falling, the floor coming up to meet me, until Jesse's hands were beneath me, lifting me towards him, yelling in my ear.

Everything was distant. Jesse's hands on me were like hands on dead limbs – I could barely feel the close of his fingers around my arms. His voice in my ear was muted, like I was swimming underwater and he was calling to me from the surface, his words meaningless and mangled, too far away to be heard.

He shook me, hard, and everything sharpened. The feel of the floor beneath my feet. The throb of my pulse in my veins, quieter now as my breathing slowed, as the world came into focus again.

Chapter Twenty-One

Markham

As soon as he saw her, he knew. She reminded him of his mother, the way so many women did, but this one in particular had a gleam in her eye, sweet and predatory at the same time, that peculiar gift women had for being two things at once.

He was sitting in a booth of a new bar he'd followed her to, one that was still shiny and new in the eyes of Gloam, not yet tarnished with frequent use and the taint of boredom. Everything was shaded in tones of black, white and steel, lit garishly by the strobe of the overhead lights.

She looked older than her true years. A memory of her resurfaced – one where she'd sat in their home, legs crossed, her eyes on Matt even as she chatted to his mother. The lipstick mark on her wine glass, and then, later, the same lipstick stamped on Matt's mouth. His mother, pretending she didn't see. Matt, so confident in his hold on Angie that he didn't bother wiping it off.

Markham watched her feign not to notice his attention. He was patient. He had nothing but time tonight.

She propped herself against the bar, her back to it. She was pretending to survey the room, but her eyes sought him too often, her gaze lingering too long. He knew she was waiting for him to approach, to offer her a drink, but instead he sat, waiting on her, knowing she would come.

Ten minutes into their game, she finally gave in and sauntered towards him, hips swaying beneath her dress, her high heels making her legs look impossibly long. She slid in beside him without asking, her thigh brushing against his. Her left hand came to rest next to his, the glint of her diamond bright beneath the blinking lights.

There was the possibility that she would know him, of course, despite the time which had passed, and the deliberate changes he'd made to his appearance. A jolt of adrenaline shot through him.

"Hi," she breathed into his ear. Her lips brushed his earlobe, and he wondered if she'd left a lipstick mark there, a slick of red against his skin.

He turned to her, smiling. The deep V of her neckline drew his eye and her laugh told him she'd caught him looking.

"So. Come here often?"

Her eyes were deep pools of blue, ringed with too much eyeliner. This close, her skin wasn't the smooth landscape it had seemed from a distance. She was wearing too much foundation, and the pores she'd tried to disguise, were emphasised, instead.

He leaned back, slinging his arm over the back of the booth, careful not to touch her.

"Isn't that my line?"

A waitress appeared, her hair blue and her apron spotless. She was snapping gum so loudly he could hear the *pop pop pop* over the music. "Get ya something?"

They ordered beers, and the banter kept on, until Markham felt he'd reeled her in just enough. He ran his thumb along the soft skin from her throat to her chin, holding her gaze. That was all it took.

***

Her tongue was in his mouth. He pressed her against the brick of the building, wishing that they were at her place, or some scum of a hotel room, instead of in this back alley. Could he do it here? It was a dead-end street, and the feel of her beneath his hands was heightened by the dark. The thought of it, of doing it and leaving her here, to be found by anyone, made him more eager. Rougher. She gasped as he yanked her dress up around her waist, his fingers skimming between her thighs. She wore nothing else underneath.

Her hands groped for his zipper. In the dark he could pretend for just a moment that she was someone else. Just for an instant he could lose himself in her, his mind a blank slate. He wanted to touch her, but his hands moved up, skimming over her breasts and then, brushing her throat. His fingers slipped around the back of her neck, as if to pull her closer. Her breath was against his cheek, hot and gasping. His thumbs found the tender spot between her collar bones and pressed gently – *testing, testing.* Her breath stalled, then came faster, and she pressed herself into him, loosening his grip on her throat. *She likes it.* The thought flooded him, blotting out everything else. His hands found her throat again, and this time he closed his fingers around her. It was too dark to see her face, but the way her body stilled, and then came alive again, wild and kicking, made it clear she realised the situation was not what she'd first assumed.

She gurgled, trying to scream, and he squeezed just enough to cut her off. The sting of her nails against his skin as she tried to claw her way out of his grip felt inconsequential. A sharp pain as the pointed toe of her shoe caught him in the shin. All these things seemed removed from him. The only thing he could think of, could feel, was the tautness of his fingers around her throat, the pressure of his hands against her as he tightened them. Something dripped into his eye, stinging. His hands were aching, the feeling creeping up his wrists and into his arms. He was tiring.

His hands opened of their own accord and the sound of her body hitting the pavement, the crack of her skull against the ground, sent a surge of adrenalin through him. He waited for her to get up, to spring to her feet and run, but there was no movement. He knelt beside her, his hands feeling in the dark until he found her face, turning it until he was sure her mouth was against his ear. He couldn't feel the exhale of her breath against his cheek, and it was difficult to hear much over the sudden thud of music coming from a nearby apartment block. He rose, turning to leave. The music above stopped as suddenly as it started. He caught the barely audible gasp she let out, and the rasp of clothing against the ground as she struggled to consciousness.

He whipped around. A light snapped on inside one of the apartments above, leaking enough light for him to make out her flailing form. She coughed and wretched, trying to rise, managing only as far as her hands and knees.

Without thinking about it, he lifted his booted foot as high as it would go and brought it down with a savage force. His foot landed squarely on her neck, shoving her face down into the pavement, the audible crunch of her nose loud in the sudden silence. He flipped her over, onto her back, his hands at her throat again. He held on until his hands ached, long after he was sure she was dead. Finally, he released her, standing over her and wishing for more light, so he could really see her face. The satisfaction of a job well done.

One less on the list. More to go.

Tomorrow, when the sun rose and light filled this street, she would be discovered. She could be just another body found in the bowels of Gloam, another botched robbery or love affair gone wrong. Except for the ring. He slipped it off her finger, tucking it away in the small front pocket of his jeans. He slid out his small pocketknife, his keys jangling as he withdrew the small blade. He felt around for her hand, turning her palm upwards. The point of the knife sank eagerly into the skin. The warm trickle of blood was his reward.

Chapter Twenty-Two

Harlow

JESSE WAS WAITING FOR me at a permanent food stall just outside my apartment, munching on what looked like a kebab. I suppressed a shudder. Synthetic meat.

I touched his shoulder and he turned towards me, gesturing to the kebab. "Ever tried this? Tastes like sawdust and plastic."

I took the counter seat beside him. "Why eat it then?"

He reached for a paper serviette from the dispenser in front of him, wiping the grease from his fingertips. "Street food is all the same. I make decent money but if I had to buy from those supermarkets which stock the real thing, I'd be broke in a month. And the decent restaurants only deal with certain clientele—you know—the kind who have money and contacts."

I thought of my date with Denny. The amazing food, what each item had cost. The bottle of wine alone was worth one well-paid job. I wondered what someone had to do to make those kinds of contacts, what kind of favours drew that kind of VIP treatment. Lending a listening ear seemed meagre, compared to the feast we'd consumed.

I'd slept soundly the night before. So soundly, I'd woken with a start, at first unsure of where I was. Dreams of Denny had lingered as I'd dressed for the day, the phantom feel of his hands on me felt real, as if he'd really spent the night in my bed.

Jesse looked at me, a slow smile growing on his face. "You get laid last night?"

"Jesse!" I swatted him in mock outrage. He waggled his eyebrows suggestively. "Did you?"

"I was hardly in the mood for that given the whole run-in with the Natives, and my swooning episode."

"Would've done you good, I say."

He motioned to the food sweating beneath the glass counter. "Eaten today?"

I shook my head. The owner of the stall, overhearing us, motioned to his wares hopefully. Not wanting to be rude, I smiled politely, then turned away from him, hoping that my silent refusal would be enough. I slid off the stool, motioning to Jesse. "Let's go. We've got a job, right?"

Jesse consulted his phone, looking at the message he'd received from a client with the details of the job. "Yeah. We need to go to the corner of Klein and Springside. Apparently, there's a house there which needs checking out."

"What are we looking for?"

"Signs of recent habitation. We're trying to trace someone who owes money to the client and has evaded them several times. This was their last-known address, although our client thinks they've already jumped ship. We're to look for any clues as to this person's whereabouts. Got your piece?" I pushed aside the light denim jacket I was wearing to show him my Sauer strapped to my hip. "Good. Let's go."

It didn't take long for us to find the place, and it was exactly as the client had described. White, peeling paint, faded green shutters. The tiny yard in front of it was littered with trash. A bicycle, one tyre flat and the other missing, blocked the short walkway leading to the front door. Picking it up and putting it aside, Jesse swung the rusting gate open, the hinges screaming in protest.

I drew my weapon, my eyes trained on the house. I studied the windows, tattered curtains visible through the glass, checking that no one was there, watching us approach the house. Nothing.

We moved to the door, and I reached for the handle, turning the old-fashioned knob slowly, glancing back at Jesse to make sure he was ready. At his nod, I pushed the door inward, the door swinging open silently. Silence. I stopped just inside the house, my pistol pointing inward, sweeping the inside of the house from side to side, watching for movement and attuned to any misplaced sound. Jesse followed behind me, stepping to my side. The light coming in from the windows was patchy and dull, casting the interior into shadows.

It was a single storey, and from our place at the door I could see nothing but a half bathroom with a toilet and a sink. A short hallway led to the rest of the house. We would have to turn a blind corner to assess the situation, and my pulse sped up, throbbing through my veins.

Jesse took the lead, stepping as quietly as he could, avoiding the empty beer cans and scattered bottles, sidestepping the stinking takeaway containers. Everything was coated with a layer of dust, suggesting that no one had lived here for some time. I kept to Jesse's side, and we rounded the corner with our weapon pointed ahead. My eyes darted around, searching for movement or any signs that someone else was here, but nothing but rotting furniture and a filthy kitchen greeted us. There was another hallway to the left of the kitchen, which I assumed was a scullery of sorts. I took another step, my toe connecting with a glass bottle I hadn't seen, sending it skittering across the tiled floor, spinning into the kitchen island and shattering.

I stilled. A faint rustle. The drag of a foot against the floor.

Someone stepped out from the hallway, a man wearing a balaclava and dressed in black from head to toe, a pistol clasped between his outstretched hands. He hesitated, as if unsure of his target. His pistol wavering between the two of us, and I fired, my finger finding the trigger before I could even form the thought. My shot buried itself in the wall just behind the gunman's ear.

He returned fire, the *pop pop pop* of the gunshots deafening. I heard the muffled thump of Jesse's body hitting the floor. Fear swept an icy trail down my back, but I couldn't turn, couldn't take my eyes from our assailant.

I raised my weapon and fired off a second shot, my mind a feverish mess, silently begging the powers that be that my shot would hit true. The gunman toppled backwards as the bullet buried itself in his left shoulder. The crash as he fell reverberated through the room but I barely heard it as I knelt beside Jesse, my hands moving over him, my brain unable to register the lack of blood or the signs of injury. It was only when he batted my hands away, half laughing and half wheezing, that I realised he was unharmed.

I rose and crossed the room in three strides and pointed my pistol at the gunman's face. I could hear his ragged breathing as he struggled to draw breath, his hand pressed to his wound, the blood seeping between his fingers. He kicked his heels weakly in an attempt to move away, his eyes fixed on my gun.

"Who are you?" He tried to roll over, but I stuck my foot out, forcing him to stay on his back. He groaned.

I leaned over him and snatched the weapon from his free hand, letting it fall to the floor before I kicked it away. It spun to the far corner of the room with a clatter. I reached for the balaclava and yanked it off, expecting to know him, to recognise his face. But he was a stranger.

His blond hair was matted with sweat and clung to his forehead, his staring eyes blue and wide. I examined his clothes, my gaze roaming his body rapidly, not wanting to allow him more than a few seconds to attempt to escape. Nothing noteworthy.

Jesse came up behind me, his piece drawn and pointed at the gunman.

"Know him?"

I shook my head, baffled. "Why would I?"

Jesse leaned forward and pressed the barrel of his gun against the man's forehead. "You tried to shoot me. Explain, or your brains are going to be decorating this floor."

The man shook his head, his eyes moving to me, pleading.

I kicked him in the side, hard. I was rewarded by a grunt of pain.

I felt Jesse looking at me, as if in warning, but taking my eyes from our assailant, even for a moment, felt like too much of a risk.

"Talk!"

"I was hired." His voice shook, and I realised he was younger than what I'd originally thought. Late teens, or early twenties at best.

"By whom?"

"I don't know."

"Was it through a fixer?" Jesse's voice was calm, but his body vibrated with tension. He was coiled, poised to pull the trigger at the slightest provocation.

"I don't... I don't think so. He approached me at a club. He never gave me his name. He was wearing a mask."

"What club?"

"Red of Hearts."

I felt Jesse twitch beside me. I risked the briefest of glances at him and saw that his pallor had turned a chalk white.

"Who was the target?"

The stranger groaned. The hand pressed against his wound was tacky with blood. He, too, looked pale. Too pale.

"He didn't give names. He gave me a description. Based on that—" He stopped, gasping a little, his mouth opening and closing like a fish on dry land. "The target was you," he finished.

Jesse went silent, his grip on his weapon easing, as if in shock. I turned back to the man, knowing we needed to call both the cops and an ambulance, and once that happened, our chances of finding out anything more was unlikely.

"What did he look like?"

"I told you! He was wearing a mask."

"Tall? Short? Colour of his hair, his eyes? Any tattoos or scars? Anything at all?"

"He was tall. Taller than him." He motioned to Jesse. "Dark hair. No tattoos or any other markings that I noticed."

"Please..." He gestured to his wound. "I need help. Call the cops. I don't care. I don't want to die!"

Jesse gave a hard, derisive laugh. "Don't worry, kiddo. You won't be dying any time soon." He moved closer to the stranger, his nose nearly touching his. "You better have told us everything. If I find out you held out on us, I'll be extracting information from you in a far more painful, persuasive way." Jesse removed his knife from his boot, giving our assailant a good look at the blade. He stepped back, holstering his gun and carefully sheathing the knife. "You got a phone?"

The stranger nodded.

"Good. Use it to call the cops yourself, or the ambulance. But you keep us out of it, you hear? Tell them whatever you want, but we weren't here." Jesse motioned to me. "Let's go."

Chapter
Twenty-Three

Markham

HE CONSIDERED THE TIMELINE tacked to his wall. It had developed into a spider's web of information – their names, where they lived, where they'd been for the past few years. He'd managed to keep track of only a handful of them – the others had moved out of Gloam, to small cities and even smaller towns. Some had disappeared altogether. Those were the ones who angered him the most, and at first, he'd tried to find them. But he'd been met with too many dead-ends, and finally had to acknowledge that they were forever out of his grasp. His energy was better spent on those right here, the ones he had a chance of reaching.

He touched the picture of one, running his fingers along the line of the scarlet X mark slashed across her features. Gone. Both her and Skylar. He had another three, their smiling faces waiting for their mark, and then, he would deviate from his plan for his final act. He would reel her in by taking something of hers she would want back. *Someone.* He smiled. He'd planned the details for taking the others for years, waiting for the right moment, knowing his timing was crucial.

He'd always hoped she'd reappear, and when she did, it was as if he'd willed it, and the universe had granted him this last thing. She would be the one who tied them all.

Harlow

We left the building with our bleeding assailant still inside it, and despite the mass of humanity teeming on the sidewalks, Jesse walked at such a clip I had to run to keep up, muttering my apologies as I bumped into people as I tried not to lose sight of him.

"Jesse!" I caught his shoulder, pulling him up short, panting. The crowd surged around us, enveloping us in clouds of sweat, soap, perfume and smoke, a noxious blend of scents. "What the hell? What happened in there?"

"Not here," he muttered. He pulled me into the closest diner, sliding into a patent leather booth near the door, his gaze trained on the street outside.

I waited, sensing he needed time to think.

When he spoke, his voice was low, and I had to lean in to hear him. "The Red of Hearts is a kill club."

"A what?"

He waved an impatient hand in the air, tension vibrating off him. "A club people go to when they want someone dead. When they want to find a hired killer. Anonymously. They all wear masks. No details are given beyond the details of the victim. Payment is done in cash."

"You mean…"

"Someone wants me dead. Paid good money for me to be dead."

He shook his head and leaned back into the booth. "Why does this all feel connected?"

I felt the same, although I couldn't say why. That feeling I'd had before crept up again. That the answers I needed were right in front of me, and I was failing to understand.

"A hit? But why?"

Jesse's skin looked pasty beneath the florescent lights of the diner. It hurt me to see it, to see the strain he was under, and it struck me then, ridiculously for the first time, that I really cared about him. That he was my friend, and that I'd nearly lost him just minutes before. I closed my eyes against the possibility of what could've happened.

I reached across the table and took his hand, hesitantly at first, unsure of how he would feel about the contact, and then, when he squeezed, I held tighter, trying to communicate all that I felt.

My phone rang then, and I reached for it, breaking the contact.

I glanced at the screen, frowning. I glanced at Jesse. "It's Carter."

When I answered, Carter didn't bother with pleasantries. He barked an address, which I frantically motioned to Jesse to take down on his phone, repeating the details out loud.

"Come now," he barked, and ended the call.

★★★

The crime scene had been cordoned off. Dozens of people stood at its perimeter, gawking, snippets of their conversations drifting towards us as Carter muscled his way through the crowd. Cops were gathering at the edges of the spectators, asking politely, and then less so, for them to disperse. Those who weren't quick enough to follow orders were rewarded with force, and I watched with distaste as a man who took exception to being manhandled threw a punch at a cop, missing and careening into two other men nearby. A brief scuffle ensued, ending in two arrests.

Two cops appeared and escorted us beneath the crime scene tape, and around a corner which led to a dead-end street. A woman lay there, half her body in the gutter, the flies already gathering.

She lay face down, her dark hair sticky with blood. Her arms were thrown out at either side of her, her legs obscenely parted, as she'd been arranged after she was killed.

Carter moved closer. "Is this how she was found?" One of the cops, a visibly junior one, was hovering nearby, and at the sound of Carter's voice, he jumped. Why the hell was someone this lowly ranked at a crime scene like this? Where were his seniors?

"Y-y-yes." He stuttered, looking desperate to be anywhere else but here.

Carter stepped to the woman's side, snapping on gloves as he did so. He rolled her over gently, and her face, when I caught sight of it, brought a ball of bile up my throat and into my mouth. I slapped a hand against my mouth, willing the vomit back down. I swallowed, and my throat burned with its acrid trail.

The woman's face was bloodied and swollen. Her features were lost in the damage done to her face. Her throat was obscenely mottled with bruises, her eyes bulging.

"Carter. What a surprise to see you here." My attention snapped from the victim to a swaggering officer approaching us, his black uniform spotless, his smile insincere.

I realised with a small shock that I recognised him.

"Detective Madden," Carter said. Neither man offered their hand to the other. They eyed one another, sizing each other up. Detective Madden broke the contact first, his gaze moving to me. I waited for the recognition, but none came.

He motioned to me with his chin. "Bringing your girlfriends to crime scenes now, are we? Whatever would your wife say?"

I glanced swiftly at Carter. *Wife?* He kept his eyes on Madden, his face darkening.

I stepped forward, holding out my hand. "Harlow. You're investigating my father's death?"

The arrogant smirk fell from his face, as he seemed to scramble to pull my features from the recesses of his memory.

"Ah…yes. Harlow. Of course." He took my hand and pumped it a little too enthusiastically, as if to make up for his memory lapse. He looked slightly panicked, as if he still wasn't sure who I was. Anger bubbled in me. I, a private citizen and newbie merc, was doing more than this asshole who had trained in law enforcement and pledged his loyalty to the public.

"Perhaps you need to be keeping a closer eye on your cases, Madden, instead of lurking around ours." Carter said it mildly, without even looking at the detective, his attention drawn back to the victim.

Madden bristled. He took a step forward, his body coiling. Carter matched him until they were toe to toe. I was about to attempt to intervene, when we were joined by two more cops, both wearing the lower-ranked uniform of blue.

Their arrival broke the tension. Both cops looked at me as if for guidance. I said nothing. The weighted silence grew, until finally the shorter of the two spoke.

"Detective Madden. We were told to report to you." As he spoke, his eyes moved to the woman, and he visibly blanched. *Jesus. More juniors. Couldn't this fucking city afford higher ranked cops?*

"You've been misinformed, gentlemen. This is our case. And our turf. I was personally called in," Carter said. Whether that was true or not, I couldn't tell. The complexity of the justice system in this place seemed so complicated that it wasn't worth learning.

Madden glared at Carter. The junior cops shifted uncomfortably, their eyes darting between the two men. I sighed inwardly. All this posturing was tiring, and ridiculous.

"Look, whatever rivalry you guys have going I can respect, but—" I gestured to the woman - "we have a victim whose body is ripening in the sun, and we don't need any more people muddying up the crime scene."

I shifted my gaze to Madden. "You should have plenty to keep you busy. Like finding my father's killer and Chloe's attacker. It's been weeks and I haven't heard a thing from you, or any of your minions." I flicked my fingers in the direction of the other officers. "Clear out. We have work to do."

Madden looked apoplectic with rage, his eyes bugging out of their sockets. Out of the corner of my eye I caught Carter's smirk.

"Who do you think you are, telling me where and how to do my job?" Madden's voice was pitched loudly enough to draw unwanted attention from the busy street beyond. The last thing we needed was to have to deal with onlookers.

"If you were doing it, you wouldn't be standing here, now would you?"

For a disjointed second, I was sure he was going to hit me. I tensed, my hand moving to my Sauer, my fingers brushing its familiar coolness.

Madden turned abruptly and strode away, leaving the junior cops to stare after him.

I nodded to them. "Gentlemen."

They scuttled off in the wake of their superior, their footsteps fading as they disappeared from view.

Carter let out a low whistle. "Remind me to never get on your bad side."

"What a prick," I muttered. Unexpectedly, I felt on the verge of tears. Tears of rage, but that didn't matter. The humiliation which rose in me at the idea of Carter seeing me cry forced them back.

I knelt beside the woman. Carter wordlessly handed me gloves, which I snapped on. I glanced up at him only when I was sure my eyes were clear. "May I?"

He nodded. I gently lifted her left hand, turning the palm towards me. Sure enough, an X was carved into her flesh. I turned her hand around, my gaze falling on her ring finger. A faint white shadow where her ring would've been. I closed my eyes against the storm of emotions which filled me. Pity for the victim. Sympathy for her loved ones. The delicate, burgeoning hope that this killer was the same one who had murdered Pop. Because if it wasn't, I'd spent weeks chasing down the wrong lead.

I rose, pulling off my gloves, careful to turn them inside out and keep the blood they were stained with contained.

Someone called Carter's name, but I heard it only faintly. I stared at the woman's body, at her battered face. Her eyes were blue. She wore expensive-looking jeans, and a loosely buttoned red blouse. The heels she'd been wearing had come off her feet. Black, pointed stilettos. I imagined her striding in those shoes, head held high, confident and assured in a place she thought she knew.

"Harlow." Carter's voice brought me back. He motioned to a man. He held a camera in his hands, and for an incomprehensible moment I thought he was a journalist, here to photograph the woman for a story, like a vulture at a kill site. Then I took in his uniform and realised they were here to process the crime scene.

I stepped aside, clamping down on my emotions, hoping I seemed all business. Detached, despite the flies settling on the woman's body.

***

I followed Carter back around the corner, the street beyond coming into view.

The crowd hadn't thinned at all – if anything, it had grown, the sidewalk completely overtaken by the sea of humanity. Several people had their phones out, photographing the stretch of street leading to the alley, or messaging people, their fingers flying over the keyboards of their phones in their haste to spread the news. God. This city. The longer I lived in it, the more I hated it.

We pushed our way through the throng until we reached Carter's car, but once inside, the crowd closed around us again, and it seemed impossible to steer the car through without endangering any of the gawkers.

"Let's wait a bit. They'll lose interest soon and go back to wherever it is they came from."

I turned in my seat to face Carter. "Who called you to the scene? Was it another cop?"

Carter shook his head. "I have a contact who works the crime scene as a reporter. I called him when we first started investigating this case, asked him to look out for any cases with strangulation and the Natives' mark."

"What if we're wrong?"

"About what?"

"About the murders being connected. What if we're chasing down the wrong killer?"

Carter was quiet. The way he didn't quite meet my eyes made me think this possibility had occurred to him, too.

"We could be."

I thumped the dashboard, wanting to scream until my throat ached and my voice was lost.

"How are we going to know for sure? We could chase this for weeks more, maybe even months. And all the while, the one who really killed Pop could leave town, or maybe they already have, and everything I've done up until now would be for nothing."

Carter reached out and gave my shoulder a squeeze. "We can't know for sure. This killer, whether they're the same one who killed your father, or not, still needs to be caught."

Carter started the car, even though the crowd hadn't thinned at all. He gunned the engine, and when no one took any notice, he laid on the hooter, and several people jumped out of the way, forcing those around them to move as well.

"I can't rule anything out right now. Once we've interviewed people in the area, and checked out the street cameras, if any were operational, we'll know more."

We inched forward, people reluctantly parting to allow us through. Finally, we were free of the mob and moving along the street. I looked out of the window, watching as we passed several more apartment blocks, a sex bar, and two food stalls. The skyscrapers ahead loomed over us, sentinels to the never-ending activity of the city.

I turned away from the window. "It's been weeks. I've accomplished so little since I arrived here, besides keeping a roof over my head and..." I swallowed. "And nearly getting a friend killed."

"What?" Carter barked. His eyes strayed from the road for a second too long, causing a passing car to blare their horn as we drifted into their lane. Carter corrected sharply, pulling us back to our side of the road.

I stared down hard at my hands, wondering if I was ever going to find peace, if the pieces to this puzzle would ever be found. "I need answers, and I need a break in this case. I know it sounds awful, but I don't want your attention to stray too far from my father's case. I know you have others you need to work on."

I relayed everything to him – about my meeting with Mr X, and Jesse and my close shave with our unknown assailant.

Carter said nothing until I was done. When he spoke, he seemed to be choosing his words with care.

"Neither of you knew him?"

I shook my head. "I've never seen him before."

"You sure?"

I threw my hands up in exasperation. "What's with you and Jesse? He asked me the same thing. Why would I know the guy? I wasn't the target anyway. Didn't you listen to the story? He was after Jesse."

"In all the years Jesse has been a merc, and then a mentor, he's never been on a hit list. Then you arrive, he becomes your mentor, and he's got a mark on his back."

I twisted in my seat to face him. Heat rushed through me, the feel of it a pulse behind my eyes, making my head pound in time to my heart. "What are you saying, exactly? That this is my fault?" My voice was loud in the cramped space. I wanted to draw back, to calm the hot thread of anger in my veins, but I was too far gone now, the idea of control laughable.

Carter glanced at me briefly, his dark eyes unreadable.

"Did I say that?"

"The insinuation was clear enough. You didn't have to say it."

"You're missing the point, Harlow." He reached out and put a hand on my shoulder, squeezing gently. I resisted the childish urge to shrug him off.

"What I'm saying is maybe the connection is you, and not Jesse. That the attempted hit on Jesse has something to do with this case."

Carter drummed his fingers against the steering wheel, his eyes on the road.

"Seen anything strange since you arrived in Gloam?"

I barked a laugh. "Yeah, where do I begin?"

He waved a hand impatiently. "Specifics, Harlow."

"Like what?"

"Feeling like you're being watched. Or that you're being followed. Anything like that?"

With a start I thought about the feeling of being followed when I'd gone to the laundromat. The glimpse of the insignia on the jacket of a retreating stranger. The note. I'd somehow forgotten about it. I glanced down at the jeans I was wearing. Were they the same ones I'd been wearing that day? I shifted in my seat and searched my pockets. I pulled a crumpled piece of paper from my right one, my heart a hammer in my chest. Wordlessly, I held it out for Carter. He took it and scanned it briefly. "Where did this come from?"

"I was at the laundromat. It was the morning of the same day we found Skylar. I'd dropped my clothes there for a wash. When I went back, I found the note stuck to the door of my machine."

"This was written by someone who knows you. Or of you."

"That doesn't make sense. I don't know anyone here. We left years ago. The only time I've ever been back was the night of—" I couldn't finish. The words caught in my throat. I thought of Chloe. Of Pop. That feeling of relief when we'd arrived in The Sands. That feeling of safety that had proved to be utterly false. My eyes burned with the onset of tears.

"I need to think on it. There's a connection somewhere here. We're missing it. Once we figure it out, I feel like everything else will fall into place." Carter said.

He patted my arm awkwardly.

"That unexpected meeting with the Natives gives us a clear direction to go in. We find this Tower Mason. And we see if it leads anywhere."

I found my voice again, grateful that Carter had said nothing about my swell of emotions. Right now, I couldn't bear for him to say anything, to watch him struggle to find the right words. Maybe that was just it – that he understood my loss to some degree. He understood what it was like to feel like you'd known someone, only to be shown that you hadn't known them at all.

"Just like that? You think it's going to be that easy?"

"No. But I'm a good PI, Harlow."

He glanced briefly at me again.

A motorbike roared past us on the left, overtaking us illegally. Carter swerved to avoid him, rolling down his window to shout obscenities that the driver couldn't hear over the roar of the traffic. The wind from his open window blew into the car, hot and stale with exhaust fumes.

He closed the window again, shaking his head sheepishly. "You would think that after all this time here, I'd be used to the range of assholes that live here. You want to know the truth? I sometimes fucking hate this place." I smiled a little at that. The exact thought I'd had just minutes earlier.

He pulled up outside the apartment block where his office was, but instead of unbuckling his seatbelt and getting out of the car, he turned to me, his expression serious. "You know I've been a PI for a long time. It's not a life that allows for much personal time, or a personal life, really." His hands were gripping the steering wheel tightly, his knuckles whitening. "That crack Madden made about my wife? We're separated. Neither of us has ever filed for divorce, even though we've been apart for nearly a year now."

He turned to look out of the windshield, his eyes following a woman who was walking past with a tiny, ridiculous dog whose rhinestone collar glinted in the sun. He stared without really seeming to see her.

"We had a son. He was five years old when I found him in an abandoned warehouse, his arms bound behind his back. He'd suffocated. They'd put a plastic bag over his head and left him to die."

His voice cracked. He drew a deep breath, fighting for composure. I placed a hand on his arm, letting it rest there. Returning the arm squeeze, knowing there was nothing to say.

"If I'd only listened to my wife, Hunter would be alive, but I was too stubborn. Too proud."

The car was starting to bake from the outside heat. Carter opened his window, although the hot breeze that blew in did nothing to cool the interior of the car.

"I was after a drug kingpin, who'd been terrorising the streets for years. He had so many contacts, with the gangs, with the cops, with everyone who was anyone in the criminal underworld. He had a stranglehold on the drug trade, and he'd made enemies. But no one was willing to go after him. He was known for killing off the families of those who crossed him. When his case landed on my desk, I knew it wasn't something I could bypass. I needed a break in my career, one which would bring my name to the forefront."

I could only see Carter's profile, but his pain was etched into the line of his jaw, into the tension of his mouth and the way he held his chin – rigid, stoic. "My wife kept telling me our family would be no different, that in pursuing this case I was putting her and Hunter in danger. But I was convinced the cops would protect them, and that once I had that lowlife behind bars we'd be untouchable. I was wrong."

When he turned to me, his cheeks were wet. The tears ran unchecked, and in his intense vulnerability Carter had never been more human to me, more relatable. He swallowed and ran his palms over his face.

"Our marriage couldn't survive the loss. We tried for years, but Hunter's death was always there, a wedge between us. She never said it, but I know she blamed me." He drew a shuddering breath. "Your father and I became partners soon after. He stood by me through it all – the funeral, my anger, my dissolving marriage. Frank was the only person who stood in the wreck of it all without flinching."

My vision blurred. The tears I'd successfully held back before now fell. All I'd heard about Pop since I'd arrived in Gloam was a version of him I'd never known, nor ever thought I could believe had existed. The person Carter was describing was the one I'd known. The man who loved with no spaces between. The man who made you feel like the world wasn't hostile, or ugly, or broken.

"I'm telling you this because we could be hunting the same killer, or it could be two completely unrelated killers. Either way, it doesn't matter to me. I'll catch them both if I must." He stopped, his throat working. "Hunter dying that way made it clear to me. I could fall into a pit of despair and convince myself that Gloam was beyond redemption, that humanity was broken in a way that could never be fixed. It would've been easier to believe that. To wallow in the senselessness of my son dying so needlessly. To rail at the brutality of it. But that wouldn't do his death justice."

The car was starting to feel like an oven. Even with the windows wide open, the breeze which blew in was hot and stale, and did nothing to relieve the heat. I ignored the trickle of sweat which ran down my spine.

"Every day someone in this city dies, or loses someone, all in the name of people taking things which don't belong to them or making the coin to buy more meaningless stuff. If people like me, who can make a difference but choose to do nothing, then all those things will be true. But I still believe in this place. In people." He turned to look at me. "I'm going to catch this guy. Or both of them, if it turns out not to be the same killer. I won't let this lie. I can't."

He unbuckled his seatbelt then, reaching for the doorhandle and stepping out of the car. I sat there a little longer, thinking over the story he'd told me, over everything he'd been through. The two of us weren't as different as I'd thought, and his pain felt familiar, almost like my own. It bonded us in a way where our priorities aligned, where I truly had someone in my corner, because he had as much meat in the game as I did.

I exited the car and joined him on the pavement. We looked at each other, and an understanding passed between us.

I squeezed his shoulder. "Thank you for telling me that. For trusting me. But mostly, for giving me hope."

Chapter
Twenty-Four

Markham

HE LOOKED AT HER face, frozen in horror for eternity. She hadn't seen it coming. It had started out innocently enough. She'd ordered a drink, he'd offered to pay for it, and she'd laid her hand on his arm, lightly stroking with a weird familiarity, as if confident he wouldn't object. A black diamond on her left hand, the gem like a black eye staring blankly up at him.

He'd followed her there, of course. She was next on his list. When Matt had still been involved with the Natives, before he'd been so disgraced, they'd lived in an upmarket, sprawling apartment. She'd been their neighbour. Close enough to hear the screaming, the shattering of glass. But, like everyone else who knew them, she said nothing. Did nothing.

"Nice ring." Her fingers stilled on his arm.

"That a problem?"

He forced the words to his tongue, even as the acrid taste of them burned. "Not if it isn't for you."

She pulled her hand away, her expression growing dark. "My husband is never home. Rich, self-absorbed and arrogant as hell. The only person he loves is himself."

She'd been married back then, too. Even as a young boy, Markham had sensed the undercurrent. But he'd been too young to understand it.

She made as if to rise, and for a long moment he thought about letting her. Maybe he didn't have to do it again. Maybe he could conquer this, the same way an addict goes into recovery.

Instead, he pulled her back to him, so close the length of their bodies pressed together.

Placated, her fingers found his arm again, stroking. Her touch became longer and more insistent with each stroke, and he couldn't remove her fingers from his skin, even as he burned with the contradiction of wanting more and needing her to stop. She'd watched him as she did it, studying his face. He kept it deliberately blank. Any indication of discomfort now would tip the scales.

"Something wrong?" She smiled, the expression somehow feline, like a cat regarding a mouse it had cornered, one which had no hope of escape.

Forcing a smile, and to maintain eye contact, he leaned away from her, shifting back from the heat of her body so he could look at her directly.

"I'm new to the city," he lied. He allowed his gaze to fall from her face to the pleasing swell of her cleavage. He waited for her to rear back in revulsion, for her to be offended, but she smiled, slow and suggestive, and then a laugh escaped her, full and lovely, and he felt the tension slip from his body like a discarded coat.

They spent hours talking and dancing. He offered her more drinks and watched as they slipped down her throat one after the other. Watched as she got progressively more drunk, while he sipped his water.

Close to midnight, she pressed into him, her lips at his ear. "Take me home?"

She followed him out to the curb where his bike waited – a relic from his childhood, and the only tangible thing he'd taken from that time, the only gift his mother had ever given him that he'd held on to.

She climbed behind him without hesitation, the sweetly spiced scent of her perfume drifting over his shoulder, her hair falling between them and brushing the back of his neck. She locked her arms around his waist and pressed into him, and he allowed the pleasure of the sensation to wash over him, blotting everything else out.

They drove through the muggy warmth of the city, its buildings, lights and billboards passing by in a blur of colour and grime.

They arrived outside his apartment block, its grey façade not dissimilar to the infamous prison just outside the city limits. It was the reason he'd nearly kept looking for something else, but space in this city was both scarce and expensive.

She swung off the bike with ease and grace, tossing her wind-blown hair with an easy laugh. He fell into place beside her, and she grabbed his hand, pulling him along to the front door of the building, seeming neither to notice nor care about its appearance.

They raced up the stairs like children, laughing and out of breath, until they reached the fifth floor, and he led her to his door. Before he could put the key in the lock, she pushed him against the door and kissed him, her tongue hot and ready, seeking and probing. His head swam, and he felt himself tighten with desire, locking his arms around her and pulling her into him until the space between their bodies was no wider than a breath.

He broke the embrace and unlocked the door, pulling her in after him. Even in his fog of desire he knew that nosy neighbours would not be welcomed, and this place had walls made of paper. They kissed again, falling over furniture and knocking over a side table, and she was laughing into his mouth, her breath warm and tasting of the last cocktail he'd bought her. Her hands moved to his belt, unbuckling it with quick and sure fingers, and then unbuttoning and unzipping his jeans and taking hold of him. She alternated between strokes and gripping, and then, just when he thought he couldn't hold back a moment longer, she stepped away, her eyes locked on his, and slowly began to undress. Her blouse came off over her head, and she stood in a lacy bra which was black and barely there. His mind snapped back out of its state of smog to absolute awareness. He didn't want the memory to surface, but it rose anyway to the forefront of his mind. His mother, in a lacy black bra, as she rose and fell to the rhythm of the man beneath her, her face turned towards him but her eyes closed. The crescendo of their cries and his hot shame when they'd realised he'd been standing there all along.

Desire drained from him like water swirling down a drain. Seeing the change, she stopped, confused. He zipped and buckled himself back in, not daring to look at her but feeling her eyes on him, hot and questioning.

"What happened?"

He finally looked at her and something in him gave way. He crossed the distance between them in one stride and his hands were around her throat, a gentle squeeze, and then a little harder. She stared at him with liquid eyes, at first confused and then darkening with fear. She struggled, kicking out at his shins and clawing at his hands. He let go, stepping back, his breath heaving in his chest, the sweat dripping down his sides. She stared for a second and then turned and ran for the door, surprisingly quick in her inebriated state and her impractical shoes.

He watched idly as she struggled with the door, pushing against it instead of pulling it towards her, too panicked to realise her error. He felt strangely calm, as if he had all the time in the world to keep her from throwing the door open and disappearing into the night.

"Wait," he called after her. She only increased her efforts to get the door open, and as he reached for her, she managed to wrench it open. He lunged for her, and caught her by the hair, wrapping the silken strands around his fist and yanking. She howled. *Good god, the neighbours.* He yanked harder and pulled her back into the apartment, slamming the door shut. She screamed again, kicking out her feet like a wild horse, connecting with his knee. A bolt of pain seized his leg and he gritted his teeth against the throb which thrummed up his shin.

"Hey, hey, just stop." She glared at him with wild eyes, her mouth drawn into a line of terror, and another memory surfaced, one he'd forgotten about. The sharp shrill of his mother's scream as Matt had punched her squarely in the face. The scrabble of her hands and feet on the wood floor as she tried to move out of reach. The sound she'd made when he'd grabbed her by the hair, pulling her to her feet while she sobbed and begged. Something closed inside him. That door within him, where he could peek at the possibility of being someone else, had slammed shut.

"I'm sorry. I didn't mean to scare you. I was just trying something out." He tried for a coy smile and hoped it didn't look as stiff as it felt. She stared, mute. Her breathing filled the room, the inhale and exhale harsh and loud in the space between them. Sweat had formed at her hairline. One bead joined another and traced a damp line down her cheek. He touched it, gently, feeling a thrum of power washing over him. She flinched but otherwise remained unmoving. His thumb moved to her mouth, tracing the shape of her lips, and something in her relaxed, her body forgetting its tension in one audible release.

"I just thought you would like that kind of thing. Please stay. Don't go."

He pulled her towards him again, and she came willingly enough. The weight and softness of her breasts against his chest brought on the fog again, and for a few more moments he was lost in her, the feel of her, the experience of another's body against his own.

Her tongue found his and her hands moved to his belt, bold and insistent once again. She had her hands on him when the break happened again, and this time when he locked his hands around her throat, he knew the precise pressure it would take. Her eyes bulged and she writhed and tried to scream. He couldn't take his eyes off her, how alive she was, how hard she fought for her small life, and how in the end, the life didn't drain out of her, but simply went out, like a lightbulb splintered beneath a fist.

Chapter
Twenty-Five

Harlow

CARTER PRESENTED ME WITH a stack of crime scene photos, a grisly gift. They were the same ones I'd gone over before, but with the events which had unfolded since, I hoped to see them with new eyes. The stacking of victims was becoming unbearable. It felt like the killer was moving faster between kills, the periods between each one shorter. The idea of another death, because we couldn't catch this guy, sat like a monkey on my back, tormenting me with its burden.

Skylar had been killed at home. I laid her photograph in front of me, staring at Skylar's face. Open and smiling, like she had something to live for. I thought of her little boy, the one who'd been missing from the apartment when we found her. Carter had put out missing posters and asked in the area. The trail was cold. No one had seen anything, or if they had, no one was talking.

Vivienne had been found in an alleyway. I consulted the photos I'd taken on my phone, the only ones we had for now. We were still waiting for the official ones, although no one seemed in a particular hurry to supply them. I'd walked into Carter's office to him railing at the unfortunate soul on the other end. He'd hung up so violently I was sure he'd crack his phone's screen.

I studied Vivienne's face, shutting out the emotion which rose in me at the sight of her broken and bloodied nose, of the bruises beneath her eyes. It was impossible to say what she'd looked like before this. I couldn't picture her in her life the same way I could Skylar. Maybe that was because she'd been found this way – dumped in a street to be discovered, her corpse treated no better than garbage.

I pulled out the third stack of crime scene photos, the ones taken of the Jane Doe from all those years before. She too, had been found in a public place, as if her killer had wanted her to be found. Like he was displaying them. *Look on my work!* I shuddered. The gap between her death and those of Sklyar and Vivienne's was a decade. It seemed a stretch to connect them, despite the similarities between the murders.

If I kept Pop and Chloe out of it, what did these three women have in common? Two dumped on the streets, one found lying peacefully on her bed at home. There was the MO, sure, but how was he choosing them? Were they random? Was the common thread as thin as them all being women? Was he meeting them all in the same place perhaps? The possibilities were endless. My head swam with them, each one as important as the other, all of them impossible to eliminate. There were too many unknown factors and not enough information we were sure of.

The screech of Carter's phone startled me. He snatched it up before it could ring a second time. He listened for a few moments, his face going rigid with shock. He murmured his thanks and then hung up.

"Jesus, Harlow. There's another one."

***

She'd been left in a dumpster on a busy street, her body left on a pile of trash. The killer hadn't bothered to cover or hide her, but left her in plain sight, waiting for her to be discovered. A passerby walking his dog had found her. Carter's ever-faithful contact had called it in immediately, and once again, we were on site before the cops.

Her body wasn't bloated yet, but her body had stiffened. She wasn't long dead. Her short black dress had ridden up to reveal her thighs, milky white.

The smell of the decaying trash surrounding her was so strong I clamped my nose shut with my fingers. I had to reach over her body for her left hand, struggling to turn her palm towards me, fighting against the tautness of her muscles. I managed to rotate her wrist just enough. Her palm was tacky with the incision of the X marked into her flesh. No ring, either. My gaze travelled to her throat, where the bruises marred her once lovely skin.

"Harlow, you should be wearing gloves." Carter's voice was quiet. He came to stand beside me but made no move to examine her.

"My contact said she was reported missing last night. Her husband called it in less than two hours ago."

"How could she have been reported missing last night if her husband only called it in this morning?"

"He wasn't home, apparently. It was called in by a friend when she failed to show up for the dinner they'd planned."

"Two bodies in twenty-four hours." I turned to look at Carter. "The gap between each murder is closing. The next one could already be dead."

Carter dragged his hands down his face, scrubbing at his cheeks with such fury I winced. "He's accelerating. Taking more risks. Planting this body where there's no doubt it'll be found."

"Fuck, Carter. We've got to catch this guy." My voice was unsteady.

Carter looked up at the buildings around us. All of them were apartment blocks, towering so high above the streets their shadows cast a grey pall below.

"How far do you think someone can drag a body without being seen?" He pointed to the pavement and street around the dumpster. "See any blood?"

I turned in a slow circle, examining the ground. It would be difficult to see blood against the black of the asphalt, but it would definitely show up on the pavement. I took my time, stepping away a few metres and then retracing my steps, then doing the same in the opposite direction. Nothing.

"There should've been blood. From the cut on her hand," I said.

"Exactly."

"You don't think she was killed here?"

"It seems unlikely. It's a busy, public street." He pointed down the road. "There are three bars further along this street. Even in the early hours of the morning, there would've been people around. Dumping a body and then taking the time to carve the mark into her palm seems risky, even for our killer."

"Carrying a body along a street from wherever he killed her seems even riskier."

"Which is why I think he killed her in this area. Maybe at his place. Or hers."

I stepped towards her, snapping some pictures with my phone, sure to get a photo of her marked hand, her absent ring. The bruises mapping her throat.

The warble of a police siren pierced the air, and then fell silent as it pulled into an empty space nearby. Two cops got out, ambling towards us. Both seemed unfazed by the corpse in the dumpster. Their attention was on us.

"Carter." The older of the two held out his hand to shake Carter's. When his hand had lingered too long without being taken, he withdrew it, clearing his throat awkwardly.

"Detective Madden sent us. He'll be on his way shortly. He asked that if we found you here…" He trailed off as he finally seemed to notice me. "What's a civilian doing here?"

Carter stepped forward and took the front of the cop's shirt in his fist. His movements were slow and deliberate, the promise of violence vibrating off him. "You tell Madden that if he wants to work a crime scene, he better come himself. I don't take orders from the likes of you."

He gave the cop a small shove, just hard enough to make him stumble. The cop recovered quickly, his face growing pink. His colleague said nothing, but took a step back, out of Carter's immediate reach.

"You two can make yourselves useful by making your way to those bars down the street and interviewing the staff there. We'll work the apartment blocks. If Madden wants a report from us, he can speak to me himself."

The cops scuttled away without a word. I bit my lip against the unexpected giggle that was rising in my throat. Carter glanced at me, quirking an eyebrow, a small smile pulling at the corner of his mouth. I bit down harder. Laughing here, with this woman's body nearby, felt gruesome, like dancing naked on someone's grave.

Carter jutted his chin at the nearest apartment block. "Let's start there, shall we?"

I followed him through the door into the building, the air ripe with the mingled smells of trash and cooked food.

"Carter, there must be over a hundred apartments in this building. We can't interview everyone who lives here."

"Let's just start and see what we find. People's memories fade with the passing of time. Leaving it for a few days could mean a lost opportunity."

We climbed to the first floor. Carter raised his fist and knocked, but after several attempts with no reply, we moved on. Six more unanswered doors, until finally, his knock was answered by an elderly woman, her frame dwarfed by Carter's height.

"Yes?" She'd opened the door only a crack, the safety chain still in place.

"Ma'am. I'm sorry to bother you. I'm a PI—Carter Reach—and this is my colleague, Harlow Novac. A body was found in the dumpster in your street. Did you hear, or see anything unusual last night?"

Her eyes found me, narrowing suspiciously. "I ain't answering any of your questions until you produce some ID, sonny." Even as she spoke to Carter, her gaze remained on me. "And you. ID, or no questions."

Carter took out his badge and showed her through the gap in the door. She nodded, satisfied, then beckoned me to the door. "And you?"

"I'm a merc, ma'am. I don't carry that kind of ID."

"That so? Well then you can wait out here while your friend asks me his questions."

Carter held up a placating hand. "We don't need to come in. I only have a few questions."

The woman paused, undecided. "Fine," she snapped. "Make it quick. I'm missing my show."

"Did you see or hear anything suspicious last night or early this morning?"

"You mean aside from the usual banging, shouting and cursing?"

"Yes ma'am." I could see Carter was working hard not to smile.

"Just that neighbour of mine coming home at an ungodly hour, as usual. That bike of his makes such a racket you can hear it from half a block down." She tapped her left ear. "I ain't deaf yet, you know. Then I heard him coming up the stairs, but he wasn't alone. He had a lady friend." She waggled her eyebrows suggestively, and I had to turn away to hide the expression on my face. "They were laughing and...well, you know. Looked like they were in for a good time."

Carter's body language had changed. I stepped forward, unable to hang back any longer. "Did you happen to see what she looked like? The lady friend?"

The woman glared at me. "Was I talking to you?"

"Please. It's important."

She huffed, then continued. "I only caught a glimpse of her back as she went into his apartment." She pointed at a door further down the corridor. "She had dark hair. Long. Wearing a black dress. High heels. That's all I saw." Carter and I exchanged a look. This felt like it. The moment we'd been waiting for. A breakthrough. A clue. Maybe even our killer, just a few feet away.

I pointed to the door she'd indicated, wanting to be sure. "That's your neighbour's apartment? Number twenty-eight?"

She nodded curtly. "Good day, you two. I believe I've done my civilian duty and now I'd like to be left in peace." I caught the door before it closed, the palm of my hand against the rough wood, my foot wedged in the gap. She glared at me.

"Do you know his name? Your neighbour?"

"Markham," she said shortly. I withdrew, and she closed the door sharply, just short of a slam.

Carter and I crossed to the door, and I knocked on it, hard. It was near impossible to hear anything over the pulse of my blood in my ears, a drumbeat of fear and anticipation.

I knocked again. Still no answer.

I turned to Carter, my disappointment turning rancid in my mouth.

"Kick in the door?" I meant it, even though I framed it as a question.

"Even PIs and mercs have to have their limits, Harlow. We can't go breaking people's doors down without cause."

"You heard what she said! She saw the victim—"

"Harlow. She saw the back of a woman's head. A black dress and heels. You could go into the first bar down the road and probably find half a dozen women who fit that description. It's not enough. We'll need to come back."

I couldn't make my feet move. I wanted to launch myself at the door, claw at it, kick at it, scream through it until I either forced my way through, or it was opened from the inside.

"He could've heard our conversation. He could be hiding in there!"

Carter reached for my arm and pulled me away, steering me back the way we had come.

"I'm going to go back to the crime scene. You go to my office, carry on with the case files. Call me if you find anything or something comes to you."

"What about Madden?"

"Don't you worry about him. I'll deal with it. Go."

He pressed the keys of both his car and office into my hand. "I'll catch a ride."

***

When I arrived back at Carter's office, it was past midday.

I sank into my usual chair, sweating in the afternoon heat, my head crammed with thoughts that ran loops in my mind, like small children set loose in a toy store.

I took my phone from my pocket, swiping through the photos, my eyes lingering on the victim's face. Untouched. You could almost believe she was asleep, but for the marks at her throat.

"They were all married." I said it aloud, imagining I could see the words floating on the air, shifting and coming back together into something which made sense. All married. Was that the link? What did it mean?

An idea formed. One which I couldn't believe we hadn't thought of before, one which felt like it had been right there, waiting to be revealed.

I searched for Carter's number and called him, the line ringing three times before he answered.

"Carter. Do you think they were having an affair with the killer? Or a one-night stand?"

He was quiet for so long I thought we'd been cut off. "Carter?"

"It's a very real possibility. And something else to link them all. But it doesn't do anything to link your father's murder to the others. It means he's going to be even more difficult to trace."

"Because the husbands didn't know."

"Exactly."

I blew out a breath, frustrated. "What's the most likely place for people to meet? Bars? Clubs?"

"Sure, especially if they're married and want to keep it that way."

"There's also the possibility that they weren't affairs."

"What do you mean?"

"Maybe they were seduced. Tracked. Targeted specifically."

"For what reason?"

"For the purpose of killing them."

"What are you saying? That our killer is the morality police and he's punishing these women for cheating on their husbands? With him, no less?"

My mind was racing, but the thoughts were running around in circles, careening into each other and making it hard to think clearly. I was onto something, but I wasn't sure what just yet.

"Plenty of killers from the past have played the morality police. Killing prostitutes because they were sinners. Taking young girls who were considered promiscuous in a bid to punish them."

Carter was silent. "I'll think on it. You might be on to something."

"Any news from your side?"

"No. Madden arrived soon after you left. Mad as a cat stuck in a tree. But he's agreed to leave his juniors here to watch the apartment, and call when whoever lives there arrives home."

"You think he's really going to do that?"

"I do. I think seeing you at the last crime scene has actually had an effect. He asked about you. Said he'd be in contact soon."

"Do you think he's found anything?"

"He didn't say."

"I've got to go. Don't stay there too late. You need your sleep." He paused. "I hope I don't have to tell you this, but the streets aren't safe after dark."

I laughed. "The streets are never safe. Anyway, I'm a merc, Carter. What do I have to be afraid of?"

"Even a merc can die from a bullet. Go home before dark."

Chapter Twenty-Six

Harlow

I'D MEANT TO FOLLOW Carter's advice, but as I was gathering my things, I thought of the emptiness of my waiting apartment, and felt a prick of loneliness. I slid my phone from my pocket and considered my options. Only two, really, if I was after real companionship. I opened my contacts. *Denny. Jesse.* I hadn't spoken to Jesse in a while. He was the safer bet, although what I was really after I wasn't going to get from Jesse, but it was probably better that way. I dialled his number, listening to the drone of it ringing as I grabbed my stuff and left the office, locking the door behind me. I let it ring several times before hanging up.

Without considering it too much, I dialled Denny's number, not expecting him to pick up. I figured he was either at work or resting on his day off.

The ringing stopped. "Harlow." His voice, warm and inviting, even over the phone line. Why hadn't I given this more thought?

"Busy?"

"No. You?"

There was a sudden expectation between us, tangible and weighted. One I could feel through the clip of his words, the exhale of his breath, as if he'd been holding it.

"Come over?"

I said it before I could reconsider. I didn't want to think. I wanted to finish what we'd started. I wanted the feel of him. A way to erase the images of the women. A way to forget how little progress I'd made, and how the answer to the killer was so close – too close for me to see clearly.

"Yes."

"Be here in half an hour."

I hung up before he could reply.

★★★

I'd had just enough time to shower and dress before he knocked at my door. I opened it slowly, swinging it open an inch at a time, revealing myself to him in glimpses. His smile lit me from the inside, heat building in my belly.

He stepped inside without a word, the door closing us in the confines of my apartment, sealing us off from the rest of the world.

We came together in a collision of limbs, lips and fingers. His kiss erased every thought from my mind, my body taking over, wanting only the feel of him against me, our bodies fused together. He reached for my t-shirt, pulling it over my head. I'd intentionally not worn a bra. I pressed my bare breasts against him. He groaned into my mouth. I took his hands and covered my breasts with them, guiding his fingers around the nipples, teasing them until they stood erect. His kiss deepened, our mouths melding together.

He lifted me off the floor then and crossed over to my bedroom, collapsing with me onto the bed sheets. His mouth left mine and he trailed his tongue along my throat, taking his time, pausing between my breasts. Slowly, excruciatingly, his tongue found one nipple, and then the other, his hand slipping between the folds of my shorts and then my underwear, one finger slipping inside me. I gasped, rising to meet him, but he pulled away, teasing me.

I reached for a handful of his shirt, gripping it to stop him from moving away, and he obliged, sliding along the length of my body, unbuttoning my shorts and taking my underwear along as he slid my clothes down my legs, leaving me bare to his touch.

He was still fully dressed. I reached for the button and fly on his jeans but he pushed my hands away, suddenly rough. He caught my wrists in his right hand, pushing them over my head, pinning me to the bed. I looked at him, catching his gaze. In the low light of my bedroom he looked feral, his face contorted. I froze, ice trickling down my spine. I bucked beneath him forcefully, and his eyes cleared, his expression relaxing. He pulled me to him so I was straddling him. I resisted for just a moment, tensing against his hold. He tipped my chin back and kissed my throat, a long, lingering kiss which melted my resistance and started a trail of fire which burned its way down to my belly.

My hands slipped beneath his shirt, the feel of his muscled chest and the warmth of his skin making me hungry for more. I yanked at his shirt and threw it to the floor, exploring his chest and then his back. He lay me down, pulling off his jeans and underwear, and entered me with no warning, the force of it making me gasp.

I rode him, my breath coming so fast the room swam around me, until we both peaked, our bodies slick with sweat, the details of the room drifting back into focus.

"Denny." It was the first word either of us had spoken. My hands were still gripping his shoulders, his arms still encircling my waist. He eased out of me and held me at arm's length, smiling. He traced the shape of my mouth with his thumb, dipping briefly into my mouth, brushing my tongue.

"Harlow. You should call me more often." His throaty laugh was deep and rich, and I felt the vibration of it through his chest.

"I was growing old waiting for your call." I wanted to bite my tongue off as the words left my mouth. The last thing I wanted was to come off as needy, as the girl who'd been waiting at the phone. I was aware that right now might not be the best time to be getting involved with someone. I slid off his lap and onto the bed, pulling the sheet with me, raising it to my breasts to cover them, feeling like an idiotic schoolgirl.

How many times had he done this? He was a barman, after all. Cute and unthreatening. Boyish, even. I was sure that every woman who encountered him sensed the same thing I did – that beneath his carefully curated image there was something else, something delicious and withheld, ripe for the picking.

I could feel him looking at me, but I couldn't bring myself to meet his gaze. I was sure he could read my thoughts, that I was as transparent as glass.

He touched me lightly, his finger tracing a path along my arm, from my shoulder to the tip of my index finger, slipping it into his mouth, his warm lips closing around my skin. He traced the tip of my finger along the length of his tongue. My eyes were drawn to his then, and his gaze was molten.

He pulled me to the edge of the bed, parting my thighs, his tongue slipping between my folds. I buried my hands in his hair, gripping hard, heat searing through me, my thoughts turning to smoke.

Chapter Twenty-Seven

Markham

HE SAT ACROSS FROM Dr Black. She was in her usual comfy armchair, while he sat in the middle of the faded plaid couch, his feet planted on the floor. It felt too much like a social visit for him to recline against the backrest. How was he supposed to relax, anyway?

She regarded him in silence. She sat unmoving, her eyes on him, her hands comfortably folded in her lap, waiting. He'd been to dozens of them over the years. It was the one thing his mother had tried to do right. She'd tried to get him help. *Instead of leaving the bastard.* Still, he had to give her points for effort.

He met her eyes, and she smiled warmly. There was no trace of impatience in her face. She had no tics that he'd ever seen. No fidgeting. No sighing. Very little shifting. No playing with her hair or tapping her fingers against the arm of her chair. She just...sat. Like she had all the time in the world. He supposed she charged by the hour, and not by the result of the session, so for her, the outcome of this session was the same. She would still get her coin, whether he wept and confessed his sins, or didn't say a single word for the next fifty minutes. He'd done exactly that the first time he'd come to her. She'd asked him a single question, and when he'd rebuffed her, she'd smiled politely and sat waiting for him to say more. When he didn't, neither did she.

He looked at the small digital clock on the table beside her. He'd only been here for ten minutes. *Do I really want the help? Can I be helped?*

He saw it all again in his mind's eye. The screaming, the feel of his hands around Matt's throat. The sound of his mother's head hitting the table, then the floor. Crack. Thud. The blood. The warmth of her cheek, even as the life had seeped out of her. It was funny how this event, although followed by multiple other deaths, was the one which stuck in his mind. He hadn't expected to miss her, or to feel regret, but he did. Matt had been the one he was after. His mother had been an unfortunate bystander. He'd hoped that with Matt gone, they'd be able to rebuild. Now he would never know.

"Markham?"

She'd spoken. He looked up. He considered her. She was the best out of the therapists he'd seen over the years. He believed she'd sincerely tried to help him. But now he knew. There was no escape. No exit door. He could kill and throttle and strangle and watch the life go out of a dozen more bodies, and never escape what he was. What Matt and his mother had made him. What life had made him. What nature had given him from the moment he was conceived. He'd convinced himself that if he followed the trail of blame, if he snuffed them all out, he'd be able to see clearly. He'd be able to clear away the clutter that hid his path, and he'd be able to turn away, finally at peace. No one else would be hurt by their indifference. No other small boys would know the sharp slice of loneliness, the unbearable thought that they were somehow unlovable.

"I know we like to play this game of who can stay quiet the longest. And normally I'm happy to participate. But today you seem to really have something to say." She paused. "So tell me."

"My mother is dead."

Sympathy filled her eyes. He wanted it but didn't at the same time. He wanted to be seen, to have his life acknowledged as something worth the fight, but he hated pity. "Do you want to tell me what happened?"

The truth was there, right on the tip of his tongue. He could spill it all. She would call the cops, as duty demanded. He'd go to jail, and maybe that was truly the only remedy for him – to lock away this part of himself in a cage made of steel and iron, so that he would no longer have to fight what he really was.

He regarded his hands. Big. Long-fingered. His mother had had small, compact hands, roughened by years of washing dishes and doing laundry. Did he get his hands from his father? Did his mother even know for certain who his father was? Did it even matter now? Would knowing him have made any difference? All he'd ever been told was that his father was a drunk.

If Matt was a barometer for her taste in men, he was sure his father would've been the same. The last thing Markham had needed as a boy was another violent and useless drunk.

"Do you believe people are meant to repeat what happens to them in childhood?"

"Cycles of abuse are known to repeat themselves. The abused becomes the abuser. But it doesn't have to be that way. Believing in fate is a way to make ourselves believe we have no control, but that's not completely true. We have control over how we react to what happens to us. We can choose who we want to be." She fixed him with that unnerving stare. "Do you believe you're meant to repeat what's happened to you?"

He wanted to laugh. A belly-busting, rib-aching laugh. He couldn't choose who he wanted to be, any more than a dog could choose to bark. It just *was.*

The truth dissolved on his tongue. "I always knew he would kill her. And now he has."

Dr Black twitched in her chair. "You're saying your stepfather killed your mother?"

"And then himself."

He laughed.

★★★

Back outside, Markham stuffed his hands into his pockets, considering the outside of Dr Black's building. He knew he wouldn't be back. Watching her usual composure melt away at his lie, how easily she'd believed him, made him realise he'd gotten all he could from her.

He surveyed the street. Just lately, he'd felt the prickle of eyes on his back whenever he was outside of his apartment. Maybe it was paranoia setting in, which had been plaguing him ever since he'd offed the last one. He knew he'd messed that up. He'd gotten caught up in the moment of taking her home, of the thrill of her cluelessness, of how everything fell into place so neatly. He was loath to think about just *how much* he'd enjoyed it – how she was a woman who had likely been touched by Matt, too. Sullied.

He pushed the thought away, burying it in the same place as the others he didn't want to examine too closely. Leaving her body out in the open like that had been cocky. Maybe he'd expected to be caught earlier.

Maybe he'd hoped *she* would figure it out sooner, be smarter about following the trail of breadcrumbs he'd left for her. Just when he'd thought perhaps he'd need to kill another one, even though his list had been whittled down to the ones he couldn't track down, he'd heard her. Her voice just outside his apartment, and one of a male he couldn't identify. It wasn't Jesse. She spoke his name, and it fell into place. *Carter.* He'd had to squash the urge to laugh out loud. It had all come full circle now. It couldn't have worked out more perfectly than if he'd planned it himself. She was close now, close enough for him to draw her in, close enough for the kill. The final play in his plan.

He turned in the direction of his apartment. It was a dump, but at least there he didn't feel like he was a bug under a microscope. He broke into a quick walk, brushing past people without a backward glance or apology, and soon enough he was climbing the stairs. He stopped. The door was ajar, leaning drunkenly on its hinges. It had been kicked in with such force, that the one hinge had come completely loose. For the first time since moving here, he regretted not carrying a weapon. He stood, listening intently for any movement from inside, but it was quiet. He stepped cautiously towards the doorway; his eyes trained into the parts of the living room he could see.

He inched into the room, careful not to disturb anything, or make a sound. The place had been trashed. Books had been torn from the shelf and scattered around the room, several of them missing pages. Kitchen drawers hung open like mouths, some of their contents upended on the floor. His heart was pounding in his chest, filling his ears with the sound of it, as he pictured the hidden compartment inside his cupboard. He strode to the bedroom, no longer caring how much noise he made. He shoved his hanging clothes aside, and reached upwards, his hand feeling for the small drawer that popped open with the flick of a hidden latch. The relief which flooded through him when he realised it was untouched was so heady he had to sit down or risk passing out.

He sank to the floor, drawing deep breaths. Black spots were moving in his field of vision, and he wondered if he was going to pass out after all. He pressed his palms hard into the floor, trying to ground himself, to will his body to stay conscious. He hadn't felt fear like this in so long, and he'd never wanted to feel that way again, but here it was, brushing against his skin, drawing him close, imprisoning him in its cold embrace.

He was so deep in his own thoughts that he missed the scuff of shoes against the floor, the quiet rustle of movement. It was only when the cool metal of a gun's muzzle met his temple, that he realised he was in danger.

Chapter
Twenty-Eight

Harlow

"No Rich. For god's sake I don't need you to come!" I was nearly shouting down the phone, but I couldn't help it. I listened to him babble on about me coming home, about how Ma needed me, and I closed my eyes against the pain that was building in my chest. He always knew how to get under my skin, how to get me to cooperate. I hated him for it. I pictured Ma at home, the loss of Pop weighing her down, glueing her to her favourite chair. I thought of her listening for his voice, for his footsteps, and then realising all over again that he was gone, that those sounds were forever lost to her. When she went to bed, and woke in the morning, did she still reach for him, forgetting for a moment that he wouldn't be there?

"Low. Hey! Are you listening to me?"

"Rich. Like I said. There's no reason for you to come here. Ma needs you." There, have a go at your own game.

A sudden pounding at the door made my stomach lurch into my mouth. "Hold on," I said into the phone.

"Who is it?"

"It's Rich." His voice came from the phone as well as outside my door.

I swung it open and stared disbelievingly at the sight of my brothers on my doorstep, both of them grinning.

"What the hell are you two doing here?"

They parted then, to reveal Chloe. The bruises at her throat were gone. Her eyes were clear and bright, her grin like the sun slipping out from behind a cloud, warming me.

I pulled all three of them to me at once, trying to get my arms around all of them, laughing, even as the tears slid down my face.

We stood in the hallway like that for a long, warm moment. My irritation was gone, replaced by a sense of home I hadn't felt since I'd left The Sands.

I finally released them, swiping at my tears, waving them in.

I could tell from their stiffening backs as I followed them in that my surroundings shocked them.

I grew uncomfortable as their silence went on. I watched them take in the details – the peeling paint, the hanging door of the kitchen cupboard. The cracked tiles, and the burn mark on the stovetop, which, no matter how much I scrubbed at it, refused to budge or fade. I cringed inwardly. I knew this place was awful. But I spent so little time here it seemed pointless to look for another, better place, whether I could afford it or not.

"Low. I know home isn't exactly paradise but this place... it's like a crackwhore den." Rich said. I sighed inwardly. Not one to pull any punches, my brother.

"If you're here to try to persuade me to come home, you're wasting your breath."

"Actually, we're only here as Chloe's escorts."

I glanced at her in time to catch her eyeroll and grinned. "Are you staying?"

Chloe nodded. "Although I was hoping for better accommodation than this." Her smile took the sting out of the comment. The thought of having her here, a piece of home, filled me with such joy I thought I'd burst from it. But just as quickly as the feeling rose, it turned sour.

"Chlo—I'd love you to stay. But—"

She cut me off with a look. "Don't say it's dangerous. We know. You've been here for weeks now. We knew we couldn't get you to come home. So, we thought you could use some company." She batted her eyes. "So here I am."

I hugged her again, breathing in her scent of desert and shampoo.

"And you two?" I said to my brothers. "You're surely not going back today?"

Rich and Charlie exchanged a glance. "Actually, we hoped we could stay the night and make our way back tomorrow," Rich said. The idea of having all three of them here with me was too good to pass up.

I smiled at them. "Of course." I swept my arm around the living room. "Although I've only got a couch."

Charlie squeezed my shoulder briefly. "That's good enough. Rich can take the floor."

We all laughed at Rich's look of outrage.

***

I would've preferred to take Chloe anywhere else but to The Dive. I hadn't heard from Denny since that night. It seemed he had a pattern, and I didn't want to be that woman who was endlessly available to him, while all he had to do was wait for me to show up, but Chloe was not to be dissuaded.

"Why not?" she asked. She was standing in front of the tarnished vanity mirror in my bedroom, sweeping mascara on to her lashes, making them look longer and thicker than ever. I'd always said that she'd make the perfect mascara model.

I scrabbled for an excuse. She misunderstood my expression and lowered the mascara wand, her attention fully on me. "Is it because of what happened after the last time we were there?" I hated to admit it, but it was tempting to say yes. I couldn't bring myself to do it.

"No, I..." Did I really want to tell her about Denny? Was there really anything to tell? I felt it then; the hot tingle at the thought of him and his hands on me, the press of his body against mine, the delicious heat. The memory of his tongue trailing my skin, the feel of him inside me.

Chloe's expression sharpened, and I felt like I'd spoken out loud.

"Ooohhh," she drawled. "Is it what I think it is?"

I said nothing, but the slow crawl of blood into my cheeks gave me away.

She clapped her hands, jumping up and down like a kid.

"A guy! Right?"

I turned my back on her and started sorting through my clothes to find something to wear, doing my best to avoid looking at her. "Let's just get ready, okay? I'm sure the guys are already champing at the bit."

Rich and Charlie were equally appalled and enthralled by The Dive. Rich's outrage at being searched at the door and forced to part with his piece and Charlie's open-mouthed gawking at the dancers on stage made Chloe and I giggle like the girls we used to be.

I tried to keep my eyes from the bar as my brothers hustled to buy the drinks, and Chloe and I found an empty booth, a cigarette still smoking in an ashtray on the table, the pleather still warm from the recent departure of other patrons.

Chloe slid in next to me, shoving the ashtray as far down the table as it would go. "So – that cute barman still here?"

The mention of Denny drew my gaze to the bar. I couldn't see past the bodies queuing for drinks, and I wondered if he was working that night. The thought of him not being there made my stomach sink.

Richard and Charlie arrived back laden with drinks. Richard slid one across to me, its tiny umbrella bobbing, the sweet tang scent of it familiar. "The barman who helped us said he knew you would like this." My gut squeezed painfully. He was here after all. Had he been on the lookout for me?

"A regular here, huh?"

I ignored the burning curiosity in Chloe's gaze. "Mostly business. But I've gotten to know one or two people who work here, sure."

I sipped my drink, feeling its cool sweetness slide down my throat, doing my utmost to keep my attention on Chloe and my brothers. I felt like a schoolgirl who'd purposely put herself in the path of the boy she liked, making it look like a coincidence. He knew I was here, so the game was up. My showing up like this would seem like a move – the last thing I'd wanted him to think.

Chloe bumped against me playfully, nearly spilling my drink. "You're quiet. Want another drink?"

"I'm barely done with this one." Chloe grabbed my hand, either not hearing me or pretending not to, and dragged me to the bar. The crowd had thinned for the moment, giving us the room to move right to the front of the bar, Chloe making a beeline for Denny. I didn't know what expression my face was wearing, but when he caught sight of me, his face lit into a smile, his gaze warm and beckoning.

"Harlow." The syllables of my name from his mouth drew me in, like an invisible thread between us. He glanced only briefly at Chloe. Was I imagining it, or did his smile cool a few degrees at the sight of her? "Chloe. Good to see you up and at it."

She smiled flirtatiously at him, cranking up the wattage to the max, but he barely seemed to notice. His eyes were on me, his attention a pinprick of focus as he took me in.

I felt, rather than saw, Chloe glance from me to him. Without looking at her I knew she'd put the pieces together, and with that, she squeezed my arm briefly. "You get the drinks, Low. I'm going to pay a visit to the ladies' room." She was gone before I could ask her what she wanted.

"Got visitors, I see." He leaned across the counter of the bar towards me, even though the stage was empty and the music muted. I caught the scent of his soap, clean and slightly antiseptic. He'd brushed his hair back from his forehead, and the white shirt he wore was clean and crisp. I pictured undoing each button, slowly, one at a time, watching his face change with every inch of skin I uncovered.

"My brothers. And Chloe. Who you know."

It felt as if all the words in the world had deserted me. My mind was blank to even a single syllable. All I wanted was to reach across and touch him, draw him to me as if we were the only two people in this place.

His smile grew knowing beneath my gaze, but I suddenly felt bold, like I didn't have to hide, or pretend. It was only when Chloe returned that I was able to pull my gaze from him, a tingling warmth flooding my body.

"Still no drinks?" She waggled her eyebrows at us, and we all laughed, the tension breaking.

Denny handed us the beers for my brothers, another cocktail for me, and a gin and tonic for Chloe. The music ramped up again as a dancer took to the stage, her heels looking too high to walk in. She strutted on regardless, the jewels of her bikini catching the light. Chloe and I turned to watch her, the din of the crowd growing as the girl started her routine.

We took our drinks from Denny. When he handed me mine, his fingers lingered against mine, the briefest brush of skin against skin. I forced myself to follow Chloe. We returned to my brothers, who were watching the girl on stage, their eyes glazed, startling to attention when we dumped their beers on the table, both of us laughing.

We talked about inconsequential things, skirting around the subject of Ma, and actively avoiding talking about Pop. It was an unspoken agreement – that tonight was for us. No talk of death, or killers, or what might've been.

Looking back, I wish now we'd spoken about those things. It might've prevented what came next.

Chapter
Twenty-Nine

Markham

IF HIS CHILDHOOD HAD taught him anything, it was how to fight. The muzzle against his temple stilled everything in him, his pulse slowing, his surroundings coming into sharp focus. He raised his hands, slowly, to show they were empty. He could only see the assailant in his peripheral vision, making out the fact that he was well over six feet, and muscled. He wore a leather jacket, despite the heat. Markham knew instinctively that it would have the insignia of the eagle at the back. He'd anticipated this day ever since he'd left his childhood home. It had taken longer than what he thought, but here was one of them, looking for Matt, no doubt.

"What do you want?" he asked quietly. It felt essential not to startle the gunman. One wrong move and Markham would have a bullet lodged in his brain.

When the stranger spoke, his voice matched what little Markham could see of him – rough, deep, raw.

"I need information."

"You want to know where Matthew is, right?"

The pressure of the muzzle slackened somewhat. Markham resisted turning and attempting to take the gun from him. Timing was essential.

He took the silence as assent. "He's dead."

His meaty hand landed on Markham's shoulder, forcing him around, the gun now pointed at Markham's forehead. Sweat dampened his armpits. His stomach roiled. He wondered if this was what the women had felt when his hands had gone around their throats, and they'd realised that the harmless barman they'd enticed was a predator who'd failed to bare his teeth.

"You lie!" the gunman hissed.

"Lying wouldn't be in my best interest right now. And I can tell it isn't what you wanted to hear, but it's still the truth. He's dead."

"What about that pig he was dealing with?"

"Carter Reach, right?"

A barely perceptible nod.

"He's a PI now. I can take you to him. I know where his offices are."

When the gunman didn't move, Markham chanced coming up on his knees, as slowly as he could. "I could take you to him now."

The gunman hesitated, and it was all Markham needed. He raised a fist and drove it into the gunman's crotch. The gun fell from his hand and Markham grabbed for it, the cool steel in his hands for only a second before the gunman recovered just enough to lunge for it. The room reverberated with the shot.

Chapter Thirty

Harlow

RICHARD AND CHARLIE LEFT the next day, hungover and haggard. I watched them drive away with a mix of love and regret, a part of me wishing I was in the car with them, returning home. But I wasn't done with this city yet.

Having Chloe with me was strange. I'd grown used to the quiet of living alone, of stepping into a space that was only mine. Now her things were strewn everywhere, her clothes taking over the cupboard, her makeup scattered on every available surface in the bathroom. It felt like we were young girls again, revelling in the opportunity of a sleepover.

She wanted to accompany me on my visits to Carter, but I couldn't bear to take her with me. I didn't want her to see the crime photos or read the reports on the killings. I needed the time to focus, and Chloe was not someone to be put quietly in a corner. I also didn't want her to see what could've happened. It was one thing to talk about it, but something else to hold the evidence in your hands, taking in the details of exactly what she'd narrowly escaped.

"Come on, Low. I'm here to help." I glanced at her in the mirror briefly, pausing mid-brush, dribbling toothpaste into the sink. I spat and swiped at my mouth, knowing I'd have no peace until I mollified her.

"Chlo. I told you. I can't take you along."

"Then why am I here?" She folded her arms across her chest, looking so much like the little girl she'd once been I couldn't help smiling.

She softened a little. "What?"

"Nothing. You're just cute when you're annoyed."

"Arg. What am I supposed to do all day?"

I motioned towards the kitchen, and the crusted dishes in the sink. The pile had grown considerably since her arrival last night. "Clean?"

She scowled. "I'm not here to play maid to you."

"When I'm back later I promise I'll go over everything with you. That's where you can help. We can brainstorm. Talk things over. I need a new set of eyes on this, but I can't have you at Carter's office. He barely tolerates *me*." That was part of it, but certainly not all of it. I was afraid to allow her too close to this. Having her in Gloam already felt like dangerous ground.

"Yes, but you forget that everyone loves me." She flashed a smile, batting her eyelashes.

I laughed. "That shit doesn't work on me."

She sighed. "Fine. I'll clean. You'll be back this afternoon, otherwise I may just be making my way back to The Sands and leaving you high and dry."

***

I was on my way to Carter's office when my phone lit up with an unknown number.

I answered, but before I could even say hello, the voice on the other end spoke. It took me only a second to recognise his voice, and my pulse jumped with a mix of nerves and hope.

"Miss Novac."

"Mr X."

"I haven't heard from you, which I assume means you've nothing to report."

"Not yet, no."

"In that case, I have good news. Tower Mason was seen yesterday, going into a building downtown. He wasn't seen coming out. I need you to go there, now."

He recited an address which I memorised. Something about it sounded familiar, although I couldn't say why.

"Report back when you have something."

The line went dead.

I called Carter, but there was no answer. I hung up and called Jesse, and this time he answered.

"Kid! Sorry I didn't return your call the other day. Got caught up."

"Jesse. I got a call from Mr X. A lead on Tower Mason. I need you to come."

"Where?" I gave him the address.

"Meet you there. Don't go in without me."

***

When I arrived, Jesse was already waiting. One look at the apartment block and I realised why the name had sounded so familiar. It was the same one where the latest victim had been found. The apartment block where the old lady had pointed us to the door of her neighbour. I caught Jesse up on the details while we moved inside. He paused at the stair landing, his gaze travelling up the flights.

He shook his head. "There must be more than twenty floors, Harlow. How are we going to find this guy?"

"Easy. Start where Carter and I left off."

I led him to the door we'd stood at, passing the old lady's apartment, the sound of the blasting TV clear enough to hear every syllable of the show she was watching.

"You knock," Jesse said. "I'll hang back, cover you. Just in case."

I raised my fist and knocked; my other hand close to my Sauer. I didn't expect anyone to answer, but just as I was about to knock again, the door opened. The sight of the man in the doorway turned my blood to ice.

"Denny?" It was Jesse who had spoken. I couldn't move my tongue. It felt pasted to the top of my mouth, as if I'd eaten glue.

Jesse stepped back, his gaze moving along the corridor. "There must be some mistake. We're looking for a guy named Markham." He pointed at the old lady's door. "Your neighbour said he lived here. Do you know him?"

I wanted to scream at Jesse. I wanted to grab him and shake him until he knew what I now knew. I wanted to share the knowledge, to ease some of the burden from my own shoulders, so I wouldn't feel like my knees were going to buckle.

Denny's smile was taut; brittle enough to crack. He kept the door open only enough to allow his torso through, the view of the apartment beyond blocked by his body.

"Your neighbour said your name is Markham." The words fell out of my mouth before I even knew I was forming them. My gut was clenched so tightly I felt like I was going to be sick. I glanced at Jesse, who just looked puzzled.

We'd overlooked something so obvious. It was the thing I'd been trying to remember, the detail which had eluded me, the one which I'd kept locked away with my other memories of that time. Now, looking at him, the fog cleared. The boy I could now see behind his adult features. The one in Matt's basement. The boy they'd rarely brought along. *Markham.*

Jesse was turning towards me, his expression changing when he really looked at me. A fury was building in me. My mind felt black with rage, my hands shaking with the effort of keeping myself together. I thought of the woman he'd been with, the woman he'd taken home. The latest victim. We'd found her in a dumpster just days before. He'd touched me after that, touched me with the same hands.

I couldn't think clearly. My thoughts crowded together, losing their shape and definition, their images blurring until only one emerged. Where was Tower Mason?

I threw myself at him, my rage making me stronger. We collided. My weight was no match for his, but I caught him by surprise, forcing him back a step, revealing a slice of the room beyond. I withdrew and threw myself at him again, trying to push him back just enough to allow me to slip in behind him.

This time he was ready. His hands closed around my arms in a grip painful enough to still me.

"Harlow, stop! What the hell is wrong with you?"

Was I wrong? Could I possibly be wrong?

"Who's Denny?" I whispered.

He shook his head, his hands softening around my arms. "I am."

"Who's Markham?" I held up a hand to stop him from replying. "Let me guess. Also you?"

I shook free of his hands, feeling like my skin was burning where he'd touched me. A burn that would brand me, a circle of fingers. Like those bruises around those women's throats. I shuddered, the floor swaying beneath my feet.

"Harlow. It's not what you think. Let me explain."

Jesse was beside us now. "Let's go."

I was about to protest. About to ask about Tower Mason, but Jesse silenced me with a look. We turned away and walked, with Markham's protests following us down the hall, his words fading as I took the stairs two at a time, wanting only to escape the sound of his voice as it trailed after us.

Chapter Thirty-One

Markham

IT HAD NOT BEEN a part of the plan, of course, but here they were. She'd tracked him to his place. From the moment he'd heard her and Carter outside his door, he knew it was only a matter of time. What had possessed him to answer the door, when he'd known that nothing good would be on the other side, he didn't know. Maybe he was tired of pretending. Maybe it was time for him to embrace his true nature, to shed his Denny persona. He'd tried. Tried to get help, to allow Denny to take over, to really slip into the role of the nice, unthreatening barman. There was a part of him who had really wanted a chance at a normal life. A family of his own. A woman he could love. That was all gone now.

A thought which had occurred to him that night he'd seen Harlow at the bar with her brothers and Chloe surfaced. A seed of an idea, which now bloomed into fullness. He would need a way to draw Harlow back to him. She wouldn't come willingly, but it was going to be more fun this way. She'd have no choice but to come, knowing she would be moving within his reach, knowing she would be in danger. But that was her nature. He'd learned that much.

First, he had something else to attend to.

Harlow

I knew I should go home. Chloe was waiting, and I'd promised I'd be home in the afternoon. Instead, I ended up in a hovel pretending to be a bar, somewhere in the heart of the city. Jesse had to drive my car, leaving his bike abandoned on Denny's street. My hands were shaking too much, my legs weak with adrenaline.

Jesse ordered me something strong and sweet. I drank it without protest. It blazed down my throat and into my belly, making my head swim pleasantly. I was only vaguely aware of my surroundings. One moment it was just me and Jesse, and the next, Carter was there, his massive hands swallowing mine, his grip steady and warm.

"She's in shock," Carter said. Who was he talking about? It didn't feel important. I drifted, my mind loose from its anchor, the chair beneath me as insubstantial as air.

"Harlow!" Jesse's voice was sharp and loud, cutting through the fog.

His face came into focus. "Did you hear what Carter said?"

I forced myself to concentrate on his words. "What?"

Carter was still gripping my hands. He squeezed gently, shifting my attention to him.

"They found Tower Mason."

Hope flared in me.

"His body was found in the apartment. The one you and Jesse were just at. Whoever did it left the door wide open. Just walked out."

"It was Denny." I shook my head hard, wanting to never say that name again, wanting to dislodge it from my brain so I never spoke those syllables again. "Markham."

I buried my face in my hands. "Oh god. How did I not see it? How could I be such an idiot?"

"You couldn't have known. Hell—I've been going to The Dive for years, saw the kid most times I was there. Never made the connection. Because he made sure there was no connection to be made. No one knew him in Gloam. It's been years since he lived here. Matt was a disgraced member. He was using the X mark to throw us off the trail, making us think it was a gang member." Jesse was babbling.

"He left a note." Carter took his phone out and opened his photo app. The image was of Tower's corpse, the note spattered with blood, the handwriting neat and concise. *It was me.*

The last residue of whatever shock I'd been feeling drained from me then, replaced with a fury so complete I wanted to scream until my lungs gave out. "He's taunting us." I slammed my hand against the table, making the glassware jump.

"We need to call the cops."

Neither Jesse nor Carter moved. I grabbed for Carter's phone, but he caught my hand, forcing me to look at him. "You know it won't do any good. You know that. You've already had first-hand experience on how ineffective they are, how little of a shit they give. We have to go after him ourselves."

I sagged against him, my anger giving way to a bone-deep wave of despair. "Do you think it was him? Who killed Pop?" I said it so quietly I wasn't sure he'd heard me.

"There's only one way to find out." Jesse was rising, Carter following suit.

Only then did I think about Chloe.

"I need to go home first."

"There's no time," Carter said. "We have to go after him now. He's already left his apartment, and I'm guessing with him leaving Tower's body there, he's got no intention of coming back. He's already on the run."

"Chloe is there. At my place. I need to send her home. I'll call my brothers. You go to his apartment; see if he left any clues. I'll meet you there."

***

The door of my apartment was ajar. It had clearly been kicked in. I held the Sauer out in front of me, stepping through the doorway slowly. The coffee table was lying on its side. The couch was askew, as if someone had lunged across it. Shards of glass glinted on the floor, water dampening the throw rug. The bedroom door was closed. I moved around the glass, stepping over the floorboard which always creaked, my eyes glued to the bedroom door.

"Chloe?" No answer. "Chlo?" My denial that he was here, that he'd come for Chloe, that I was somehow back to where I'd started was so strong I could almost convince myself it was true. My fear crowded it out, my blood beating such a violent pulse I could taste it in my mouth.

My fingers brushed the door handle. I hesitated, listening. Muffled breathing. The soft shift of feet on the floor. I pushed the handle down, kicking the door wide.

Chloe was on the bed. Her hands and feet were bound behind her in a hogtie so brutal she had no choice but to lie on her belly, her head lifting only high enough for her enormous eyes to meet mine. She screamed, but the sound was muffled by the thick dishcloth he'd used to gag her. He held a knife to her throat. *The same one he'd used on the women?* The thought turned my knees to liquid. I fought to stay upright. I couldn't fail Chloe now. Not again.

"Drop it," Markham snapped.

Playing for time, I took another step into my bedroom. Two more long strides, and I'd be at the foot of the bed. "It's loaded."

"I'll take my chances. Drop it. And stay where you are. No closer."

I looked at Chloe, trying to read her expression. Tears had tracked their way down her cheeks, leaving a black mascara trail on her skin. She didn't seem hurt, aside from the discomfort of being bound. I knew what I had to do.

"Let her go. She has nothing to do with this, right?"

As I said it, the pieces I'd been trying to put together changed formation, and slotted in. All along, the answer had been right under my nose.

"You weren't after Chloe, were you? Or my father."

He smiled, the expression devoid of all warmth, all humanity, like a grinning skull.

"I've been waiting for you to figure it out. It took you longer than I thought. You would've worked it out far sooner if you'd remembered me."

He gestured to my gun. "I'm not saying it again."

I bent and slid it across the floor. It spun across the tiles, coming to rest at his feet.

He picked it up, placing it on my bedside table. All thoughts of trying to retrieve it flew from my mind when Markham moved towards Chloe, the knife still in his hand. I screamed, about to throw myself at him, until I realised he was cutting her free.

She flopped onto the bed, then rolled to the floor and crawled towards me, struggling to stay on all fours.

"Hey!" Markham's voice was quiet, but commanding. Chloe stopped. She was panting, her eyes fixed on me, her face pinched.

He'd picked up my pistol and beckoned me to him. The thought of his hands on me filled my mouth with bile, and I struggled against the urge to gag.

I crossed the room to him, trying to block out Chloe's protests of terror. I knew that only one of us would leave here. He would not take someone else I loved.

His fingers closed around my left wrist; his grip so tight I gasped. If I could only get him out of here, or give Chloe the chance to run, then whatever happened after that didn't matter. I closed my eyes for a moment, thinking of Pop, of home. Of Ma, Rich and Charlie. The heat of The Sands, relentless and comforting. I thought of Chloe and I as young girls, holed up in her bedroom, talking about growing old, about our futures.

"Markham." His real name felt like poison in my mouth, but I had a part to play.

I placed my fingers on his, gently pulling to ease the pressure. "Hey. You're hurting me." I said it quietly, looking into his eyes, hoping I'd buried my fear and revulsion so far down that he wouldn't be able to see it. "Let Chloe go. Do what you want with me. You're a good guy, right? A good guy who's just made some mistakes."

He grabbed me a second time, closing his fingers around my face and squeezing until I thought my teeth would shatter in my mouth. I instinctively dug my nails into the skin of his hand until he released me, yelping. He started at me as if I were a beloved dog who had bitten him.

"You think you can play me? Tell me what I want to hear? Do you think I'm an idiot?"

"No. That's why you called yourself Denny, isn't it? To try to make a fresh start? To be someone else?" Even as I said the words I thought of how he'd duped me. How he'd hidden this side of himself underneath the dazzling layers of charm and charisma. How easily he'd fooled us all.

Markham was the one. He'd killed those women, and he'd killed my father. I'd slept with the man who had taken my father's life, who had strangled him to death just outside our home and left his body in the dirt. My skin crawled with revulsion. I wanted to scratch until I bled, until I could purify myself with my own blood and wash away every trace of him, every memory of his touch. I wanted to launch myself at him and claw, kick and punch until he was nothing more than a bag of bones, meat and blood.

Instead, I sank towards the floor, his grip on my wrist loosening as the unexpected pull of my weight slipped me from his grasp. Could I crawl away? Pull Chloe to her feet and run? He was too close. One of us would get a bullet in the back of the head.

Cool metal pressed against the back of my neck. "Get up." I rose slowly. "Turn around." I turned to face him, looking past the barrel of the gun to Markham, taking in the set of his jaw and the strained lines of his forehead. I met his eyes. They were wild and...*afraid*. He looked like a little boy who fallen asleep and then woken to find he was alone, abandoned and forgotten. His head was cocked to the side, as if he was listening for something only he could hear. His hands shook, and the gun kept straying off target, away from my face and to a spot just over my shoulder.

"Markham." I waited for his eyes to focus on me. "I don't blame you. It's not your fault. I know you didn't mean to kill my father. I know you killed those women because they deserved it. You were doing the world a favour, doing this city a service. You've had so much happen to you that was beyond your control. Am I right?" I waited for his response, holding his gaze. It was only a guess. It wasn't as if he'd shared anything real about his life. But I remembered how Matt had treated him, how, even when he was so young, barely a teen, he'd walked around with eyes that were so haunted it was difficult to hold them for too long, for fear you'd lose something of yourself in them.

If I was wrong, I knew this was possibly the last few breaths I would ever draw.

His eyes seemed to clear, as if wherever he'd been in his mind, he'd come back from. He focused on me. Tears formed and streamed down his face, but he seemed unaware of them. "I wanted to stop." Slowly, he lowered the gun. I considered my options. Try to disarm him? Run for the door? Both those scenarios presented the danger of Markham shooting me or Chloe in the back.

I'd been gone too long. Soon, Carter and Jesse would come looking for me. The idea of two more people that I cared about in this room and within arm's reach of Markham made my head swim with panic.

I breathed deeply. My gut told me that the only way forward was by gaining Markham's trust, by keeping him calm. So many times, I'd ignored my natural instincts and disregarded my inner voice. All along, this had been my downfall. Not trusting myself.

He sank onto the edge of my bed, keeping hold of the gun but pointing it down, into the floor. I took advantage of that second of distraction and turned to Chloe. *Run,* I mouthed. When she rose, her feet skittering noisily against the tiles, I expected him to raise the gun and shoot her, but he didn't even look up. She ran for the door, and only when she disappeared from view did I allow myself to believe she was safe.

I sank beside Markham, slowly sliding an arm around him. He reminded me of a cagey animal. His body was taut, as if ready to attack. I carefully slipped my arm around him. When he seemed fine with that, I gave him a gentle squeeze, forcing my repulsion at the feel of him down into the pit of my stomach, making it roil.

He pressed his knuckles into his eyes, still gripping the gun. I watched his hand tighten around the pistol. "Markham. Put the gun down. It's loaded."

He laughed then, the sound brittle and low. "So you said. That's the point though, isn't it?"

"Are you really going to shoot me? Add me to your list?" I asked. There was no accusation in my words. I said it as if it wasn't even a possibility, that I knew he could never do something so heinous.

I hoped my words would convince him to put the gun aside, but he simply relaxed his grip. He raised his head. "You *were* on my list. The final one. The one to close the circle." He closed his eyes tightly, squeezing them shut like a child afraid of a monster. "I didn't want to kill any of them. I've tried to stop. But I couldn't. I could only see my mother when I looked at them. Women who would produce sons that they didn't want and didn't care for. They'd create more men like me."

He shuddered beneath my arm, as if suddenly cold.

"Do you know what it's like to be a prisoner in your own body? In your mind?" His body shook beneath my arm. "I wanted to be Denny. He was supposed to be what saved me."

He stood up abruptly. "I want you to come with me." He motioned with the gun, his grip on it firm again. "Maybe if I show you this, you'll understand."

I rose, feeling unsteady on my feet. I swayed a little, feeling the room dip and spin. It felt impossibly hot. A cold sweat had formed a film on my skin, and I sat again without meaning to, pressing my forehead into my cupped hands, my breathing rapid.

"Hey." His hand on my shoulder. I wanted to tear it from me, rip it off from his wrist and watch the blood spurt. The room spun, tilting sickeningly. Acid rose in my throat. I gritted my teeth, willing myself not to vomit.

"Let me help you." His voice, soft and soothing, his touch gentle.

He lifted me until I was on my feet, holding me steady. His fingers on my arm, resting there, keeping me upright. I concentrated on sinking my feet as deeply into the floor as I could, anchoring myself to the ground. The room slowed, and the clod of vomit in my throat crawled back down, a scorpion retreating to its den.

"Let's go."

He led me out of the apartment, down the stairs, to the street and to his car. My eyes roamed the streets, looking for Chloe, relieved when I didn't find her. I'd lost all track of time – how much had passed since I'd parted ways with Carter and Jesse?

287

It was a rare grey afternoon, the clouds hanging heavy over the city, obscuring the tops of the skyscrapers. Markham kept the gun trained on the small of my back, following so closely behind me it was mostly hidden between the press of our bodies.

We stopped at the car door. As he fumbled with the keys, I thought of running, just taking off. The streets were thronged with people. He wouldn't have a clear shot of me. Would he just shoot madly into the crowd, hoping to somehow hit his target?

He finally unlocked the passenger door and motioned me in. He closed the door after me. He hesitated. He had to cross over to the other side to get in the driver's seat. It would take half a minute, at most, but that would still be enough time for me to open my door and make a run for it. As he watched, I tugged at my seatbelt and pulled it across my chest. The gesture, as I'd hoped, seemed to reassure him, and he crossed in front of the car to his side and got in, locking the doors before strapping himself in.

He moved into the traffic, took several turns, and then followed the stretch of highway leading away from Gloam, to the south. It was a route I was unfamiliar with, and once we were out of the snarl of the city, I lost my bearings completely. He drove within the speed limit, his previous agitation gone. He rolled the window down, letting the outside air in, and propped his elbow on it, as if we were taking a casual drive just for the pleasure of it. I studied him surreptitiously from the corner of my eye. He looked different now, now that I knew the truth. I could see beneath the shiny veneer of his good looks, of his cultivated manners and practised humour. I thought I'd become more worldly as I'd been absorbed into the fabric of Gloam, but I'd failed to see all the markers which should've been obvious. I'd missed them all.

I stared out the window, at the barren land with its bitter soil which yielded nothing at all. At the occasional stand of houses, clustered together as if for protection from the outside world. Their yards were similarly cluttered with rusting bicycles and discarded furniture, the curtains drawn tightly against the prying eyes of the world.

He took an offramp that led us to a small neighbourhood. The houses were better maintained, their yards paved with walkways and flanked by small beds of flowers. A few small children were kicking a ball in the street, and only gave way to the car when Markham honked. The oldest one raised his middle finger in response, and Markham gunned the engine, loud enough for the kid to think better of his actions and to scamper away with the rest.

We pulled up to a house soon after, and I felt a jolt of recognition. A paved walkway of grey stone led to the front door. A blue door.

"Why have you brought me here?" I asked it without thinking what my question would reveal.

"To show you. To explain." He spread his hands in front of him, as if offering me something. "I'm not a monster. I know it must seem that way, but monsters are made, don't you think?"

He was babbling. It felt like his tenuous grip on reality was slipping. Like the world he lived in his mind was solidifying, blotting out the real world like a cloud passing over the sun. Sweat dripped down my spine.

People like to talk about moments. The moment they knew they were in love. The moment they could sense danger. The moment they took a misstep. The problem with these moments is they're always recognised only in hindsight. There was so much now I wish I'd known when I'd made the decision to leave The Sands for Gloam. I would've done it all differently.

"You recognise it, don't you?" He prodded me with the gun, no longer bothering to hide it, even though out of the corner of my eye I saw the neighbour's door open, and then hastily close again. Would they call the police? Had they seen the gun?

"Why would I recognise it?"

He grabbed my arm, rough enough for it to hurt. He spun me to face him, bringing the gun to beneath my chin, pressing it into the soft flesh. "I'm not some child you can patronise. Are mercs trained like cops? As in, in a dangerous situation, you do everything to not upset the crazy?"

He was right. The time for placating was over, and I sensed that if I wanted to live through this, I needed to give him the very thing he'd fought all this time for—power.

"I recognise it."

"How?"

"From the intel Jesse and I stole for a job."

His quick exhale told me he hadn't expected that.

"Why are you asking me this?"

"I've suspected for the last while that you knew something. You were working with Carter, after all. I did some research on him. Some big-time cases. Including the one which got his son killed."

Clouds were rolling in, thick and fast. Thunder muttered in the distance, the sun disappearing behind a fat, grey cloud, the day instantly darkening.

He was forcing me up the walkway now. A broken cord of police tape fluttered, rising and then coiling at our feet, a yellow plastic snake. The door was unlocked, which surprised me, and he pushed me inside, closing the door on the outside light, plunging us into murky shadows. All the curtains were drawn, and it took my eyes a few seconds to adjust. The whole house smelled like rot, the stench of decay hanging in the air, as if the house itself had absorbed the scent of death.

Another smell permeated the air, and when we entered the kitchen, it grew, so dense it was almost visible. It was coming from the fridge, its door partially open, old food rotting within its walls. It was obvious the power was out and had been for some time. The dimness inside seemed to bother Markham, and he yanked the small, tattered curtain over the kitchen window open, allowing in a weak grey light that did little to dispel the shadows.

My phone began to ring, the sound strident in the weighted silence of the house.

"Hand it over. Now."

I slipped it from my pocket, glancing briefly at the flashing screen. Carter. Markham took it from me and ended the call, cutting off the ring tone mid-trill. He turned it off, the screen going black.

I could make a run for it. His back was to me, the gun pointed down. Maybe he was inexperienced with a gun, and his shot would go wide. I could bolt for the street, scream for help. A moving target was difficult to hit, even for more experienced gunmen. I thought of the neighbour twitching her curtain to see outside, and how quickly she'd closed it again. I had the sinking feeling that I wouldn't get any help from her, or any of the neighbours, at that. They seemed used to trouble and wanted no part of it.

I took one step towards the door, indecision slowing me. Markham swung the gun back in my direction, and his face looked like that of a stranger. It was contorted with rage, his skin pulling across his features so tightly I could imagine his skull beneath. The empty eye sockets, the skinless cheeks.

"Sit!" He motioned to the kitchen table. A stain which was surely blood had absorbed into the wood. Just one small spot on the left corner. I grazed it with my fingertip, thinking of the police report. How Angela's cause of death had been ruled as a head injury due to a fall. I shuddered.

Markham followed my gaze. "She fell. I was going for him, but she got between us." His jaw clenched, and I flinched against the sound of his teeth gnashing together. "She was always getting between us. You want to know the ultimate irony of my life? She never got between us to protect me. It was to keep him from me. When I was old enough and big enough to stand up to him, she stood in my way. But when I was just a little kid getting beat on by my stepfather, she stood by and let it happen."

I couldn't look away from his face. It was desolate and lost, and I could see the boy he once was beneath the man he'd become. I thought of my own childhood. How I'd always felt safe. We were loved. When you're a child your world is small, and you never think that your experience isn't the norm, that your family isn't the same as everyone else's. To imagine that was impossible. It was to admit that the world was cruel and random.

He'd laid the gun down on the table, relinquishing it for the first time. He lowered his head to his folded arms, the sound of his sobs growing until it filled the room and blotted out every other noise. I touched his shoulder, carefully. When he didn't pull away, I moved closer, slipping my arm around him. I should've felt revulsion for him, and I had, but right now I could only pity him. Pity the boy he'd been, and how different things might've been for him if he'd been handed different cards.

I looked at the gun, easily within my reach. Picking it up would mean making a decision. My life or his. He was the same as the rest of us. No matter the misery of our lives, we fought when threatened. I wanted another way out of this. Not one which ended in more violence and another death. I wanted something else. Something that could close the cycle and end the murders. I didn't want any more blood on my hands.

He raised his head, his eyes red and swelling, his face damp. I touched his scarlet cheek, a light brush of my fingers. I could no longer see the man who had killed my father. Who had strangled those women. Now I could only see the man beneath it all, who'd wanted so badly to rise above his circumstances, to not be the monster he'd been told he was.

"Markham, I want both of us to get out of this alive. You know you'll need to pay for what you've done. You can't walk away from this. But you can be redeemed. You can admit what you've done, take ownership for it. That's within your power."

"I'm so sorry." He said it so quietly I only just caught his words. "I wish I could've been different. I wish we'd met in another time."

"Like parallel lives? Or reincarnation?"

He smiled, sadly. "I think in my next life I'm likely to come back as a roach. That would be justice."

He pushed the gun towards me. "I know you came here because you wanted to find your father's killer. You found him. So do what you came to do. Avenge him."

I didn't pick it up at first. "I want to know why."

"Why?"

"Why my father?"

"You said it yourself. I wasn't after him."

"You were after me."

"Yes."

"Why?"

"Do you know what happened to my family after you were recovered? They were ruined. Matt was always a violent man, but after Carter and your father found you, and you and your family disappeared, Matt's reputation with the Natives went to shit. None of them trusted him again. He was kicked out of the gang. We lost all our money, our friends, our contacts."

He pushed the Sauer into my hand. "I needed someone to blame. It was you. My anger at my mother was always pointless. She was never going to change. You were an outsider, and that made it easier."

He lowered himself into the chair across from me. "All those women I killed? They were all from my past. Women who knew Matt was hitting me, abusing my mother—none of them ever did a thing to help us. They needed to pay. And they did."

When he looked at me again, his face was different. Shuttered. Like everything he'd just said to me had been spoken by someone else, someone who was no longer there. As if his façade at playing Denny had simply run its course, and all that was left was a killer.

I raised my gun, its familiar weight in my hand comforting. It was still loaded. I pointed it straight at his face. His gaze remained on me, unwavering, unafraid. My finger moved to the trigger. I thought of Pop, of his body left for us to find. I thought of Chloe, whom he'd tried to kill once, and who he'd threatened earlier today, using her as a lure to reel me in. I thought of the other women, strangled and bludgeoned because Markham had deemed them unworthy of their lives, black marks on society. My finger tightened. I thought of the mess such a close shot would cause; his blood spattering the wall behind him, his body slumping to the floor. How he would die in the house he'd hated, where he'd lived with people who had never loved him.

The door swung open with a bang, and a shot rang through the room.

Chapter Thirty-Two

Harlow

HAD I PULLED THE trigger? Carter was standing in the doorway, his handgun pointed at Markham. But Markham was no longer there. He was sprinting for the door, and Carter was trying to reload. Markham shoved past Carter so roughly Carter lost his footing, stumbling further into the room. I was dazed. Was I still even holding my gun? My hands didn't feel like they belonged to me, the contact between them and my gun feeling far away, as if I'd disconnected from my body.

Carter hesitated. "Are you hurt?"

I shook my head, frantic at the possibility of Markham escaping. "Go!" I yelled.

Someone was shouting, and with a start I realised it was Jesse. His voice came from outside, but I couldn't see him. There was a dull thud, the sound of solid flesh connecting, and then the *rat-tat-tat* of gunfire.

I tightened my grip on my Sauer and rushed through the door.

Jesse had intercepted Markham. He sat squarely on Markham's chest, his piece pointed at his forehead, his knees pinning Markham's arms at his sides. They were both panting. Carter stood over both of them, nearby enough to pose a threat, but not close enough to be within Markham's reach should he manage to wriggle free.

At my approach, Markham's eyes rolled towards me, his gaze locking on mine. I studied the planes of his face. One which had become so familiar to me. One I'd opened beneath like a flower turning towards the sun. I'd wanted so much for him to be the man he'd been as Denny that I'd ignored all the warning signs beneath. Had he been that skilled at hiding, or had I just ignored them? Had I been so greedy to have someone who wasn't from my old life, who didn't know about my father or my past, that I'd bestowed on him characteristics he didn't have?

"We're not that different, you and I." Jesse moved to shut him up, but I held up a hand to restrain him.

"We've both been disappointed by the people in our lives. Let down. Fooled into thinking we would be protected, loved, safe. We were lied to."

I wanted to feel anger at his words. At his comparison that somehow, we were the same. Just weeks ago, that anger would've been blazing and righteous. Anger was the easier emotion. One which fuelled, which drove. All I felt now was sadness.

"You're right about one thing. We were both lied to. That's where the similarity ends." It was only because I was looking at him that I saw it coming, but I was still too late. He bucked beneath Jesse, unseating him enough to pull out the knife he'd had pinned behind his back, and bury it into Jesse's chest. Shock washed over me, and it was like someone had poured lead into my limbs. I couldn't move.

Carter was yelling something, rushing to aid Jesse, pressing his palms into the scarlet flood which was spurting from his chest.

His lips moved, and I could hear his voice, but to make out his words felt as impossible as gouging out my eyes.

The only thing I could focus on, was the sight of Markham's retreating back against the fall of the sun, his silhouette nothing more than a moving shadow disappearing from sight.

***

I sat at a café window, watching the street as people passed. It was a grey, murky morning, the low-hanging clouds allowing only the briefest glimpse of the sun. More than anything, I wanted to leave this place. I wanted to return home, but no one had heard from or seen Markham for weeks. I kept waiting for news, convinced that any moment now there would be a report of a sighting, but it was as if he'd simply disappeared that day, down that side-street. As if he'd pulled a magic disappearing act. I rose from my seat, cradling my paper coffee cup with the remnants of my latte. I drained the cup and tipped it into the dustbin on my way out, pulling my coat closer to my body. It was an unseasonably cold day, the wind like ice against my cheeks. Maybe I could change my mind. Pack my stuff and go home today. Surprise my brothers and Ma and pick up my life where I'd left it. But Markham's disappearance wasn't something I could let go. It itched at me from the inside, an itch I could never scratch. He would never stop. I'd hoped for news of his death – an unfortunate accident, a bar fight. Maybe he'd tried to kill someone who'd turned the gun on him. A shape formed in my mind then. I knew so much more than I did when I'd first come to Gloam. Like how to find people who didn't want to be found. Everyone left a trail, no matter how well they covered their tracks.

Carter

She'd been gone for weeks. Her phone would ring – a small solace – but I was only ever met with her voicemail on the other end. She'd vanished, and with every day which passed, my imagined scenarios grew worse.

Her family hadn't heard from her either. I'd reported her missing, for the good that had done. Jesse had been combing the streets, despite his doctor's orders to take it easy. He'd employed the services and the connections of both Mr X and Evans, but both had come up empty.

No one had seen or heard from her. She'd vanished. Her and Markham both.

I arrived at my offices late that morning. When I stepped through the door, something gave way beneath my foot, and I slid wildly, my arms pinwheeling. An envelope lay on the floor, now bearing the imprint of my boot. Other than that, it was blank. No address, no name.

I turned it over. It was unsealed, and slim. I lifted the flap, slipping out a photograph.

It was face down. I flipped it over.

A body, the face clearly visible. One cheek swollen, one eye black, but still recognisable. His hand had been arranged next to his face, his palm facing upwards, an X carved into it. At the bottom of the photo, was a scrawled H.

A Word from the Author

So much goes into writing a book. If you enjoyed this one, I would love it if you could leave a review on Amazon and/or Goodreads. It can be short and sweet – no essays necessary! For those of you who do, thank you.

Please click or visit the links below to leave your reviews:
Amazon:
https://mybook.to/S2QP
Goodreads:
https://www.goodreads.com/book/show/214622243-gloam

If you'd like to keep in touch and see what I'm up to, you can join my mailing list here:
https://www.jenniferwithers.com/
I offer exclusive freebies to my subscribers, and being on my list means you're the first to hear about new material and promos.

Acknowledgements

First, my husband, Stuart. If there's anyone who understands obsession, it's you. Thank you for being my biggest supporter, and for doing life with me. I love you.

For my little boy, Tristan. You're still too small to read this my love, but one day, I hope you will. Thank you for being my greatest teacher, and for being all you are.

My family – my Mom, Tina, my siblings, Mike and Trace, my sister-in-law, Melanie, and my nieces and nephews – Mark, Michayla, Lola, Amy-Lee and Luke. Let us never forget how lucky we are to have each other. I love you guys immensely.

Michelle Carstens – a fellow old soul and someone who gets me to the depth of my bones. Thank you for being my person.

Ania Kamerski – for all the work on my author photos and so much more. Our friendship started as an unlikely one – and has never failed to surprise me since.

For all my other friends who I've not named here – for your love and support – there are no words. Thank you.

Lastly, and most importantly, to the readers of this book. I hope you enjoyed the ride. Without you, this book would just be words on a page. Thanks for joining me.

About the author

Jennifer started out her writing career as a spunky 7-year-old banging away at her mother's old typewriter. One BA in English Studies later, she decided to pursue her writing career, such as it was, more seriously, which led to many unfinished drafts and plenty of artist angst. A few writing courses, seminars and workshops later, she wrote and published her first novel, The War Between. Jennifer lives in Pretoria, with her husband and 6-year-old son, and plans to write a novel a year from here on out (scout's honour).

www.ingramcontent.com/pod-product-compliance
Lightning Source LLC
Chambersburg PA
CBHW032207190626
46810CB00019B/2169